Buckingham Smith

Narratives of the Career of Hernando de Soto in the Conquest of

Florida

As told by a knight of Elvas, and in a relation by Luys Hernandez de Biedma factor of

the expedition

Buckingham Smith

Narratives of the Career of Hernando de Soto in the Conquest of Florida
As told by a knight of Elvas, and in a relation by Luys Hernandez de Biedma factor of the expedition

ISBN/EAN: 9783337293550

Printed in Europe, USA, Canada, Australia, Japan

Cover: Foto ©Andreas Hilbeck / pixelio.de

More available books at **www.hansebooks.com**

Bradford Club Series.

NUMBER FIVE.

NARRATIVES

OF THE CAREER OF

HERNANDO DE SOTO

IN THE

CONQUEST OF FLORIDA

AS TOLD BY A KNIGHT OF ELVAS

AND IN A RELATION BY

Luys Hernandez de Biedma

FACTOR OF THE EXPEDITION

TRANSLATED BY

BUCKINGHAM SMITH

NEW YORK

M DCCC LXVI

Entered according to Act of Congress, in the year 1866,

By John B. Moreau,

FOR THE BRADFORD CLUB,

In the Clerk's Office of the District Court of the United States
for the Southern District of New York.

SEVENTY-FIVE COPIES PRINTED.

PUBLICATIONS

OF THE

BRADFORD CLUB.

THE BRADFORD CLUB.

UNDER this designation, a few gentlemen, interested in the study of American History and Literature, propose occasionally to print limited editions of such manuscripts and scarce pamphlets as may be deemed of value towards illustrating these subjects. They will seek to obtain for this purpose unpublished journals or correspondence containing matter worthy of record, and which may not properly be included in the Historical Collections or Documentary Histories of the several States. Such unpretending contemporary chronicles often throw precious light upon the motives of action and the imperfectly narrated events of bygone days; perhaps briefly touched upon in dry official documents.

The Club may also issue fac-similes of curious manuscripts, or documents worthy of notice, which, like the printed issues, will bear its imprint.

> " These are the
> Registers, the chronicles of the age
> They were written in, and speak the truth of History
> Better than a hundred of your printed
> Communications."—*Shakerly Marmyon's Antiquary.*

WILLIAM BRADFORD—the first New York Printer—whose name the Club has adopted, came to this country in 1682, and established

his Press in the neighborhood of Philadelphia. In 1693 he removed
to this City—was appointed Royal Printer—and set up his Press
"at the Sign of the Bible." For upwards of thirty years he was
the only Printer in the Province, and in 1725 published our first
Newspaper—*The New York Gazette.* He conducted this paper
until 1743, when he retired from business. He died in May, 1752,
and was described, in an obituary notice of the day, as "a man of
great sobriety and industry, a real friend to the poor and needy, and
kind and affable to all." He was buried in Trinity Church Yard, by
the side of the wife of his youth; and the loving affection of
relatives and friends reared a simple and unostentatious Monument
to his memory.

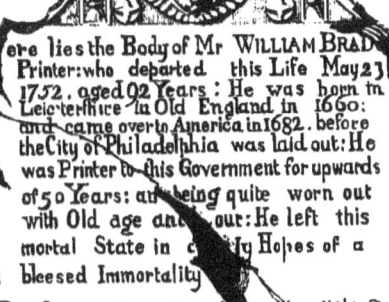

ere lies the Body of Mr WILLIAM BRAD
Printer: who departed this Life May 23
1752. aged 92 Years : He was born in
Leicestershire in Old England in 1660:
and came over to America in 1682. before
the City of Philadelphia was laid out: He
was Printer to this Government for upwards
of 50 Years: and being quite worn out
with Old age and out: He left this
mortal State in d ly Hopes of a
blessed Immortality

Reader, reflect how you'll quit this Stage
You'll find but few attain to such an Age
Life's full of Pain: Lo; here's a Place of Rest.
Prepare to meet your GOD, then you are blest
Here lies also the Body of Elizabeth, Wife to
the said William Bradford : who departed
this Life June 8 1731. aged 68 years.

LIFE OF SOTO.

HERNANDO DE SOTO, whose name is conspicuous among the early enterprises of discovery and conquest in both American continents, was born at Xeréz, in the Province of Estremadura. He was of good origin; his blood what is called noble in Spain, and so derived from the four quarterings of ancestry. In his early youth, probably in Sevilla, at the time the splendid armament was prepared at the royal cost that conveyed Pedrárias to Castilla del Oro, Soto joined the Governor, as one, perhaps, of the fifteen hundred men whom he conducted. In the year 1514 he arrived at Nombre de Dios, a little while after Balboa, looking from Panamá, made discovery of the South Sea, which Magallanes afterwards called Pacífico.

Soto, under Francisco Hernandez de Córdova, was one of the first settlers of what was afterwards known as Leon in Nicaragua. He was early sent to drive Gil Gonzalez Dávila from that territory; but he being still young, and with little military experience, Dávila, under pretext of treating, rose upon him at daylight. Although his men made brave resistance, they were overcome by a much feebler force, losing a large amount of gold with their arms. The danger of keeping so many prisoners induced the victor to set them at liberty at the end of three days, restoring their property, having first made sure of their peaceful return to Leon.

Subsequently, Francisco Hernandez, finding a large number of men unemployed about him, and an abundance of every material for his design, strove to bring about a revolt, intending afterward to ask of the King the government of the country. For having

B

opposed the measure, with a dozen others, Soto was seized and sent to the fort at Granada. With nine men, the Captain Companon went to his relief: and, having liberated him, took the field, armed and on horseback, where he awaited Hernandez, who, although he had sixty men, would not venture a conflict, knowing that his person would be sought out over every other. Not long afterwards, Pedrárias captured his ambitious lieutenant and beheaded him.

Towards the year 1524, Hernando de Soto, Francisco Companon, and Hernan Ponçe de Leon resided in the same town, associates in all that they possessed. They were wealthy, and in the respectability of their standing were equal, as also in their rank in life. Having good apportionments of Indians, they employed them profitably as herdsmen, and in gathering gold. Of Companon we hear little. He died early: and in the will of Soto, made many years afterward, a number of masses are ordered to be said for the repose of the soul of that Captain.

Such are some of the brief and scattered notices found in the old books respecting the early days of the future Adelantado of Florida. The incidents are blended with the subjugation and settlement of Central America, as the history of his later years is inseparably connected with that of the conquest of Peru.

While Pedrárias governed Castilla del Oro, he transferred the capital of the Province across the Isthmus, from Darien to Panamá, on the ocean which, in the year 1513, his predecessor had beheld. From this point, in the course of years, small expeditions were fitted out by the colonists, to go southward by sea for traffic, and on discoveries. Andagoya was another explorer; and, in 1524, Pizarro followed the coast, in sight of the Andes, to the ninth degree of latitude south of the equator. The result of these enterprises was the evidence of the existence of the precious metals in large amount among the natives, and of emeralds, with the knowledge of an extensive, populous, and opulent Indian empire.

Pizarro, supplied with means by the friends who had before assisted him, taking with him the portion of gold that belonged of right to the crown, with specimens of the cotton and fabrics of the region which he had visited, as also of the jewels, plumes, and people of Tumbez, went to Spain to ask for the government of

that country. While absent, in the year 1529, his friends, fearing
that the enterprise might be taken in hand by Pedrárias, applied to
three of the richest citizens of Leon to take part in it with Pizarro
and his companions, Luque and Almagro ; and they received the
word of Hernan Ponçe that either he, Soto, or Compañon would
come to Panamá for that purpose, and there await the arrival of
their leader.

Pizarro returned, bringing with him four brothers, born, like
himself, out of wedlock, and one, Hernando, legitimate. Luque and
Almagro, who had found the means and given him their assistance
(the former as the agent of a silent partner), were not pleased with
the addition to their numbers of this kindred of the new Adelantado,
although for Luque, who was of the Church, a bishopric had been
provided. Almagro remained inactive until Pizarro promised to
assist him to a government as extensive as the one conceded, when
the territory should be won, and that the treasure, slaves, and
effects of every nature, acquired by him, should be shared among the
three; and that nothing should be asked of the King in behalf of the
brothers until the fulfilment of these stipulations. At this junc-
ture, Ponçe arrived with two cargoes of slaves. The vessels were
added to the common stock on condition of paying their charter, the
bestowal on Ponçe of one of the largest apportionments of Indians
that should be made, and appointing Soto to be captain of troops,
and governor of the principal place the invaders might occupy.

One hundred and eighty-five capable men embarked, with thirty-
seven horses, the men bearing bucklers made of the staves of wine-
barrels, almost impenetrable to either dart or arrow. Almagro
remained to collect and bring away any other forces that might
arrive. After a few days' navigation the Spaniards landed, and de-
spoiled the unsuspecting inhabitants of Quaque of twenty thousand
pesos' worth of gold and a large amount of precious stones. The vessels were immediately sent to take back the news and bring more
men and horses.

The troops remained in quiet seven months, scourged by a sharp
and novel disease. At that time a vessel arrived with some additional
strength, when, relying upon the promise of soon receiving more, the
army was put in motion. The Indians, alas! soon began to have a

different impression of the white men from that before received;
they were now discovered to be neither good nor averse to rob-
bery; but false, cruel, and destructive. The object was to reach
Tumbez; but the invader had little idea of the vast forces that the
contending brothers, Guascar and Atahualpa, Princes of Peru, had
marshalled, though, fortunately for him, in view of each other they
regarded his arrival as a matter too trivial for present thought.

On the mainland near the Island of Puná, where the Spaniards
lived for a long while, the force was joined by Belalcázar, with a
company of thirty men and twelve horses; and in the year 1531,
Hernando de Soto arrived with two ships, bringing infantry and cavalry. The original force, which had been wasting away by a strange
malady, being thus strengthened, the Commander, believing that
the people of Tumbez were sufficiently gratified by the outrages
they had been allowed to commit on those of Puná to give his men
a friendly reception, determined to remove to the main. Oppor-
tunely a note was found in the hands of one of the Indians of that
city, written by a Castilian left there on the occasion of its discovery,
which ran: "Ye who shall come to this land, know that there are
more gold and silver in it than there is iron in Biscaya." The greater
part of the soldiery, however, only laughed at the paper, as a device
to give them encouragement.

The Spaniards were astonished at the ruin of the city, wrought
by war with Puná, and, it was said, by pest; but the sorest disappointment was felt by those from Nicaragua, who thought they
had exchanged a paradise for disease and desolation. Some Indians,
seeking to save their property, drew near to the strangers, and in
conversation spoke of Cuzco, Vilcas, Pachacamac; of edifices having
ceilings of gold and silver plate—news ordered to be immediately
spread throughout the camp. Not to remain in idleness, the troops
ranged the arid country in the hot sun; discovered a river in a
green vale, over which passed the great highway of the Incas;
and visited a royal caravansera, where they drank from the cool
waters.

Cautious in advancing the next step, only after consultation
with the officers was it resolved to make reconnoissance about the
skirts of the mountains, where were said to be masses of population,

and, if possible, to find Chillemasa, the lord of Tumbez. This duty being intrusted to Soto, he directly set about to perform it, with a company of sixty cavalry and a small body of foot. Shortly after, Juan de la Torre came back, saying that he had fled from the Captain, who proposed to mutiny with that troop, and return upon Quito. The Commander passed over the intelligence delicately, and Soto, having proceeded with his guides as far as Caxas, came back. He spoke of having seen large edifices, and numerous flocks of the sheep and camels of the country. Among the articles of plunder that were displayed, the soldiers were particularly pleased with some tablets of fine gold. A portion of the royal road of the Inca Guaynacapa, for its grandeur, had awakened the highest admiration. The inhabitants, astonished that these people should venture so far away from their companions, united for their destruction; but coming hand to hand, many of the Indians were left dead, while they did little injury.

The people, at hearing the report from Soto, were delighted, and began to receive with less distrust the story the Indians had told of the magnificence of Cuzco, in which the great lord held his court and was served from urns and beakers of gold; where the country was productive and populous; the fanes lined with the precious metals—a tale they had before attributed to the fancy only of their General. Still, there were those who did not believe in the reality of such riches; and Francisco Ysaga is recorded as one who gave his steed to procure releasement from the service. Nor should we smile at the incredulity of what might have been a swine-herd of the *dehesas* of Estremadura; since, a few years earlier, in the reign of Ysabel, the sacred mass-bells were of bronze, and the sceptre of Castilla, which waved Colón westward, to throw open the Portals of the Ocean, was light, and only silver-gilded. The prisoners brought by Soto were questioned, and the objects of spoil being carefully considered, it was thought best to establish on the spot a permanent foothold. This, formed of invalid soldiers, was the town of San Miguel, which became finally seated at the junction of several rivers, in the broad and fertile vale of Piúra.

Hernando de Soto now went forward with a troop of horsemen, to observe the passing of Atahualpa, who, with a large force, was rumoured to be marching from Quito to Caxamalca, to oppose his brother, advancing from Cuzco. The army was found to be very large, and the Spaniards, at sight of it, quailed in view of the poverty of their numbers. Atahualpa, on the other side, having heard about the invaders, through the stories in circulation, sent a lord to see what people they might be. Wheresoever this emissary went, the Spaniards were supplied with subsistence from that moment less willingly than before. Having attired himself in the costume of a countryman, he set out to visit the camp. With a basket of guavas as a gift, he presented himself before the Chief, to excuse the Cacique of Mayabelica for having failed in rendering him obedience; but Pizarro, displeased, cuffed the *Orejon*, who thereupon returned to the Prince, speaking disparagingly of what he had discovered. He said the intruders scarcely numbered two hundred men, were the wash of the sea, had beards, were thieves, and went about carried on a kind of sheep, like that of Callao. After hearing this statement, Atahualpa gave himself no more concern about the strange people.

While the invaders paused to make the new settlement, information was diligently sought concerning the political difficulties of Peru, the customs of the inhabitants, their arms, manner of fighting, and their military force. The treasure in hand having been divided, the General borrowed of his friends and sent a large sum to Almagro, renewing to him the assurances of good faith, and urging that the forces at his disposal should be sent; for he had suspected that it was the desire of his companion to push his own fortunes at a distance, and Pizarro stood in need of his liberality, energy, and promptitude.

In September, 1532, the troop took its departure from San Miguel, in quest of Atahualpa—who, having proved successful in repeated battles over the forces of the legitimate heir of the crimson *borla*, held him pent up in Cuzco—and, on the third day, it stopped in the valley of Piúra, to learn more particulars, and make further preparations. The entire force now consisted of only sixty-seven cavalry, with a hundred and ten infantry having swords and bucklers, some with crossbows, and three or four bearing fire-arms. The crossbow-men, numbering twenty, were placed apart, under an officer. The Commander now boldly proclaimed that if there were any who would go back they might return to the town, where servants would be allotted them to labour, the same as had been provided for others who remained there; for the fame of the Indian strength had alarmed the timid, and it was desirable to have those only who were willing to go forward, trusting more to the valour of a few than to the show of many.

Thus provided, the army began its march, the boldness of the leader well sustained by the courage of his companions. The way was found to be open and undefended, left so purposely, it was supposed, to allow them to march as far as they would from support. Words of peace and greeting were continually received, with gifts from Atahualpa. A message was returned, to say that the Spaniards were marching to his assistance, and to make known to him from the Vicar of Christ, and from the great temporal prince, the King of Castilla and Leon, that there is a God in heaven and on earth.

After many days, the Spaniards arrived where from the direct road to Chincha one forks to Caxamalca, which was chosen, though less favourable than the other to movement, and where there were natural defences. The men were told that the success of the enterprise was dependent on action; to keep the other road, where they should be lost in time and place, was not the way to their object; and that, after all, men have to die, with this difference, that some leave a name to be famous, while others are forgotten. Stimulated by this address, and reminded that in such a cause, when the Holy Faith is to be planted, Christians should look for divine assistance, the soldiers declared their wish to be led, and that, when the occasion should present itself, they would be mindful of their duty.

After a journey through vales at the foot of the ridge, the troops were allowed to rest a day before ascending. Forty cavalry and sixty infantry were selected with which to advance, intrusted to the experience of guides, leaving the rest in charge of the luggage. The way was steep and difficult. Fortifications were passed, and places that might have been favourably held stood vacant. The war between the brothers alone seemed to awaken interest and occupy the attention.

After several days' march, through a region cold from elevation, in the beginning of the year 1533, Caxamalca being at hand, the force was drawn up in three divisions. The place the Inca occupied was exactly ascertained, as well as the strength and position of his troops. On the evening of the 14th of November, the Spaniards entered the town, but found it nearly uninhabited. In the midst of a great plaza, within a triangular wall, were only some women in houses, who gave utterance to their sympathy for the fate that to them appeared to await the strangers. Nothing anywhere presented a welcome, or bore a friendly aspect.

A messenger sent to Atahualpa did not return; and it was thought proper that his army should at once be scrutinized. Hernando de Soto, in the character of ambassador, went, attended by fifteen horsemen, to gain the presence of the great monarch, and ask a grant of leave for the General to appear before him, and deliver the words sent by the King. From a tower the Indian tents were seen extending the distance of more than a league, that of the Prince rising in the midst.

At this time Hernando de Soto was in about the thirty-third year of his age. In person he was of moderate size, with breeding and manner becoming his condition. A fine equestrian, he was also skilled in the use of arms. Passing along on his charger, he leaped the banks of a water-course, and amid an astonished multitude rode up to where the army lay. In number it was estimated at thirty thousand strong—the divisions composed of archers, slingers, lancers, and mace-men. He reached the royal tent, and, his presence being announced, the chief inmates appeared. Atahualpa, accompanied by a retinue, sat on a rich stool, the imperial tassel decorating his forehead. In a low voice, with eyes fixed on the ground, he required that the Christian should be asked his purpose. He was told that the General of the white men had sent him salutations, and an invitation to sup with him in Caxamalca, or, if that could not be, then to dine the next day. The Inca bade him take back the royal thanks, and promised to come the next day: he afterwards added that he should be attended by his army, but that it need excite no apprehension. At this moment, Hernan Pizarro coming up with an equal number of horsemen, hearing what was said, made obeisance to the Inca. He declared that his Highness would be very welcome, even though he should bring his men armed, for nothing so delighted Spaniards as military spectacles. Atahualpa, understanding this person to be the brother of the General, raised his eyes and said, that from the banks of the Turicara the *Curuca* had sent him an iron collar, with word that, for the ill-treatment the Caciques had received from the white men, he had killed three of their number and a horse. Pizarro denied the charge, called Mayabelica a great knave, and declared that, even though the Chiefs had been treated badly, the people there were as so many turkeys, and all on those plains were not enough to take the life of a single horse. The conversation having ceased, beautiful women handed drink of maize to the Prince and strangers, in golden cups. Soto, remounting with *donaire*, coursed his steed in the royal presence. He skirmished, he charged, wheeled, curvetted, and, returning, halted so nigh to the royal stool, that Atahualpa felt the impatient blast of the nostrils of the beast, and the heat of his strength; still the native remained as composed as though he were accustomed to such pastime. Calling to him some people who had fled, he reproved their timidity, telling them that in the country whence those animals came, they were like the sheep in Peru. The time, until the morning, was spent on both sides in watchfulness and care. The captains visited the guards, the soldiers made every thing ready, and passed words of encouragement. Indian priests offered sacrifices, uttering supplications in their temples to the Sun. A squadron of men, apt in the use of the *lazo*, were added to the warriors.

The next day Atahualpa, in slow and imposing procession, marched up to where the impatient Spaniards were expecting him within the walls; and thence he sent word to their commander to tie his horses and bloodhounds, or otherwise he should come no farther. With a body of eight thousand men, he shortly afterward entered the plaza, in the middle of which Pizarro awaited him, having fifteen chosen men, armed with sword and buckler. The Friar Valverde went forward, exhorting the Inca to peace. He held up a cross and presented a Bible, in which he said the commands of God were inscribed. The Prince took the book, turned it over, examined the leaves, and cast it aside, telling the

c

friar to bring back the treasure and the thousand things of which
the inhabitants had been robbed.

At this moment a shout arose from the warriors, which was followed by the beating of drums; Pizarro then waved a white shawl,
the signal preconcerted for action. Thereupon Captain Pedro de
Candia caused a gun to be fired, and directly began the discharge of
the arquebuses, followed by the blast of trumpets and roll of kettle-
drums, carrying consternation and fearful panic among the native
host. The charge of horse succeeded. Detached bodies, issuing
from several directions where they had been concealed, were led
upon the defenceless squadrons by Hernan Pizarro and Soto; while
the infantry, under Belalcázar and Mena, joining in the war-cry of
"Santiago," attacked them with sword and crossbow. The General
approached the litter, and, with his band, struck down the bearers;
these were directly replaced, and they again by others, who took
successively the posts of the fallen: first one and then another
soldier rushed upon Atahualpa, till Pizarro interposed for his safety;
Two thousand Indians were slain within a brief period of time, no
one pretending to offer resistance. The spoil was immense. Jars of
silver, jewels of gold, and rich stuffs, strewed the ground. Many
Curacas were killed about the royal litter; many princesses and
priestesses were taken, as well as the wives of nobles.

The Inca, pondering upon the mutations of fortune, observed that
within a day, as it were, he was a victor over Guascar, and himself
was vanquished. Seeking to extricate himself from present troubles,
the unhappy Prince appeared only to have fallen lower in misfortune.
He reckoned on the avarice of the white man, but had not calculated his possible perfidy. Thinking to regain his liberty at a price
so extraordinary that when named the payment was considered
impossible, he secretly ordered his brother to be drowned in the
River Andamarca, incited to this course, not unlikely, by the policy
of Pizarro. The room, nevertheless, which was the measure of the
purchase-money, was duly filled from the gold and silver of Cuzco,
of its temple, *guacas*, or receptacles of deceased kings, and from the
oratories. The Inca, notwithstanding, was still detained. In the
mean time, Almagro, who had been made field-marshal by royal
commission, approached the city, and after being greeted on the

road by his old comrade, who came out to meet him, he went
directly to call upon the prisoner.

The treasure did not long remain undivided. In the allotment,
Almagro probably shared with Pizarro according to their agreement; the Lieutenant-General, Hernan Pizarro, took the second
portion in magnitude, and Soto the third, in amount twenty-three
thousand five hundred and thirty-two *pesos*, each of the value of an
ounce of pure silver.

About this time there were rumours of a purpose on the part of
the Inca to bring war upon the Christians. They appear, however,
to have had no better foundation than the tales of servants and the
apprehensions of timidity, if they were not altogether produced by
the Adelantado, in seeking a pretext to place the succession to the
borla in question, by the failure of both pretenders to the empire.
Taking occasion of the absence of Hernan Pizarro on a mission to
Spain, Soto and Guevara, with some others, were sent to ascertain
the truth of the report, that an army was to be found at a distant
point; but before they could get back to make known the falsity of
the news, which had before been suspected, Atahualpa, on a variety
of charges, and with the sanction of the Dominican Valverde, was
beheaded. The officers, on their arrival, reproached the Chief for
the wantonness and excess of the action. Some had sought the
society of the Prince, being interested in him through his admi-
rable conversation, in which they discovered a strong understanding
and an acute intellect. In those personages he might have found
friends. Soto, whom the Adelantado had just before made lieutenant-general, was one of the gentlemen who had most pleased the
captive, having at times, with chess and dice, relieved some of his
heavy hours.

With the death of the two Princes, government was suspended,
and society became entirely disorganized. Distant Provinces and
late territorial accessions withdrew their allegiance: old lords re-
gained their possessions, or new masters usurped them. Law was
at an end. Life was nowhere safe for the Indian: the highways
became infested with thieves, as the mountains with robbers. The
downfall of the extensive monarchy was complete. It had lasted,
from its rise, according to some computations, nearly four centuries;

but the perfection and extent of the public works on the soil attest
for its civilization a much higher antiquity. In extent, along the
sea, it measured from nigh the equator, southward, a distance of
about thirty-five degrees of coast.   One of kin, on the side of
Guascar, was permitted to receive the crimson tassel.

The Spaniards, having tarried seven months in Caxamalca, advanced towards Cuzco with the newly appointed sovereign, Almagro
conducting the vanguard. As they passed through Yanamarca, there
lay the unburied corses of three thousand men, slain in a contest
between the native factions. Approaching the beautiful valley of
Xauxa, the Marshal was directed to advance with Soto and other
officers. After traversing some distance they met a large body of
Indians, who bade them begone from their country, and charged
them with the murder of their King. The stream was crossed, the
Indians dispersed, and the Spaniards, weary of killing, returned to
find that Pizarro had arrived. Provisions, deposits of fine cloth,
and a large amount of gold in a temple, were the booty.

Belalcázar had been sent to command in San Miguel. Finding
himself with considerable force from Panamá, he became ambitious
to go back to make the conquest of Quito. A rumour prevailed that
the Indians to the north were preparing an independency; and this,
joined to the news brought by the late comers, that the Adelantado
of Guatemala was making ready to subdue the Provinces of Quito,
was enough to satisfy any scruples that might exist in the con-
science of a *conquistador* as to what should be his proper course in
the face of such temptation; so that when importuned to undertake
the adventure, Belalcázar found no difficulty in acceding to the
desire of his men, who believed the treasure of Caxamalca was as
nothing compared with that of Quito, where the Court once had
been held. One hundred and fifty well-appointed infantry and
cavalry were got in readiness to march; but, as the event proved,
to contend with no other enemies than cold, hunger, and severe
fatigue.

Hernando de Soto went forward from Xauxa with sixty cavalry
towards Cuzco. The soldiers distrusting their abilities to cope with
the Indians in sight, and the Captain, who was considered to be a
man of no less judgment than courage, finding himself surrounded,

addressed his men. He declared their only safety to be in giving battle; that their enemies were preparing, counting the strength they should meet, and increasing their numbers every hour. The Spaniards had hitherto met the inhabitants of the plains: these people were the Ayllos, living on the first ascent to the mountains. They appeared along the heights in masses, with clubs, darts, and slings, swearing by the Sun and the Earth to destroy this band of robbers, or to die themselves. Soto went foremost into action, the Indians, with yells, holding the ground with desperate firmness. Five Christians were slain outright, and two horses. The Captain, with one other, fought his way toward the eminences. Some who fell in the passage-way impeded the ascent of the rest, until two, having dismounted, placed themselves one on either side for defence, thus enabling others to get by. With these succours, the first that passed returned to assist those advancing; when the Indians, weary of the contest, drew off to a little distance, and the Spaniards betook themselves to the margin of a brook at hand. Eleven men and fourteen horses were injured. That night Almagro reached the pass, and, sounding a trumpet, was answered from Soto. In the morning the forces united, and easily scattered the natives. This rencontre appears to have been the severest the Spaniards experienced in the subjugation of the Incas.

In the year 1534, Pedro de Alvarado, having ships in readiness on the Pacific coast of Guatemala to go on discoveries in the west, according to the royal permission, hearing of the wealth of Quito, and considering it not within the limits of country assigned to Pizarro, directed his ambitious course thither by sea, with five hundred soldiers, of whom nearly the half were mounted. Among those he brought in his company was Captain Luis de Moscoso de Alvarado, the same personage who some years later, on the death of Soto, successfully conducted the retreat of his followers down the Mississippi to the shores of Mexico.

Alvarado, having arrived with his army on the coast of Peru, near the equator, marched into the interior. For a time he met no serious interruption. Towns of importance were surprised, and large quantities of gold procured from them. In ascending the Andes, the severity of the weather caused the loss of eighty-three soldiers: many negroes and natives of Guatemala likewise perished by the way. Three and four thousand *pesos* were given at first for a horse; but treasure itself was at last abandoned among the snows, with armour, and the victims of the elements. The mountains, nevertheless, were pierced, and the Adelantado halted not far from the River Bamba.

While Alvarado thus contended with hunger and cold, toiling along the rugged ascent to Quito, Pizarro was approaching Cuzco. Having overtaken Almagro and Soto, he sent them forward to meet a force reported to be advancing. It was encountered, and soon dispersed. Mango Inca, who had been raised by the natives in those parts to be their sovereign, finding no escape, delivered himself in state to the victors. The pillage of the city took place before the arrival of the Spaniards. When Soto entered Cuzco the Temple of the Sun had been rifled, and valuables to an immense amount carried away. Nevertheless, the plate remaining was considerable. Other things than the precious metals were now neglected; from their abundance losing all esteem in the eyes of the conquerors. Even silver, for the time, appeared to be unimportant. Soto had already shodden with it the horses of his troops. Of the precious stones, they who wished took what most pleased them.

Wild was the lament of the people on the occupation of their city by the strangers. Thousands bemoaned the loss of friends and homes, crying out to their gods, and cursing the dissension of Guascar and Atahualpa, who had brought desecration to their temples, and laid waste their most cherished possessions.

The news of the arrival and march of Alvarado having come to the knowledge of Almagro, he determined at once to oppose him. He sent word to Pizarro of what was passing, and then set out for San Miguel. Finding Belalcázar gone, there were not wanting those to intimate distrust of him—that he had marched to unite with Alvarado. The resolution of the Marshal was to follow on; and he came to Quito directly after the arrival of Belalcázar, while he was yet fruitlessly searching for treasure. Having tenderly chided the Captain for leaving his post, with a part of his well-disciplined soldiery he went to look for Alvarado, and found him near the Rio Bamba.

The fading fortunes of the Adelantado of Guatemala were too manifest for him to put them at issue even with the feebler force of Almagro, whose possession already of Quito, and his well-known liberality, were more than a match for the strength of his adversary. Several days of conference ensued, in which the Marshal insisted upon nothing less than an abandonment of the expedition, and the return of Alvarado whence he came. This was finally assented to on the part of Moscoso and Cladera, with the condition that one hundred and twenty thousand castellanos should be paid to the Adelantado, in recompense for the ships, outfit, and men to be left,—terms to which Almagro acceded.

Pizarro was well pleased with the treaty; but some unquiet spirits sought to awaken distrust of Almagro in his mind, with fears of the consequences of the friendship said to exist between him and Alvarado, that had for its object to unseat him in his government. From this time begin the factions and conflicts of the Pizarros and Almagros. Some of the best minded of their companions sought to restrain them, but only with occasional or momentary success. The conduct of the brothers of Pizarro was found insufferable to many, and the arrogance of Hernando was regarded to be as lofty as his aspirations. Soto prominently attempted to quiet the gathering storm, and, failing of success, prepared to remove from the scene.

Almagro made ready to accomplish the conquest of Chili, and Soto had the promise of the post of lieutenant-general; but, dissatisfied, he withdrew at length from the enterprise. This being the condition of affairs, in the year 1535, some gentlemen and soldiers, finding themselves in good circumstances of wealth, thought to fix a limit to their desires and return to their native land, warned by the rising passions among the conquerors. The love of riches, having been satisfied, was giving way to ambition of rule; and the Indian borla, now torn in fragments, no longer held them in brotherhood, as before, for safety, wealth, and renown.

In Spain Soto appears to have resided in Xeréz, and at court, probably, he met the widow of Pedrárias, with whom he had been acquainted in Nicaragua, first cousin to the celebrated Marchioness of Moya, lady of honour and life-long favourite of Ysabel of Castilla.

With her he contracted for espousals with her daughter, named, after her, Ysabel de Bobadilla, and sent her in marriage-pledge six thousand ducats. He became a knight of the Order of Santiago. Being now in the vigour of life, he sought for a government beyond sea. His first desire was to obtain one over the country extending from Panamá to San Miguel; though he deemed that the most sterile and unprofitable territory in the New World, yet he supposed the unknown region lying to the east of Quito—the country of Canela—might be made available; and if that concession could not be secured, then he desired to have the *Adelantamiento* of Nicaragua, with the privilege of sailing west towards the Spice Islands of the South Sea, and the right to one-tenth of whatever he should discover in that direction, at his own cost.

About this time, the news of the utter loss of the armament which set out to conquer Florida having arrived, Soto obtained the grant of that country, from the River Palmas eastwardly to the "Island of Florida," once ceded to Narvaez, with the Tierra-Nueva adjoining it on the ocean, before conferred on Ayllón, having no specific limit to the northward, but geographically bounded by the Land of Estevan Gomez. Within four years from the time of landing in the country, he was to receive two hundred leagues of shore, to be selected by him from what he might conquer and colonize, where he should be Governor and Captain-General, with the dignity of Adelantado for life, and High-Sheriff in perpetuity to his heirs. Within that territory he had the right to select twelve leagues square by the sea for his possession. Fifty negro slaves, of which one-third should be female, were permitted to be taken to Cuba, and, also by him, other fifty to Florida. If a king or cacique should be taken, the Adelantado was to receive one-seventh part from his ransom and the spoil of his goods; but if he should be killed in any manner, either before or after capture, the King should receive one-half, after deducting the fifth due to the Crown. These terms appear to have been imposed to restrain atrocities such as were committed by the conquerors on the native sovereigns of México, Mechoacán, and Perú.

The better to command and afford whatever might be necessary in the progress of this great undertaking, Soto was made Governor of Cuba during the pleasure of the sovereign. In consequence, he subsequently took up stock-farms on the Island, whence to draw supplies, whether as invader or colonist—a feature in the plan of subjugation laid down with breadth to be carried out by the suggestions of experience, sustained by the General's individual resources.

It is to the testament of Soto that we are to look for more of his character than can be learned from those who have written rather of his actions than of his mind, or the kindliness of his heart. The endowments bespeak his pride, his piety, religious feeling, and magnificence: the bequests mark the munificence with which it was in his power to bestow. Portions were set apart for five maids of his wife, dependent on her kind favour; and from a source in perpetual rents, to be bought by amounts aloof from the hazards of his adventure, provision is made for marrying annually three destitute orphans, daughters of persons of his line to the fifth degree, "the poorest that can be found;" and if there should be none such, then those of noble ancestry in the same condition, "the poorest in the City of Xeréz." An equal rental is bequeathed to Doña Ysabel, and, when it can no longer avail her, to the marriage yearly of other damsels, in number and under circumstances like the first. The body of his mother, his own tomb and private chapel, his friends and dependents, with the repose of souls, are provided for.

The history of the life of Hernando de Soto while in Spain, as a man of fame and fortune, as well as of his subsequent career in America, may be read in the following account of his attempted conquest. The author, although a foreigner, has no more than any other writer allowed a word to fall from his pen disrespectful of the Adelantado. By him was he seen first in a position of affluence and splendor; then as he accompanied him thrice through the circle of the seasons, amid privations, anxieties, and bitter disappointment. If, in the course of that protracted march over the soil of our country, Soto should in instances be thought cruel,—as there were acts of severity he deemed necessary for "pacification," and the safety of his command,—they are not in excess of those of other captains of that age; nor must it be forgotten that the people of his country were as refined, enlightened, and humane as any of Europe.

D

By those who knew him was he deemed brave, prudent, and magnanimous. The estate which beckoned to his ambition was in
extent a principality, the title accessory, a marquisate. These, in
the prime of life, with still greater riches and wider honours than
he possessed, appeared to sway temptingly towards his hand.

Such is an imperfect sketch of some of the more conspicuous
passages in the life of Hernando de Soto, Captain in Nicaragua,
Lieutenant-General in the conquest of Peru, Governor of Cuba, and
Adelantado of Florida.

PROEM.

This book is a translation of the original Portuguese *Relaçam verdadeira dos trabalhos q̄ ho gouernador dõ Fernãdo de souto e certos fidalgos portugueses passarom no descubrimēto da prouincia da Frolida. Agora nouamēte feita per hũ fidalgo Deluas,* printed at Evora in the year 1557, copies of which are very rare. Two translations into English have been published at London: the earlier, made by Richard Hakluyt, was first printed in 1609, with the title, "Virginia richly valued, by the description of the mainland of Florida, her next neighbour:" the later was printed in 1686, one year after the first edition in French was issued, of which it is a translation. The book was also printed in Dutch, in 1706.

The author of the *Relaçam* is unknown. At the time of making the original publication, as appears from the printer's notice, he was yet living. No doubt, he was one of the eight Portuguese gentlemen, spoken of in the text, who went from Elvas to join Soto at Sevilla, three of whom lost their lives in Florida. In the order they are mentioned, it is perhaps worth the remark, as possibly indicating the writer, that two named Fernandez are placed last; first Benito, who was drowned near Achese, then Alvaro, a survivor.

The narrative, as an early record of the country, and condition of the inhabitants, merits attention and study. The facts are stated with clearness and evident care. It is likewise an outward picture of affairs as they stood in the camp, or appeared from the marquee of the Adelantado. Some hints of their inner working, up to the time of the death of Soto, may be learned from the *Historia General y Natural de las Indias.* Documents of the age, now published, attest the exactness of many statements, and time simply has unveiled the truthfulness of others.

The digression, giving a history of Ortiz among the Indians from whom he fled, probably the Calosa, a people living about the Capes of Florida at the earliest day,—to the country of Outina, as appears from some trace of the language of the people among whom the Spaniards landed, speaking the Timuqua tongue—is a happy union of incidents in native life, customs, and superstition.

The speeches of the Indians, however clothed in words, are after the Indian manner of thought, as they were probably rendered into Spanish by the ability of the Andaluz, long a captive among them. In more simple language, the ideas would have been brought nigher to nature.

That this account, fraught with instructive incident, has come to us untouched from the hand that wrote it, is matter for gratulation; since in two chronicles we have to lament over ruins that mark as many narratives to have existed, possessing a scope and interest not inferior to the present one. The production of Rodrigo Rangel, the private secretary of the Adelantado, afforded the material for the chapters, now incomplete, of Oviedo; and an account, composed by a captain who remained in America,—for which pictures in colours of the battle-scenes with the Indians of Florida were at one time in the cabinet of Philip II.—was the source whence Herrera drew supplies; while the dry and brief itinerary of Biedma has escaped to us undisturbed in the same official repository—the Council of the Indias. The *Florida* of the Ynca, on the same subject, belongs less to history than to romance.

To avoid confusion and error as to persons, the names of the Spaniards are given in the translation spelled in their own language, such as Soto and Añasco, instead of Souto and Dambusco. On the other hand, the reader is entitled to find the variety in the orthography of Indian proper names preserved in their irregularity, for observation and the benefit of criticism.

TRUE RELATION

OF THE

VICISSITUDES THAT ATTENDED

THE

GOVERNOR DON HERNANDO DE SOTO

AND SOME

NOBLES OF PORTUGAL IN THE DISCOVERY

OF THE

PROVINCE OF FLORIDA,

NOW JUST GIVEN BY A

FIDALGO OF ELVAS.

VIEWED BY THE LORD INQUISITOR.

FERNANDO DA SILVEIRA,

Senhor da Serzedas, great Poet and very Illustrious, respecting
the Material of this Book, and in Praise of the Author.

———————— · — ——

EPIGRAM.

He who would see the New World,
The Golden Pole,* the second,
Other seas, other lands,
Achievements great, and wars,
And such things attempted
As alarm and give pleasure,
Strike terror and lend delight;—
Read of the author this pleasing story,
Where nothing fabulous is told,
All worthy of being esteemed,
Read, considered, used.

———— ——— ——— ·· ·· ——— — ——

* We inhabit the Northern Arctic Pole, and that people inhabit the Southern An-
tarctic Pole. Golden Pole is used, because that region is rich.

FINIS

ANDRÉ DE BURGOS

ARISTOTLE writes that all, or at least most men, are given or prone to look at and listen to novelties, especially when they are of foreign or remote countries. These things, he says, enliven the heavy while they give recreation to delicate and subtile minds, that propensity moving men not only to see and hear, but, if possible, to take part in occurrences. This desire exists in the Lusitanians more than in any other people,—for two reasons: the one, because they are very ingenious and warlike; the other, because they are by nature great navigators, having discovered more land, with wider sailing, than all the nations of the earth beside. So, it appearing to me that I could do some little service to those who should read this book, I resolved to imprint it, assured, beyond its being in the Portuguese, that it is composed by a native, and likewise because citizens of Elvas took part in the discovery, as the narrative will itself disclose. What he has written I undoubtingly credit: he tells no tales, nor speaks of fabulous things; and we may believe that the author—having no interest in the matter—would not swerve from truth. We have his assurance besides, that all he has set down passed before him. Should the language, by chance, appear to you careless, lay not the fault on me; I imprint and do not write. God be your protector.

FLORIDA,
WITH THE MARCH OF
HERNANDO DE SOTO
1539 - 1544.
COMPILED BY J. G. SHEA ESQ.
Engraved for the BRADFORD CLUB New York 1860.

DISCOVERY OF FLORIDA.

RELATION OF THE TOILS AND HARDSHIPS THAT ATTENDED
DON HERNANDO DE SOTO, GOVERNOR OF FLORIDA, IN THE
CONQUEST OF THAT COUNTRY; IN WHICH IS SET FORTH
WHO HE WAS, AND ALSO WHO WERE OTHERS WITH HIM;
CONTAINING SOME ACCOUNT OF THE PECULIARITIES AND
DIVERSITIES OF THE COUNTRY, OF ALL THAT THEY SAW
AND OF WHAT BEFELL THEM.

CHAPTER I.

WHO SOTO WAS, AND HOW HE CAME TO GET THE GOVERN-MENT OF FLORIDA.

HERNANDO DE SOTO was the son of an esquire of Xeréz
de Badajóz, and went to the Indias of the Ocean Sea,
belonging to Castilla, at the time Pedrárias Dávila was
the Governor. He had nothing more than blade and
buckler: for his courage and good qualities Pedrárias
appointed him to be captain of a troop of horse, and he
went by his order with Hernando Pizarro to conquer
Peru. According to the report of many persons who
were there, he distinguished himself over all the captains
and principal personages present, not only at the seizure
of Atabalipa, lord of Peru, and in carrying the City of

2

Cuzco, but at all other places wheresoever he went and
found resistance. Hence, apart from his share in the
treasure of Atabalipa, he got a good amount, bringing
together in time, from portions falling to his lot, one
hundred and eighty thousand cruzados, which he brought
with him to Spain. Of this the Emperor borrowed a
part, which was paid; six hundred thousand reaes in
duties on the silks of Granada, and the rest at the Casa
de Contratacion.

In Sevilla, Soto employed a superintendent of household, an usher, pages, equerry, chamberlain, footmen, and
all the other servants requisite for the establishment of a
gentleman. Thence he went to Court, and while there
was accompanied by Juan de Añasco of Sevilla, Luis
Moscoso de Alvarado, Nuño de Tobár, and Juan Rodriguez Lobillo. All, except Añasco, came with him from
Peru; and each brought fourteen or fifteen thousand
cruzados. They went well and costly apparelled; and
Soto, although by nature not profuse, as it was the first
time he was to show himself at Court, spent largely,
and went about closely attended by those I have named,
by his dependents, and by many others who there came
about him. He married Doña Ysabel de Bobadilla,
daughter of Pedrárias Dávila, Connt of Puñonrostro.
The Emperor made him Governor of the Island of Cuba
and Adelantado of Florida, with title of Marquis to a
certain part of the territory he should conquer.

CHAPTER II.

How Cabeça de Vaca arrived at Court, and gave account of the country of Florida; and of the persons who assembled at Sevilla to accompany Don Hernando de Soto.

After Don Hernando had obtained the concession, a fidalgo arrived at Court from the Indias, Cabeça de Vaca by name, who had been in Florida with Narvaez; and he stated how he with four others had escaped, taking the way to New Spain; that the Governor had been lost in the sea, and the rest were all dead. He brought with him a written relation of adventures, which said in some places: Here I have seen this; and the rest which I saw I leave to confer of with His Majesty: generally, however, he described the poverty of the country, and spoke of the hardships he had undergone. Some of his kinsfolk, desirous of going to the Indias, strongly urged him to tell them whether he had seen any rich country in Florida or not; but he told them that he could not do so: because he and another (by name Orantes, who had remained in New Spain with the purpose of returning into Florida) had sworn not to divulge certain things which they had seen, lest some one might beg the government in advance of them, for which he had come to

Spain; nevertheless, he gave them to understand that it
was the richest country in the world.

Don Hernando de Soto was desirous that Cabeça de
Vaca should go with him, and made him favorable pro-
posals; but after they had come upon terms they disa-
greed, because the Adelantado would not give the money
requisite to pay for a ship that the other had bought.
Baltasar de Gallegos and Cristóbal de Espindola told
Cabeça de Vaca, their kinsman, that as they had made
up their minds to go to Florida, in consequence of what
he had told them, they besought him to counsel them;
to which he replied, that the reason he did not go was
because he hoped to receive another government, being
reluctant to march under the standard of another; that he
had himself come to solicit the conquest of Florida, and
though he found it had already been granted to Don
Hernando de Soto, yet, on account of his oath, he could
not divulge what they desired to know; nevertheless, he
would advise them to sell their estates and go,—that in so
doing they would act wisely.

As soon as Cabeça de Vaca had an opportunity he
spoke with the Emperor; and gave him an account of all
that he had gone through with, seen, and could by any
means ascertain. Of this relation, made by word of
mouth, the Marquis of Astorga was informed. He determined at once to send his brother, Don Antonio
Osorio; and with him Francisco and Garcia Osorio, two
of his kinsmen, also made ready to go. Don Antonio
disposed of sixty thousand reaes inconie that he received of the Church, and Francisco of a village of vas-

sals he owned in Campos. They joined the Adelantado at Sevilla, as did also Nuño de Tobár, Luis de Moscoso, and Juan Rodriguez Lobillo. Moscoso took two brothers; there went likewise Don Carlos, who had married the Governor's niece, and he carried her with him. From Badajóz went Pedro Calderon, and three kinsmen of the Adelantado: Arias Tinoco, Alonso Romo, and Diego Tinoco.

As Luis de Moscoso passed through Elvas, André de Vasconcelos spoke with him, and requested him to speak to Don Hernando de Soto in his behalf; and he gave him warrants, issued by the Marquis of Vilareal, conferring on him the captaincy of Ceuta, that he might show them; which when the Adelantado saw, and had informed himself of who he was, he wrote to him that he would favour him in and through all, and would give him a command in Florida. From Elvas went André de Vasconcelos, Fernan Pegado, Antonio Martinez Segurado, Men Royz Pereyra, Ioam Cordeiro, Estevan Pegado, Bento Fernandez, Alvaro Fernandez; and from Salamanca, Jaen, Valencia, Albuquerque, and other parts of Spain, assembled many persons of noble extraction in Sevilla; so much so that many men of good condition, who had sold their lands, remained behind in Sanlúcar for want of shipping, when for known countries and rich it was usual to lack men: and the cause of this was what Cabeça de Vaca had told the Emperor, and given persons to understand who conversed with him respecting that country. He went for Governor to Rio de la Plata, but his kinsmen followed Soto.

Baltasar de Gallegos received the appointment of chief Castellan, and took with him his wife. He sold houses, vineyards, a rent of wheat, and ninety geiras of olive-field in the Xarafe of Sevilla. There went also many other persons of mark. The offices, being desired of many, were sought through powerful influence: the place of Factor was held by Antonio de Biedma, that of Comptroller by Juan de Añasco, and that of Treasurer by Juan Gaytan, nephew of the Cardinal of Ciguenza.

CHAPTER III.

How the Portugues went to Sevilla and thence to Sanlúcar; and how the Captains were appointed over the Ships, and the People distributed among them.

The Portugues left Elvas the 15th day of January, and came to Sevilla on the vespers of Saint Sebastian. They went to the residence of the Governor; and entering the court, over which were some galleries in which he stood, he came down and met them at the foot of the stairs, whence they returned with him; and he ordered chairs to be brought, in which they might be seated. André de Vasconcelos told him who he was, and who the others were; that they had all come to go with him and aid in his enterprise. The Adelantado thanked him, and appeared well pleased with their coming and proffer. The table being already laid, he invited them to sit down; and, while at dinner, he directed his majordomo to find lodgings for them near his house.

From Sevilla the Governor went to Sanlúcar, with all the people that were to go. He commanded a muster to be made, to which the Portugues turned out in polished armor, and the Castilians very showily, in silk over silk, pinked and slashed. As such luxury did not appear to him becoming on such occasion, he ordered a review to be called for the next day, when every man should appear with his arms; to which the Portugues came as at first; and the Governor set them in order near the standard borne by his ensign. The greater number of the Castilians were in very sorry and rusty shirts of mail; all wore steel caps or helmets, but had very poor lances. Some of them sought to get among the Portugues. Those that Soto liked and accepted of were passed, counted, and enlisted; six hundred men in all followed him to Florida. He had bought seven ships; and the necessary subsistence was already on board. He appointed captains, delivering to each of them his ship, with a roll of the people he was to take with him.

CHAPTER IIII.

How the Adelantado with his People left Spain, going to the Canary Islands, and afterward arrived in the Antillas.

In the month of April, of the year 1538 of the Christian era, the Adelantado delivered the vessels to their several captains, took for himself a new ship, fast of sail, and gave another to André de Vasconcelos, in which the Portugues were to go. He passed over the bar of Sanlúcar on Sunday, the morning of Saint Lazarus, with great festivity, commanding the trumpets to be sounded and many charges of artillery to be fired. With a favourable wind he sailed four days, when it lulled, the calms continuing for eight days, with such rolling sea that the ships made no headway.

The fifteenth day after our departure we came to Gomera, one of the Canaries, on Easter Sunday, in the morning. The Governor of the Island was apparelled all in white, cloak, jerkin, hose, shoes, and cap, so that he looked like a governor of Gypsies. He received the Adelantado with much pleasure, lodging him well and the rest with him gratuitously. To Doña Ysabel he gave a natural daughter of his to be her waiting-maid. For our money we got abundant provision of bread, wine,

3

and meats, bringing off with us what was needful for the ships. Sunday following, eight days after arrival, we took our departure.

On Pentecost we came into the harbour of the City of Santiago, in Cuba of the Antillas. Directly a gentleman of the town sent to the seaside a splendid roan horse, well caparisoned, for the Governor to mount, and a mule for his wife; and all the horsemen and footmen in town at the time came out to receive him at the landing. He was well lodged, attentively visited and served by all the citizens. Quarters were furnished to every one without cost. Those who wished to go into the country were divided among the farm-houses, into squads of four and six persons, according to the several ability of the owners, who provided them with food.

CHAPTER V.

Of the Inhabitants there are in the City of Santiago
and other Towns of the Island,—the Character of
the Soil and of the Fruit.

The City of Santiago consists of about eighty spacious
and well-contrived dwellings. Some are built of stone
and lime, covered with tiles: the greater part have the
sides of board and the roofs of dried grass. There are
extensive country seats, and on them many trees, which
differ from those of Spain. The fig-tree bears fruit as big
as the fist, yellow within and of little flavour: another
tree with a delicious fruit, called anane, is of the shape
and size of a small pine-apple, the skin of which being
taken off, the pulp appears like a piece of curd. On the
farms about in the country are other larger pines, of
very agreeable and high flavour, produced on low trees
that look like the aloe. Another tree yields a fruit
called mamei, the size of a peach, by the islanders more
esteemed than any other in the country. The guayaba
is in the form of a filbert, and is the size of a fig. There
is a tree, which is a stalk without any branch, the height
of a lance, each leaf the length of a javelin, the fruit of
the size and form of a cucumber, the bunch having
twenty or thirty of them, with which the tree goes on
bending down more and more as they grow: they are
called plantanos in that country, are of good flavour, and

will ripen after they are gathered, although they are
better when they mature on the tree. The stalks yield
fruit but once, when they are cut down, and others, which
spring up at the butt, bear in the coming year. There is
another fruit called batata, the subsistence of a multitude
of people, principally slaves, and now grows in the Island
of Terceira, belonging to this kingdom of Portugal. It is
produced in the earth, and looks like the ynhame, with
nearly the taste of chestnut. The bread of the country
is made from a root that looks like the batata, the stalk
of which is like alder. The ground for planting is prepared in hillocks; into each are laid four or five stalks, and
a year and a half after they have been set the crop is fit
to be dug. Should any one, mistaking the root for batata,
eat any of it, he is in imminent danger; as experience
has shown, in the case of a soldier, who died instantly
from swallowing a very little. The roots being peeled
and crushed, they are squeezed in a sort of press; the
juice that flows has an offensive smell; the bread is of
little taste and less nourishment. The fruit from Spain
are figs and oranges, which are produced the year round,
the soil being very rich and fertile.

There are numerous cattle and horses in the country,
which find fresh grass at all seasons. From the many
wild cows and hogs, the inhabitants everywhere are abundantly supplied with meat. Out of the towns are many
fruits wild over the country; and, as it sometimes hap-
pens, when a Christian misses his way and is lost for fifteen or twenty days, because of the many paths through
the thick woods made by the herds traversing to and fro,

he will live on fruit and on wild cabbage, there being many and large palm-trees everywhere which yield nothing else available beside.

The Island of Cuba is three hundred leagues long from east to southeast, and in places thirty, in others forty leagues from north to south. There are six towns of Christians, which are, Santiago, Baracoa, the Báyamo, Puerto Príncipe, Sancti Spíritus, and Havana. They each have between thirty and forty householders, except Santiago and Havana, which have some seventy or eighty dwellings apiece. The towns have all a chaplain to hear confession, and a church in which to say mass. In Santiago is a monastery of the order of Saint Francis; it has few friars, though well supported by tithes, as the country is rich. The Church of Santiago is endowed, has a cura, a prebend, and many priests, as it is the church of the city which is the metropolis.

Although the earth contains much gold, there are few slaves to seek it, many having destroyed themselves because of the hard usage they receive from the Christians in the mines. The overseer of Vasco Porcallo, a resident of the Island, having understood that his slaves intended to hang themselves, went with a cudgel in his hand and waited for them in the place at which they were to meet, where he told them that they could do nothing, nor think of any thing, that he did not know beforehand; that he had come to hang himself with them, to the end that if he gave them a bad life in this world, a worse would he give them in that to come. This caused them to alter their purpose and return to obedience.

CHAPTER VI.

How the Governor sent Doña Ysabel with the
Ships from Santiago to Havana, while he with
some of the Men went thither by Land.

The Governor sent Don Carlos with the ships, in
company with Doña Ysabel, to tarry for him at Havana,
a port in the eastern end of the Island, one hundred and
eighty leagues from Santiago. He and those that remained, having bought horses, set out on their journey,
and at the end of twenty-five leagues came to Báyamo,
the first town. They were lodged, as they arrived, in
parties of four and six, where their food was given to
them; and nothing was paid for any other thing than
maize for the beasts; because the Governor at each town
assessed tax on the tribute paid, and the labour done, by
the Indians.

A deep river runs near Báyamo, larger than the
Guadiana, called Tanto. The monstrous alligators do
harm in it sometimes to the Indians and animals in the
crossing. In all the country there are no wolves, foxes,
bears, lions, nor tigers: there are dogs in the woods,
which have run wild from the houses, that feed upon the
swine: there are snakes, the size of a man's thigh, and
even bigger; but they are very sluggish and do no kind

of injury. From that town to Puerto Principe there are
fifty leagues. The roads throughout the Island are made
by cutting out the undergrowth, which if neglected to be
gone over, though only for a single year, the shrubs
spring up in such manner that the ways disappear: and
so numerous likewise are the paths made by cattle, that
no one can travel without an Indian of the country for a
guide, there being everywhere high and thick woods.

From Puerto Principe the Governor went by sea in a
canoe to the estate of Vasco Porcallo, near the coast, to
get news of Doña Ysabel, who, at the time, although
not then known, was in a situation of distress, the ships
having parted company, two of them being driven in
sight of the coast of Florida, and all on board were suffering for lack of water and subsistence. The storm over,
and the vessels come together, not knowing where they
had been tossed, Cape San Antonio was descried, an uninhabited part of the Island, where they got water; and at the
end of forty days from the time of leaving Santiago, they
arrived at Havana. The Governor presently received
the news and hastened to meet Doña Ysabel. The troops
that went by land, one hundred and fifty mounted men in
number, not to be burdensome upon the Islanders, were
divided into two squadrons, and marched to Sancti Spiritus, sixty leagues from Puerto Principe. The victual
they carried was the caçabe bread I have spoken of, the
nature of which is such that it directly dissolves from
moisture; whence it happened that some ate meat and
no bread for many days. They took dogs with them,
and a man of the country, who hunted as they journeyed,

and who killed the hogs at night found further necessary
for provision where they stopped; so that they had abundant supply both of beef and pork. They found immense
annoyance from mosquitos, particularly in a lake called Bog
of Pia, which they had much ado in crossing between mid-
day and dark, it being more than half a league over, full
half a bow-shot of the distance swimming, and all the rest of
the way the water waist deep, having clams on the bottom that sorely cut the feet, for not a boot nor shoe sole
was left entire at half way. The clothing and saddles
were floated over in baskets of palm-leaf. In this time
the insects came in great numbers and settled on the
person where exposed, their bite raising lumps that
smarted keenly, a single blow with the hand sufficing to
kill so many that the blood would run over the arms and
body. There was little rest at night, as happened also
afterwards at like seasons and places.

They came to Sancti Spiritus, a town of thirty houses,
near which passes a little river. The grounds are very
fertile and pleasant, abundant in good oranges, citrons,
and native fruit. Here one half the people were lodged;
the other half went on twenty-five leagues farther, to a
town of fifteen or twenty householders, called Trinidad.
There is a hospital for the poor, the only one in the
Island. They say the town was once the largest of any;
and that before the Christians came into the country a
ship sailing along the coast had in her a very sick man,
who begged to be set on shore, which the captain directly ordered, and the vessel kept on her way. The
inhabitants, finding him where he had been left, on that

shore which had never yet been hunted up by Christians, carried him home, and took care of him until he was well. The Chief of the town gave him a daughter; and being at war with the country round about, through the prowess and exertion of the Christian he subdued and reduced to his control all the people of Cuba. A long time after, when Diego Velasquez went to conquer the Island, whence he made the discovery of New Spain, this man, then among the natives, brought them, by his management, to obedience, and put them under the rule of that Governor.

From Trinidad they travelled a distance of eighty leagues without a town, and arrived at Havana in the end of March. They found the Governor there, and the rest of the people who had come with him from Spain. He sent Juan de Añasco in a caravel, with two pinnaces and fifty men, to explore the harbour in Florida, who brought back two Indians taken on the coast. In consequence, as much because of the necessity of having them for guides and interpreters, as because they said, by signs, that there was much gold in Florida, the Governor and all the company were greatly rejoiced, and longed for the hour of departure—that land appearing to them to be the richest of any which until then had been discovered.

CHAPTER VII.

How we left Havana and came to Florida, and
what other Matters took place.

BEFORE our departure, the Governor deprived Nuño
de Tobár of the rank of Captain-General, and conferred it
on a resident of Cuba, Vasco Porcallo de Figueroa, which
caused the vessels to be well provisioned, he giving a great
many hogs and loads of caçabe bread. That was done
because Nuño de Tobár had made love to Doña Ysabel's
waiting-maid, daughter of the Governor of Gomera; and
though he had lost his place, yet, to return to Soto's
favour, for she was with child by him, he took her to wife
and went to Florida. Doña Ysabel remained, and with
her the wife of Don Carlos, of Baltasar de Gallegos, and
of Nuño de Tobár. The Governor left, as his lieutenant
over the Island, Juan de Rojas, a fidalgo of Havana.

On Sunday, the 18th day of May, in the year 1539,
the Adelantado sailed from Havana with a fleet of nine
vessels, five of them ships, two caravels, two pinnaces;
and he ran seven days with favourable weather. On the
25th of the month, being the festival of Espiritu Santo,
the land was seen, and anchor cast a league from shore,
because of the shoals. On Friday, the 30th, the army
landed in Florida, two leagues from the town of an

Indian chief named Ucita. Two hundred and thirteen
horses were set on shore, to unburthen the ships, that
they should draw the less water; the seamen only remained on board, who going up every day a little with the
tide, the end of eight days brought them near to the town.

So soon as the people were come to land, the camp
was pitched on the sea-side, nigh the bay, which goes up
close to the town. Presently the Captain-General, Vasco
Porcallo, taking seven horsemen with him, beat up the
country half a league about, and discovered six Indians,
who tried to resist him with arrows, the weapons they
are accustomed to use. The horsemen killed two, and
the four others escaped, the country being obstructed
by bushes and ponds, in which the horses bogged and
fell, with their riders, of weakness from the voyage. At
night the Governor, with a hundred men in the pinnaces,
came upon a deserted town; for, so soon as the Christians
appeared in sight of land, they were descried, and all
along on the coast many smokes were seen to rise, which
the Indians make to warn one another. The next day,
Luis de Moscoso, master of the camp, set the men in
order. The horsemen he put in three squadrons—the
vanguard, battalion, and rearward; and thus they marched
that day and the next, compassing great creeks which
run up from the bay; and on the first of June, being
Trinity Sunday, they arrived at the town of Ucita, where
the Governor tarried.

The town was of seven or eight houses, built of timber, and covered with palm-leaves. The Chief's house
stood near the beach, upon a very high mount made by

hand for defence; at the other end of the town was a
temple, on the top of which perched a wooden fowl with
gilded eyes, and within were found some pearls of small
value, injured by fire, such as the Indians pierce for
beads, much esteeming them, and string to wear about
the neck and wrists. The Governor lodged in the house
of the Chief, and with him Vasco Porcallo and Luis de
Moscoso; in other houses, midway in the town, was
lodged the Chief Castellan, Baltasar de Gallegos, where
were set apart the provisions brought in the vessels.
The rest of the dwellings, with the temple, were thrown
down, and every mess of three or four soldiers made a
cabin, wherein they lodged. The ground about was very
fenny, and encumbered with dense thicket and high trees.
The Governor ordered the woods to be felled the distance
of a crossbow-shot around the place, that the horses might
run, and the Christians have the advantage, should the
Indians make an attack at night. In the paths, and at
proper points, sentinels of foot-soldiers were set in couples, who watched by turns; the horsemen, going the
rounds, were ready to support them should there be an
alarm.

The Governor made four captains of horsemen and
two of footmen: those of the horse were André de Vasconcelos, Pedro Calderon of Badajóz, and the two Carde-
ñosas his kinsmen (Arias Tinoco and Alfonso Romo),
also natives of Badajóz; those of the foot were Francisco
Maldonado of Salamanca, and Juan Rodriguez Lobillo.
While we were in this town of Ucita, the Indians which
Juan de Añasco had taken on that coast, and were with

the Governor as guides and interpreters, through the carelessness of two men who had charge of them, got away one night. For this the Governor felt very sorry, as did every one else; for some excursions had already been made, and no Indians could be taken, the country being of very high and thick woods, and in many places was marshy.

CHAPTER VIII.

Of some Inroads that were made, and how a Christian was found who had been a long time in the
possession of a Cacique.

From the town of Ucita the Governor sent the Chief
Castellan, Baltasar de Gallegos, into the country, with
forty horsemen and eighty footmen, to procure an Indian
if possible. In another direction he also sent, for the
same purpose, Captain Juan Rodriguez Lobillo, with fifty
infantry: the greater part were of sword and buckler;
the remainder were crossbow and gun men. The command of Lobillo marched over a swampy land, where
horses could not travel; and, half a league from camp,
came upon some huts near a river. The people in them
plunged into the water; nevertheless, four women were
secured; and twenty warriors, who attacked our people,
so pressed us that we were forced to retire into camp.

The Indians are exceedingly ready with their weapons,
and so warlike and nimble, that they have no fear of footmen; for if these charge them they flee, and when they
turn their backs they are presently upon them. They
avoid nothing more easily than the flight of an arrow.
They never remain quiet, but are continually running,
traversing from place to place, so that neither crossbow

nor arquebuse can be aimed at them. Before a Christian
can make a single shot with either, an Indian will discharge three or four arrows; and he seldom misses of his
object. Where the arrow meets with no armour, it pierces
as deeply as the shaft from a crossbow. Their bows are
very perfect; the arrows are made of certain canes, like
reeds, very heavy, and so stiff that one of them, when
sharpened, will pass through a target. Some are pointed
with the bone of a fish, sharp and like a chisel; others
with some stone like a point of diamond: of such the
greater number, when they strike upon armour, break at
the place the parts are put together; those of cane split,
and will enter a shirt of mail, doing more injury than
when armed.

Juan Rodriguez Lobillo got back to camp with six
men wounded, of whom one died, and he brought with him
the four women taken in the huts, or cabins. When Baltasar de Gallegos came into the open field, he discovered
ten or eleven Indians, among whom was a Christian,
naked and sun-burnt, his arms tattooed after their manner, and he in no respect differing from them. As soon
as the horsemen came in sight, they ran upon the Indians,
who fled, hiding themselves in a thicket, though not before two or three of them were overtaken and wounded.
The Christian, seeing a horseman coming upon him with
a lance, began to cry out: "Do not kill me, cavalier; I
am a Christian! Do not slay these people; they have
given me my life!" Directly he called to the Indians,
putting them out of fear, when they left the wood
and came to him. The horsemen took up the Chris-

tian and Indians behind them on their beasts, and, greatly rejoicing, got back to the Governor at nightfall. When he and the rest who had remained in camp heard the news, they were no less pleased than the others.

CHAPTER IX.

How the Christian came to the Land of Florida, who he was, and of what passed at his Interview with the Governor.

The name of the Christian was Juan Ortiz, a native of Sevilla, and of noble parentage. He had been twelve years among the Indians, having gone into the country with Pánphilo de Narvaez, and returned in the ships to the Island of Cuba, where the wife of the Governor remained; whence, by her command, he went back to Florida, with some twenty or thirty others, in a pinnace; and coming to the port in sight of the town, they saw a cane sticking upright in the ground, with a split in the top, holding a letter, which they supposed the Governor had left there, to give information of himself before marching into the interior. They asked it, to be given to them, of four or five Indians walking along the beach, who, by signs, bade them come to land for it, which Ortiz and another did, though contrary to the wishes of the others. No sooner had they got on shore, when many natives came out of the houses, and, drawing near, held them in such way that they could not escape. One, who would have defended himself, they slew on the spot; the other they seized by the hands, and took him to Ucita,

their chief. The people in the pinnace, unwilling to
land, kept along the coast and returned to Cuba.

By command of Ucita, Juan Ortiz was bound hand
and foot to four stakes, and laid upon scaffolding, beneath
which a fire was kindled, that he might be burned; but a
daughter of the Chief entreated that he might be spared.
Though one Christian, she said, might do no good, cer-
tainly he could do no harm, and it would be an honour to
have one for a captive; to which the father acceded,
directing the injuries to be healed. When Ortiz got
well, he was put to watching a temple, that the wolves,
in the night-time, might not carry off the dead there,
which charge he took in hand, having commended himself to God. One night they snatched away from him
the body of a little child, son of a principal man; and,
going after them, he threw a dart at the wolf that was
escaping, which, feeling itself wounded, let go its hold,
and went off to die; and he returned, without knowing
what he had done in the dark. In the morning, finding
the body of the little boy gone, he became very sober;
and Ucita, when he heard what had happened, determined he should be killed; but having sent on the trail
which Ortiz pointed out as that the wolves had made, the
body of the child was found, and a little farther on a
dead wolf; at which circumstance the Chief became well
pleased with the Christian, and satisfied with the guard
he had kept, ever after taking much notice of him.

Three years having gone by since he had fallen into
the hands of this Chief, there came another, named Mocoço, living two days' journey distant from that port, and

burnt the town, when Ucita fled to one he had in another
seaport, whereby Ortiz lost his occupation, and with it
the favour of his master. The Indians are worshippers of
the Devil, and it is their custom to make sacrifices of the
blood and bodies of their people, or of those of any other
they can come by; and they affirm, too, that when he
would have them make an offering, he speaks, telling
them that he is athirst, and that they must sacrifice to
him. The girl who had delivered Ortiz from the fire,
told him how her father had the mind to sacrifice him
the next day, and that he must flee to Mococo, who she
knew would receive him with regard, as she had heard
that he had asked for him, and said he would like to see
him: and as he knew not the way, she went half a league
out of town with him at dark, to put him on the road,
returning early so as not to be missed.

Ortiz travelled all night, and in the morning came to
a river, the boundary of the territory of Mococo, where
he discovered two men fishing. As this people were at
war with those of Ucita, and their languages different, he
did not know how he should be able to tell them who he
was, and why he came, or make other explanation, that
they might not kill him as one of the enemy. It was
not, however, until he had come up to where their arms
were placed that he was discovered, when they fled towards the town; and though he called out to them to
wait, that he would do them no injury, they only ran the
faster for not understanding him. As they arrived, shouting, many Indians came out of the town, and began surrounding, in order to shoot him with their arrows, when

he, finding himself pressed, took shelter behind trees, crying aloud that he was a Christian fled from Ucita, come to visit and serve Mocoço. At the moment, it pleased God that an Indian should come up, who, speaking the language, understood him and quieted the others, telling them what was said. Three or four ran to carry the news, when the Cacique, much gratified, came a quarter of a league on the way to receive him. He caused the Christian immediately to swear to him, according to the custom of his country, that he would not leave him for any other master; and, in return, he promised to show him much honour, and if at any time Christians should come to that land, he would let him go freely, and give him his permission to return to them, pledging his oath to this after the Indian usage.

Three years from that time, some people fishing out at sea, three leagues from land, brought news of having seen ships; when Mocoço, calling Ortiz, gave him permission to depart, who, taking leave, made all haste possible to the shore, where, finding no vessels, he supposed the story to be only a device of the Cacique to discover his inclination. In this way he remained with him nine years, having little hope of ever seeing Christians more; but no sooner had the arrival of the Governor in Florida taken place, when it was known to Mocoço, who directly told Ortiz that Christians were in the town of Ucita. The captive, thinking himself jested with, as he had supposed himself to be before, said that his thoughts no longer dwelt on his people, and that his only wish now was to serve him. Still the Cacique assured him that it was even as he stated, and gave him leave to go, telling him that if he did not, and the Christians should depart, he must not blame him, for he had fulfilled his promise.

Great was the joy of Ortiz at this news, though still doubtful of its truth; however, he thanked Mocoço, and went his way. A dozen principal Indians were sent to accompany him; and on their way to the port, they met Baltasar de Gallegos, in the manner that has been related. Arrived at the camp, the Governor ordered that apparel be given to him, good armour, and a fine horse. When asked if he knew of any country where there was either gold or silver, he said that he had not been ten leagues in any direction from where he lived; but that thirty leagues distant was a chief named Paracoxi, to whom Mocoço, Ucita, and all they that dwelt along the coast paid tribute, and that he perhaps had knowledge of some good country, as his land was better than theirs, being more fertile, abounding in maize. Hearing this, the Governor was well pleased, and said he only desired to find subsistence, that he might be enabled to go inland with safety; for that Florida was so wide, in some part or other of it, there could not fail to be a rich country. The Cacique of Mocoço came to the port, and calling on the Governor, he thus spoke:—

Most High and Powerful Chief:—

Though less able, I believe, to serve you than the least of these under your control, but with the wish to do more than even the greatest of them can accomplish, I appear before you in the full confidence of receiving your favour, as much so as though I deserved it, not in requital of the trifling service I rendered in setting free the Christian while he was in my power, which I did, not for the sake of my honour and of my promise, but because I hold that great men should be liberal. As much as in your bodily perfections you exceed all, and in your command over fine men are you superior to others, so in your nature are you equal to the full enjoyment of earthly things. The favour I hope for, great Lord, is that you will hold me to be your own, calling on me freely to do whatever may be your wish.

The Governor answered him, that although it were true, in freeing and sending him the Christian, he had done no more than to keep his word and preserve his honour, nevertheless he thanked him for an act so valuable, that there was no other for him that could be compared to it; and that, holding him henceforth to be a brother, he should in all, and through all, favour him. Then a shirt and some other articles of clothing were directed to be given to the Chief, who, thankfully receiving them, took leave and went to his town.

CHAPTER X.

How the Governor, having sent the Ships to Cuba,
marched Inland, leaving one hundred Men at the
Port.

From the port of Espiritu Santo, where the Governor
was, he sent the Chief Castellan, with fifty cavalry and
thirty or forty infantry, to the Province of Paracoxi, to
observe the character of the country, inquire of that farther on, and to let him hear by message of what he should
discover; he also sent the vessels to Cuba, that, at an
appointed time, they might return with provisions. As
the principal object of Vasco Porcallo de Figueroa in
coming to Florida had been to get slaves for his planta-
tion and mines, finding, after some incursions, that no
seizures could be made, because of dense forest and extensive bogs, he determined to go back to Cuba; and in
consequence of that resolution, there grew up such a difference between him and Soto, that neither of them
treated nor spoke to the other kindly. Still, with words
of courtesy, he asked permission of him to return, and
took his leave.

Baltasar de Gallegos having arrived at Paracoxi,
thirty Indians came to him on the part of the absent
Cacique, one of whom said: "King Paracoxi, lord of this

Province, whose vassals we are, sends us to ask of you what it is you seek in his country, and in what he can serve you;" to which the Chief Castellan replied, that he much thanked the Cacique for his proffer, and bade them tell him to return to his town, where they would talk together of a peace and friendship he greatly desired to establish. They went off, and came again the next day, reporting that as their lord could not appear, being very unwell, they had come in his stead to see what might be wanted. They were asked if they had knowledge or information of any country where gold and silver might be found in plenty; to which they answered yes; that towards the sunset was a Province called Cale, the inhabitants of which were at war with those of territories where the greater portion of the year was summer, and where there was so much gold, that when the people came to make war upon those of Cale, they wore golden hats like casques.

As the Cacique had not come, Gallegos, reflecting, suspected the message designed for delay, that he might put himself in a condition of safety; and fearing that, if those men were suffered to depart, they might never return, he ordered them to be chained together, and sent the news to camp by eight men on horseback. The Governor, hearing what had passed, showed great pleasure, as did the rest who were with him, believing what the Indians said might be true. He left thirty cavalry and seventy infantry at the port, with provisions for two years, under command of Captain Calderon, marching with the others inland to Paracoxi; thence, having united with the force already there, he passed through a small town named Acela, and came to another called Tocaste, whence he advanced with fifty of foot and thirty horse towards Cale; and having gone through an untenanted town, some natives were seen in a lake, to whom having spoken by an interpreter, they came out and gave him a guide. From there he went to a river of powerful current, in the midst of which was a tree, whereon they made a bridge. Over this the people passed in safety, the horses being crossed swimming to a hawser, by which they were drawn to the other bank, the first that entered the water having been drowned for the want of one.

The Governor sent two men on horseback, with word to those in the rear that they should advance rapidly, for that the way was becoming toilsome and the provisions were short. He came to Cale and found the town abandoned; but he seized three spies, and tarried there until the people should arrive, they travelling hungry and on bad roads, the country being very thin of maize, low, very wet, pondy, and thickly covered with trees. Where there were inhabitants, some water-cresses could be found, which they who arrived first would gather, and, cooking them in water with salt, ate them without other thing; and they who could get none, would seize the stalks of maize and eat them, the ear, being young, as yet containing no grain. Having come to the river, which the Governor had passed, they got cabbage from the low palmetto growing there, like that of Andaluzia. There they were met by the messengers, who, reporting a great deal of maize in Cale, gave much satisfaction.

6

While the people should be coming up, the Governor
ordered all the ripe grain in the fields, enough for three
months, to be secured. In gathering it three Christians
were slain. One of two Indians who were made prisoners stated that seven days' journey distant was a large
Province, abounding in maize, called Apalache. Presently, with fifty cavalry and sixty infantry, he set out
from Cale, leaving Luis de Moscoso, the Field Marshal, in
command, with directions not to move until he should be
ordered. Up to that time, no one had been able to
get servants who should make his bread; and the method
being to beat out the maize in log mortars with a one-
handed pestle of wood, some also sifting the flour afterward through their shirts of mail, the process was found
so laborious, that many, rather than crush the grain,
preferred to eat it parched and sodden. The mass was
baked in clay dishes, set over fire, in the manner that I
have described as done in Cuba.

CHAPTER XI.

How the Governor arrived at Caliquen, and thence, taking the Cacique with him, came to Napetaca, where the Indians, attempting to rescue him, had many of their number killed and captured.

On the eleventh day of August, in the year 1539, the Governor left Cale, and arrived to sleep at a small town called Ytara, and the next day at another called Potano, and the third at Utinama, and then at another named Malapaz. This place was so called because one, representing himself to be its Cacique, came peacefully saying, that he wished to serve the Governor with his people, and asked that he would cause the twenty-eight men and women, prisoners taken the night before, to be set at liberty; that provisions should be brought, and that he would furnish a guide for the country in advance of us; whereupon, the Governor having ordered the prisoners to be let loose, and the Indian put under guard, the next day in the morning came many natives close to a scrub surrounding the town, near which the prisoner asked to be taken, that he might speak and satisfy them, as they would obey in whatever he commanded; but no sooner had he found himself close to them, than he boldly started away, and fled so swiftly that no one could overtake him, going off with the rest into the woods. The Governor ordered a bloodhound, already fleshed upon him, to be let loose, which, passing by many, seized upon the faithless Cacique, and held him until the Christians had come up.

From this town the people went to sleep at the one of Cholupaha, which, for its abundance of maize, received the name of Villafarta; thence, crossing a river before it, by a bridge they had made of wood, the Christians marched two days through an uninhabited country.

On the seventeenth day of August they arrived at Caliquen, where they heard of the Province of Apalache, of Narvaez having been there and embarked, because no road was to be found over which to go forward, and of there being no other town, and that water was on all sides. Every mind was depressed at this information, and all counselled the Governor to go back to the port, that they might not be lost, as Narvaez had been, and to leave the land of Florida; that, should they go further, they might not be able to get back, as the little maize that was yet left the Indians would secure: to which Soto replied, that he would never return until he had seen with his own eyes what was asserted, things that to him appeared incredible. Then he ordered us to be in readiness for the saddle, sending word to Luis de Moscoso to advance from Cale, that he waited for him; and, as in the judgment of the Field Marshal, and of many others, they should have to return from Apalache, they buried in Cale some iron implements with other things. They reached Caliquen through much suffering; for the land over which the Governor had marched lay wasted and was without maize.

All the people having come up, a bridge was ordered to be made over a river that passed near the town, whereon we crossed, the tenth day of September, taking with us the Cacique. When three days on our journey, some Indians arrived to visit their lord; and every day they came out to the road, playing upon flutes, a token among them that they come in peace. They stated that further on there was a Cacique named Uzachil, kinsman of the Chief of Caliquen, their lord, who waited the arrival of the Governor, prepared to do great services; and they besought him to set their Cacique free, which he feared to do, lest they should go off without giving him any guides; so he got rid of them from day to day with specious excuses.

We marched five days, passing through some small towns, and arrived at Napetaca on the fifteenth day of September, where we found fourteen or fifteen Indians who begged for the release of the Cacique of Caliquen, to whom the Governor declared that their lord was no prisoner, his attendance being wished only as far as Uzachil. Having learned from Juan Ortiz, to whom a native had made it known, that the Indians had determined to assemble and fall upon the Christians, for the recovery of their Chief, the Governor, on the day for which the attack was concerted, commanded his men to be in readiness, the cavalry to be armed and on horseback, each one so disposed of in his lodge as not to be seen of the Indians, that they might come to the town without reserve. Four hundred warriors, with bows and arrows, appeared in sight of the camp; and, going into a thicket, they sent two of their number to demand the Cacique: the Governor, with six men on foot, taking the Chief by the hand, conversing with him the while to assure the Indians, went towards the place where they were, when, finding the moment propitious, he ordered a trumpet to be sounded: directly, they who were in the houses, foot as well as horse, set upon the natives, who, assailed unexpectedly, thought only of their safety. Of two horses killed, one was that of the Governor, who was mounted instantly on another. From thirty to forty natives fell by the lance; the rest escaped into two very large ponds, situated some way apart, wherein they swam about; and, being surrounded by the Christians, they were shot at with crossbow and arquebuse, although to no purpose, because of the long distance they were off.

At night, one of the lakes was ordered to be guarded, the people not being sufficient to encircle both. The Indians, in attempting to escape in the dark, would come swimming noiselessly to the shore, with a leaf of water-lily on the head, that they might pass unobserved; when those mounted, at sight of any ruffle on the surface, would dash into the water up to the breasts of the horses, and the natives would again retire. In such way passed the night, neither party taking any rest. Juan Ortiz told them that, as escape was impossible, they would do well to give up; which they did, driven by extreme chillness of the water; and one after another, as cold overpowered,

called out to him, asking not to be killed—that he was
coming straightway to put himself in the hands of the
Governor. At four o'clock in the morning they had all
surrendered, save twelve of the principal men, who, as of
more distinction and valiant than the rest, preferred to
die rather than yield: then the Indians of Paracoxi, who
were going about unshackled, went in after them, swimming, and pulled them out by the hair. They were all
put in chains, and, on the day following, were divided
among the Christians for their service.

While captives, these men determined to rebel, and
gave the lead to an interpreter, one reputed brave, that
when the Governor might come near to speak with him,
he should strangle him; but no sooner was the occasion
presented, and before his hands could be thrown about
the neck of Soto, his purpose was discovered, and he received so heavy a blow from him in the nostrils, that
they gushed with blood. The Indians all rose together.
He who could only catch up a pestle from a mortar,
as well he who could grasp a weapon, equally exerted
himself to kill his master, or the first one he met; and
he whose fortune it was to light on a lance, or a sword,
handled it in a manner as though he had been accustomed to use it all his days. One Indian, in the public
yard of the town, with blade in hand, fought like a
bull in the arena, until the halberdiers of the Governor,
arriving, put an end to him. Another got up, with a
lance, into a maize crib, made of cane, called by Indians
barbacoa, and defended the entrance with the uproar
of ten men, until he was stricken down with a battle-

axe. They who were subdued may have been in all two hundred men: some of the youngest the Governor gave to those who had good chains and were vigilant; all the rest were ordered to execution, and, being bound to a post in the middle of the town yard, they were shot to death with arrows by the people of Paracoxi.

CHAPTER XII.

How the Governor arrived at Palache, and was
informed that there was much Gold inland.

On the twenty-third day of September the Governor
left Napetaca, and went to rest at a river, where two Indians brought him a deer from the Cacique of Uzachil;
and the next day, having passed through a large town
called Hapaluya, he slept at Uzachil. He found no person there; for the inhabitants, informed of the deaths at
Napetaca, dared not remain. In the town was found
their food, much maize, beans, and pumpkins, on which
the Christians lived. The maize is like coarse millet;
the pumpkins are better and more savoury than those of
Spain.

Two captains having been sent in opposite directions,
in quest of Indians, a hundred men and women were
taken, one or two of whom were chosen out for the Governor, as was always customary for officers to do after
successful inroads, dividing the others among themselves
and companions. They were led off in chains, with col-
lars about the neck, to carry luggage and grind corn,
doing the labour proper to servants. Sometimes it happened that, going with them for wood or maize, they
would kill the Christian, and flee, with the chain on,

7

which others would file at night with a splinter of stone, in the place of iron, at which work, when caught, they were punished, as a warning to others, and that they might not do the like. The women and youths, when removed a hundred leagues from their country, no longer cared, and were taken along loose, doing the work, and in a very little time learning the Spanish language.

From Uzachill the Governor went towards Apalache, and at the end of two days' travel arrived at a town called Axille. After that, the Indians having no knowledge of the Christians, they were come upon unawares, the greater part escaping, nevertheless, because there were woods near town. The next day, the first of October, the Governor took his departure in the morning, and ordered a bridge to be made over a river which he had to cross. The depth there, for a stone's throw, was over the head, and afterward the water came to the waist, for the distance of a crossbow-shot, where was a growth of tall and dense forest, into which the Indians came, to ascertain if they could assail the men at work and prevent a passage; but they were dispersed by the arrival of crossbow-men, and some timbers being thrown in, the men gained the opposite side and secured the way. On the fourth day of the week, Wednesday of St. Francis, the Governor crossed over and reached Uitachuco, a town subject to Apalache, where he slept. He found it burning, the Indians having set it on fire.

Thenceforward the country was well inhabited, producing much corn, the way leading by many habitations like villages. Sunday, the twenty-fifth of October, he arrived at the town of Uzela, and on Monday at Anhayca Apalache, where the lord of all that country and Province resided. The Camp-master, whose duty it is to divide and lodge the men, quartered them about the town, at the distance of half a league to a league apart. There were other towns which had much maize, pumpkins, beans, and dried plums of the country, whence were brought together at Anhaica Apalache what appeared to be sufficient provision for the winter. These ameixas are better than those of Spain, and come from trees that grow in the fields without being planted.

Informed that the sea was eight leagues distant, the Governor directly sent a captain thither, with cavalry and infantry, who found a town called Ochete, eight leagues on the way; and, coming to the coast, he saw where a great tree had been felled, the trunk split up into stakes, and with the limbs made into mangers. He found also the skulls of horses. With these discoveries he returned, and what was said of Narvaez was believed to be certain, that he had there made boats, in which he left the country, and was lost in them at sea. Presently, Juan de Añasco made ready to go to the port of Espiritu Santo, taking thirty cavalry, with orders from the Governor to Calderon, who had remained there, that he should abandon the town, and bring all the people to Apalache.

In Uzachil, and other towns on the way, Añasco found many people who had already become careless; still, to avoid detention, no captures were made, as it was not

well to give the Indians sufficient time to come together.
He went through the towns at night, stopping at a distance from the population for three or four hours, to rest,
and at the end of ten days arrived at the port. He dispatched two caravels to Cuba, in which he sent to Doña
Ysabel twenty women brought by him from Ytara and
Potano, near Cale; and, taking with him the foot-soldiers
in the brigantines, from point to point along the coast by
sea, he went towards Palache. Calderon with the cavalry, and some crossbow-men of foot, went by land. The
Indians at several places beset him, and wounded some
of the men. On his arrival, the Governor ordered planks
and spikes to be taken to the coast for building a piragua,
into which thirty men entered well armed from the bay,
going to and coming from sea, waiting the arrival of the
brigantines, and sometimes fighting with the natives,
who went up and down the estuary in canoes. On Saturday, the twenty-ninth of November, in a high wind, an
Indian passed through the sentries undiscovered, and set
fire to the town, two portions of which, in consequence,
were instantly consumed.

On Sunday, the twenty-eighth of December, Juan de
Añasco arrived; and the Governor directed Francisco Maldonado, Captain of Infantry, to run the coast to the westward with fifty men, and look for an entrance; proposing
to go himself in that direction by land on discoveries. The
same day, eight men rode two leagues about the town in
pursuit of Indians, who had become so bold that they would
venture up within two crossbow-shot of the camp to kill
our people. Two were discovered engaged in picking

beans, and might have escaped, but a woman being present, the wife of one of them, they stood to fight. Before they could be killed, three horses were wounded, one of which died in a few days. Calderon going along the coast near by, the Indians came out against him from a wood, driving him from his course, and capturing from many of his company a part of their indispensable subsistence.

Three or four days having elapsed beyond the time set for the going and return of Maldonado, the Governor resolved that, should he not appear at the end of eight days, he would go thence and wait no longer; when the Captain arrived, bringing with him an Indian from a Province called Ochus, sixty leagues from Apalache, and the news of having found a sheltered port with a good depth of water. The Governor was highly pleased, hoping to find a good country ahead; and he sent Maldonado to Havana for provisions, with which to meet him at that port of his discovery, to which he would himself come by land; but should he not reach there that summer, then he directed him to go back to Havana and return there the next season to await him, as he would make it his express object to march in quest of Ochus.

Francisco Maldonado went, and Juan de Guzman remained instead, Captain of his infantry. Of the Indians taken in Napetuca, the treasurer, Juan Gaytan, brought a youth with him, who stated that he did not belong to that country, but to one afar in the direction of the sun's rising, from which he had been a long time absent visiting other lands; that its name was Yupaha, and was governed by a woman, the town she lived in being of astonishing size, and many neighboring lords her tributaries, some of whom gave her clothing, others gold in quantity. He showed how the metal was taken from the earth, melted, and refined, exactly as though he had seen it all done, or else the Devil had taught him how it was; so that they who knew aught of such matter declared it impossible that he could give that account without having been an eye-witness; and they who beheld the signs he made credited all that was understood as certain.

CHAPTER XIII.

How the Governor went from Apalache in quest of Yupaha, and what befell him.

On Wednesday, the third of March, in the year 1540, the Governor left Anhaica Apalache to seek Yupaha. He had ordered his men to go provided with maize for a march through sixty leagues of desert. The cavalry carried their grain on the horses, and the infantry theirs on the back; because the Indians they brought with them for service, being naked and in chains, had perished in great part during the winter. On the fourth day of the journey they arrived at a deep river, where a piragua was made; and, in consequence of the violence of the current, a cable of chains was extended from shore to shore, along which the boat passed, and the horses were drawn over, swimming thereto, by means of a windlass to the other side.

A day and a half afterwards, they arrived at a town by the name of Capachiqui, and on Friday, the eleventh, the inhabitants were found to have gone off. The following day, five Christians, going in the rear of the camp to search for mortars, in which the natives beat maize, went to some houses surrounded by a thicket, where many Indians lurked as spies, an equal number of whom, separa-

ting from the rest, set upon our men, one of whom fled
back, crying out to arms. When they who could first
answer to the call reached the spot, they found one of the
Christians killed, and the three others badly wounded,
the Indians fleeing into a sheet of water, full of woods,
into which the horses could not go. The Governor left
Capachiqui, passing through a desert; and on Wednesday, the twenty-first of the month, came to Toalli.

The houses of this town were different from those behind, which were covered with dry grass; thenceforward
they were roofed with cane, after the fashion of tile.
They are kept very clean: some have their sides so made
of clay as to look like tapia. Throughout the cold country every Indian has a winter house, plastered inside and
out, with a very small door, which is closed at dark, and
a fire being made within, it remains heated like an oven,
so that clothing is not needed during the night-time.
He has likewise a house for summer, and near it a kit-
chen, where fire is made and bread baked. Maize is kept
in barbacoa, which is a house with wooden sides, like a
room, raised aloft on four posts, and has a floor of cane.
The difference between the houses of the masters, or
principal men, and those of the common people is, besides being larger than the others, they have deep balco-
nies on the front side, with cane seats, like benches; and
about are many large barbacoas, in which they bring
together the tribute their people give them of maize, skins
of deer, and blankets of the country. These are like
shawls, some of them made from the inner bark of trees,
and others of a grass resembling nettle, which, by tread-

ing out, becomes like flax. The women use them for covering, wearing one about the body from the waist downward, and another over the shoulder, with the right arm left free, after the manner of the Gypsies: the men wear but one, which they carry over the shoulder in the same way, the loins being covered with a bragueiro of deer-skin, after the fashion of the woollen breech-cloth that was once the custom of Spain. The skins are well dressed, the colour being given to them that is wished, and in such perfection, that, when of vermilion, they look like very fine red broadcloth; and when black, the sort in use for shoes, they are of the purest. The same hues are given to blankets.

The Governor left Toalli on the twenty-fourth day of March, and arrived on Thursday, in the evening, at a little stream where a small bridge was made, and the people passed to the opposite side. Benito Fernandes, a Portuguese, fell off from it, and was drowned. So soon as the Governor had crossed, he found a town, a short way on, by the name of Achese, the people of which, having had no knowledge of the Christians, plunged into a river; nevertheless, some men and women were taken, among whom was found one who understood the youth, the guide to Ynpaha, which rather confirmed what he stated, as they had come through regions speaking different languages, some of which he did not understand. By one of the Indians taken there, the Governor sent to call the Cacique from the farther side of the river, who, having come to him, thus spoke :—

Very High, Powerful, and Good Master:—

The things that seldom happen bring astonishment. Think, then, what must be the effect on me and mine, the sight of you and your people, whom we have at no time seen, astride the fierce brutes, your horses, entering with such speed and fury into my country, that we had no tidings of your coming—things so altogether new, as to strike awe and terror to our hearts, which it was not nature to resist, so that we should receive you with the sobriety due to so kingly and famous a lord. Trusting to your greatness and personal qualities, I hope no fault will be found in me, and that I shall rather receive favours, of which one is that with my person, my country, and my vassals, you will do as with your own things; and another, that you tell me who you are, whence you come, whither you go, and what it is you seek, that I may the better serve you.

The Governor responded, that he greatly thanked him for his good-will, as much so as though he had given him a great treasure. He told him that he was the child of the sun, coming from its abode, and that he was going about the country, seeking for the greatest prince there, and the richest province. The Cacique stated that farther on was a great lord, whose territory was called Ocute. He gave him a guide, who understood the language, to conduct him thither; and the Governor commanded his subjects to be released. A high cross, made of wood, was set up in the middle of the town-yard; and, as time did not allow more to be done, the Indians were instructed that it was put there to commemorate the suffering of Christ, who was God and man; that he had created the skies and the earth, and had suffered for the salvation of all, and therefore that they should revere that sign; and they showed by their manner that they would do so.

The Governor set out on the first day of April, and advanced through the country of the Chief, along up a river, the shores of which were very populous. On the fourth he went through the town of Altamaca, and on the tenth arrived at Ocute. The Cacique sent him a present, by two thousand Indians, of many conies and partridges, maize bread, many dogs, and two turkeys. On account of the scarcity of meat, the dogs were as much esteemed by the Christians as though they had been fat sheep. There was such want of salt also, that oftentimes, in many places, a sick man having nothing for his nourishment, and was wasting away to bone, of some ail that elsewhere might have found a remedy, when sinking under pure debility he would say: "Now, if I had but a slice of meat, or only a few lumps of salt, I should not thus die."

The Indians never lack meat. With arrows they get abundance of deer, turkeys, conies, and other wild animals, being very skilful in killing game, which the Christians were not; and even if they had been, there was not the opportunity for it, they being on the march the greater part of their time; nor did they, besides, ever dare to straggle off. Such was the craving for meat, that when the six hundred men who followed Soto arrived at a town, and found there twenty or thirty dogs, he who could get sight of one and kill him, thought he had done no little; and he who proved himself so active, if his Captain knew of it, and he forgot to send him a quarter, would show his displeasure, and make

him feel it in the watches, or in any matter of labour that
came along, with which he could bear upon him.

On Tuesday, the twelfth of April, the Governor took
his departure, the Cacique of Ocute giving him four
hundred tamemes, the Indians that carry burdens. He
passed through a town, the lord of which was called
Cofaqui, and came to the province of another, named
Patofa, who, being at peace with the Chief of Ocute and
other neighbouring lords, had heard of the Governor for
a long time, and desired to see him. He went to call
on him, and made this speech :—

POWERFUL LORD:—

Not without reason, now, will I ask that some light mishap befall
me, in return for so great good fortune, and deem my lot a happy
one; since I have come to what I most wished in life, to behold and
have the opportunity in some way to serve you. Thus the tongue
casts the shadow of the thought; but I, nevertheless, am as unable
to produce the perfect image of my feelings as to control the appearances of my contentment. By what circumstance has this
your land, which I govern, deserved to be seen by one so superior
and excellent that all on earth should obey and serve as prince?
and those who here inhabit being so insignificant, how can they
forget, in receiving this vast enjoyment, that, in the order of things,
will follow upon it some great adversity? If we are held worthy of
being yours, we can never be other than favoured, nor less than
protected in whatsoever is reasonable and just; for they that fail of
deserving either, with the name of men can only be considered
brutes. · From the depth of my heart, and with the respect due
to such a chief, I make mine offer; and pray that, in return for so
sincere good-will, you dispose of me, my country, and my vassals.

The Governor answered that his offers and good-will,
shown in works, would greatly please him, and which he
should ever bear in memory, to honour and favour him as
he would a brother. From this Province of Patofa, back

to the first Cacique we found at peace, a distance of fifty
leagues, the country is abundant, picturesque, and luxuriant, well watered, and having good river margins; thence
to the harbour of Espiritu Santo, where we first arrived,
the land of Florida, which may be three hundred leagues
in length, a little more or less, is light, the greater part
of it of pine-trees, and low, having many ponds; and in
places are high and dense forest, into which the Indians
that were hostile betook themselves, where they could
not be found; nor could horses enter there, which, to the
Christians, was the loss of the food they carried away,
and made it troublesome to get guides.

CHAPTER XIIII,

How the Governor left the Province of Patofa,
marching into a Desert Country, where he, with
his People, became exposed to great Peril and
underwent severe Privation.

In the town of Patofa, the youth, whom the Governor
brought with him for guide and interpreter, began to froth
at the mouth, and threw himself on the ground as if he
were possessed of the Devil. An exorcism being said over
him, the fit went off. He stated that four days' journey
from there, towards the sunrise, was the Province he spoke
of: the Indians at Patofa said that they knew of no
dwellings in that direction, but that towards the northwest there was a province called Coça, a plentiful country
having very large towns. The Cacique told the Governor
that if he desired to go thither he would give him a guide
and Indians to carry burdens, and if he would go in the
direction pointed out by the youth, he would furnish him
with every thing necessary for that also.

With words of love, and tendering each other services,
they parted, the Governor receiving seven hundred tamemes. He took maize for the consumption of four days,
and marched by a road that, gradually becoming less, on
the sixth day it disappeared. Led by the youth, they

forded two rivers, each the breadth of two shots of a
crossbow, the water rising to the stirrups of the saddles,
and passing in a current so powerful, that it became necessary for those on horseback to stand one before another,
that they on foot, walking near, might cross along above
them : then came to another of a more violent current,
and larger, which was got over with more difficulty, the
horses swimming for a lance's length at the coming out,
into a pine-grove. The Governor menaced the youth,
motioning that he would throw him to the dogs for having
lied to him in saying that it was four days' journey,
whereas they had travelled nine, each day of seven or eight
leagues; and that the men and horses had become very
thin, because of the sharp economy practised with the
maize. The youth declared that he knew not where he
was. Fortunately for him, at the time, there was not another whom Juan Ortez understood, or he would have
been cast to the dogs.

The Governor, leaving the camp among the pine-trees,
marched that day, with some cavalry and infantry, five or
six leagues, looking for a path, and came back at night
very cast down, not having found any sign of inhabitants.
The next day there was a variety of opinion about the
course proper to take, whether to return or do otherwise.
The country through which they had come remained
wasted and without maize ; the grain they had so far
brought with them was spent ; the beasts, like the men, were
become very lean ; and it was held very doubtful whether
relief was anywhere to be found : moreover, it was the
opinion that they might be beaten by any Indians what-

soever who should venture to attack them, so that continuing thus, whether by hunger or in strife, they must inevitably be overcome. The Governor determined to send
thence in all directions on horseback, in quest of habitations; and the next day he dispatched four captains to as
many points, with eight of cavalry to each. They came
back at night leading their beasts by the bridle, unable to
carry their masters, or driven before them with sticks,
having found no road, nor any sign of a settlement. He
sent other four again the next day, with eight of cavalry
apiece, men who could swim, that they might cross any
ponds and rivers in the way, the horses being chosen of
the best that were; Baltasar de Gallegos ascending by the
river, Juan de Añasco going down it, Alfonso Romo and
Juan Rodriguez Lobillo striking into the country.

The Governor had brought thirteen sows to Florida,
which had increased to three hundred swine; and the
maize having failed for three or four days, he ordered to
be killed daily, for each man, half a pound of pork, on
which small allowance, and some boiled herbs, the people
with much difficulty lived. There being no food to give
to the Indians of Patofa, they were dismissed, though they
still wished to keep with the Christians in their extremity,
and showed great regret at going back before leaving them
in a peopled country. Juan de Añasco came in on Sunday, in the afternoon, bringing with him a woman and a
youth he had taken, with the report that he had found a
small town twelve or thirteen leagues off; at which the
Governor and his people were as much delighted as though
they had been raised from death to live.

On Monday, the twenty-sixth of April, the Governor set out for Aymay, a town to which the Christians gave the name of Socorro. At the foot of a tree, in the camp, they buried a paper, and in the bark, with a hatchet, they cut these words: " Dig here; at the root of this pine you will find a letter;" and this was so fixed that the Captains, who had gone in quest of an inhabited country, should learn what the Governor had done and the direction he had taken. There was no other road than the one Juan de Añasco had made moving along through the woods.

On Monday the Governor arrived at the town, with those the best mounted, all riding the hardest possible; some sleeping two leagues off, others three and four, each as he was able to travel and his strength held out. A barbacoa was found full of parched meal and some maize, which were distributed by allowance. Four Indians were taken, not one of whom would say any thing else than that he knew of no other town. The Governor ordered one of them to be burned; and thereupon another said, that two days' journey from there was a province called Cutifachiqui.

On Wednesday the three Captains came up: they had found the letter and followed on after the rest. From the command of Juan Rodriguez two men remained behind, their horses having given out, for which the Governor reprimanded him severely, and sent him to bring them. While they should be coming on he set out for Cutifachi-qui, capturing three Indians in the road, who stated that the mistress of that country had already information of the Christians, and was waiting for them in a town. He

9

sent to her by one of them, offering his friendship, and announcing his approach. Directly as the Governor arrived, four canoes came towards him, in one of which was a kinswoman of the Cacica, who, coming near, addressed him in these words:—

EXCELLENT LORD:—
My sister sends me to salute you, and to say, that the reason why she has not come in person is, that she has thought to serve you better by remaining to give orders on the other shore; and that, in a short time, her canoes will all be here, in readiness to conduct you thither, where you may take your repose and be obeyed.

The Governor thanked her, and she returned to cross the river. After a little time the Cacica came out of the town, seated in a chair, which some principal men having borne to the bank, she entered a canoe. Over the stern was spread an awning, and in the bottom lay extended a mat where were two cushions, one above the other, upon which she sate; and she was accompanied by her chief men, in other canoes, with Indians. She approached the spot where the Governor was, and, being arrived, thus addressed him :—

EXCELLENT LORD:—
Be this coming to these your shores most happy. My ability can in no way equal my wishes, nor my services become the merits of so great a prince; nevertheless, good wishes are to be valued more than all the treasures of the earth without them. With sincerest and purest good-will I tender you my person, my lands, my people, and make you these small gifts.

The Cacica presented much clothing of the country, from the shawls and skins that came in the other boats; and drawing from over her head a large string of pearls,

she threw them about his neck, exchanging with him
many gracious words of friendship and courtesy. She
directed that canoes should come to the spot, whence the
Governor and his people passed to the opposite side of
the river. So soon as he was lodged in the town, a great
many turkeys were sent to him. The country was
delightful and fertile, having good interval lands upon
the streams; the forest was open, with abundance of
walnut and mulberry trees. The sea was stated to be
distant two days' travel. About the place, from half a
league to a league off, were large vacant towns, grown
up in grass, that appeared as if no people had lived
in them for a long time. The Indians said that, two
years before, there had been a pest in the land, and the
inhabitants had moved away to other towns. In the
barbacoas were large quantities of clothing, shawls of
thread, made from the bark of trees, and others of
feathers, white, gray, vermilion, and yellow, rich and
proper for winter. There were also many well-dressed
deer-skins, of colors drawn over with designs, of which
had been made shoes, stockings, and hose. The Cacica,
observing that the Christians valued the pearls, told the
Governor that, if he should order some sepulchres that
were in the town to be searched, he would find many;
and if he chose to send to those that were in the
uninhabited towns, he might load all his horses with
them. They examined those in the town, and found
three hundred and fifty pounds' weight of pearls, and
figures of babies and birds made of them.

The inhabitants are brown of skin, well formed and

proportioned. They are more civilized than any people seen in all the territories of Florida, wearing clothes and shoes. This country, according to what the Indians stated, had been very populous. It appeared that the youth who was the guide had heard of it; and what was told him he declared to have seen, and magnified such parts as he chose, to suit his pleasure. He told the Governor that they had begun to enter upon the country he had spoken to him about, which, because of its appearance, with his being able to understand the language of the people, gained for him some credit. He wished to become a Christian, and asked to be baptized, which was done, he receiving the name of Pedro; and the Governor commanded the chain to be struck off that he had carried until then.

In the town were found a dirk and beads that had belonged to Christians, who, the Indians said, had many years before been in the port, distant two days' journey. He that had been there was the Governor-licentiate Ayllon, who came to conquer the land, and, on arriving at the port, died, when there followed divisions and murders among the chief personages, in quarrels as to who should have the command; and thence, without knowing any thing of the country, they went back to Spain.

To all it appeared well to make a settlement there, the point being a favourable one, to which could come all the ships from New Spain, Peru, Sancta Marta, and Tierra-Firme, going to Spain; because it is in the way thither, is a good country, and one fit in which to raise supplies: but Soto, as it was his object to find another

treasure like that of Atabalipa, lord of Peru, would not
be content with good lands nor pearls, even though many
of them were worth their weight in gold (and if the
country were divided among Christians, more precious
should those be the Indians would procure than these
they have, being bored with heat, which causes them to
lose their hue): so he answered them who urged him to
make a settlement, that in all the country together there
was not support for his troops a single month; that it was
necessary to return to Ochus, where Maldonado was to
wait; and should a richer country not be found, they
could always return to that who would, and in their
absence the Indians would plant their fields and be
better provided with maize. The natives were asked if
they had knowledge of any great lord farther on, to
which they answered, that twelve days' travel thence
was a province called Chiaha, subject to a chief of Coça.

The Governor then resolved at once to go in quest of
that country, and being an inflexible man, and dry of
word, who, although he liked to know what the others
all thought and had to say, after he once said a thing he
did not like to be opposed, and as he ever acted as he
thought best, all bent to his will; for though it seemed
an error to leave that country, when another might have
been found about it, on which all the people could have
been sustained until the crops had been made and the
grain gathered, there were none who would say a thing
to him after it became known that he had made up his
mind.

CHAPTER XV.

How the Governor went from Cutifachiqui in quest
of Coça, and what occurred to him on the
Journey.

On the third day of May the Governor set out from
Cutifachiqui; and, it being discovered that the wish of
the Cacica was to leave the Christians, if she could, giving them neither guides nor tamemes, because of the
outrages committed upon the inhabitants, there never
failing to be men of low degree among the many, who
will put the lives of themselves and others in jeopardy
for some mean interest, the Governor ordered that she
should be placed under guard, and took her with him.
This treatment, which was not a proper return for the
hospitable welcome he had received, makes true the
adage, For well doing . . ; and thus was she carried
away on foot, with her female slaves.

This brought us service in all the places that were
passed, she ordering the Indians to come and take the
loads from town to town. We travelled through her territories a hundred leagues, in which, according to what
we saw, she was greatly obeyed, whatsoever she ordered
being performed with diligence and efficacy. Perico,
the guide, said she was not the suzeraine, but her niece,

who had come to that town by her command to punish
capitally some principal Indians who had seized upon the
tribute; but to this no credit was given, because of the
falsehoods in which he had been taken, though all was
put up with, from the necessity of having some one
whereby to understand what the Indians said.

In seven days the Governor arrived at the Province
of Chelaque, the country poorest off for maize of any
that was seen in Florida, where the inhabitants subsisted
on the roots of plants that they dig in the wilds, and on
the animals they destroy there with their arrows. They
are very domestic people, are slight of form, and go
naked. One lord brought the Governor two deer-skins
as a great gift. Turkeys were abundant; in one town
they presented seven hundred, and in others brought him
what they had and could procure. He was detained in
going from this province to that of Xualla five days,
where they found little grain, but remained two days,
because of the weariness of the men and the leanness of
the horses.

From Ocute to Cutifachiqui are one hundred and
thirty leagues, of which eighty are desert; from Cutifa
to Xualla are two hundred and fifty of mountainous
country; thence to Guaxule, the way is over very rough
and lofty ridges.

One day while on this journey, the Cacica of Cutifachi,
whom the Governor brought with him, as has been stated,
to the end of taking her to Guaxule, the farthest limit
of her territories, conducted by her slaves, she left the
road, with an excuse of going into a thicket, where,

deceiving them, she so concealed herself that for all their search she could not be found. She took with her a cane box, like a trunk, called petaca, full of unbored pearls, of which, those who had the most knowledge of their value said they were very precious. They were carried for her by one of the women; and the Governor, not to give offence, permitted it so, thinking that in Guaxule he would beg them of her when he should give her leave to depart; but she took them with her, going to Xualla, with three slaves who had fled from the camp. A horseman, named Alimamos, who remained behind, sick of a fever, wandering out of the way, got lost; and he laboured with the slaves to make them leave their evil design. Two of them did so, and came on with him to the camp. They overtook the Governor, after a journey of fifty leagues, in a province called Chiaha; and he reported that the Cacica remained in Xualla, with a slave of André de Vasconcelos, who would not come with him, and that it was very sure they lived together as man and wife, and were to go together to Cutifachiqui.

At the end of five days the Governor arrived at Guaxule. The Christians being seen to go after dogs, for their flesh, which the Indians do not eat, they gave them three hundred of those animals. Little maize was found there, or anywhere upon that route. The Governor sent a native with a message to the Cacique of Chiaha, begging that he would order some maize to be brought together at his town, that he might sojourn there some time. He left Guaxule, and after two days' travel arrived at Canasagua, where twenty

men came out from the town on the road, each laden
with a basket of mulberries. This fruit is abundant and
good, from Cutifachique to this place, and thence onward
in other provinces, as are the walnut and the amexa;
the trees growing about over the country, without planting or pruning, of the size and luxuriance they would
have were they cultivated in orchards, by hoeing and
irrigation. Leaving Canasagua, he marched five days
through a desert.

Two leagues before coming to Chiaha, fifteen men
met the Governor, bearing loads of maize, with word
from the Cacique that he waited for him, having twenty
barbacoas full; that, moreover, himself, his lands, and
his vassals, were subject to his orders. On the fifth day
of July the Governor entered Chiaha. The Cacique
received him with great pleasure, and, resigning to him
his dwellings for his residence, thus addressed him :—

POWERFUL AND EXCELLENT MASTER:—

Fortunate am I that you will make use of my services. Nothing could happen that would give me so great contentment, or
which I should value more. From Guaxule you sent to have
maize for you in readiness to last two months: you have in this
town twenty barbacoas full of the choicest and the best to be
found in all this country. If the reception I give is not worthy of
so great a prince, consider my youth, which will relieve me of
blame, and receive my good-will, which, with true loyalty and pure,
shall ever be shown in all things that concern your welfare.

The Governor answered him, that his gifts and his
kindness pleased him greatly, and that he should ever
consider him to be his brother.

There was abundance of lard in calabashes, drawn
like olive oil, which the inhabitants said was the fat of

bear. There was likewise found much oil of walnuts, which, like the lard, was clear and of good taste; and also a honey-comb, which the Christians had never seen before, nor saw afterwards, nor honey, nor bees, in all the country.

The town was isolated, between two arms of a river, and seated near one of them. Above it, at the distance of two crossbow-shot, the water divided, and united again a league below. The vale between, from side to side, was the width in places of a crossbow-shot, and in others of two. The branches were very wide, and both were fordable: along their shores were very rich meadow-lands, having many maize-fields.

As the Indians remained at home, no houses were taken save those of the Chief, in which the Governor lodged; the people lived out, wherever there happened to be shelter, each man having his tree. In this manner the army lay, the men out of order, and far apart. The Governor passed it over, as the Indians were peaceful, and the weather very calm: the people would have suffered greatly had they been required to do differently. The horses arrived so worn out, that they could not bear their riders from weakness; for they had come all the way having only a little maize to live on, travelling, hungry and tired, even from beyond the desert of Ocute; so, as the greater part of them were unfit to be mounted, even in the necessary case of battle, they were turned out at night to graze, about a quarter of a league from the camp. The Christians were greatly exposed, so much so that if at that time the Indians had set upon

them, they would have been in bad way to defend
themselves.

The duration of the sojourn was thirty days, in which
time, the soil being covered with verdure, the horses fattened. At the departure, in consequence of the importu-
nity of some who wanted more than was in reason, the
Governor asked thirty women of the Chief for slaves, who
replied that he would confer with his principal men ; when
one night, before giving an answer, all went off from the
town with their women and children. The next day, having made up his mind to go in search of them, the Cacique arrived, and, approaching, thus addressed him :—

Powerful Lord :—

Because of my shame, and out of fear of you, discovering that
my subjects, contrary to my wishes, had chosen to absent themselves,
I left without your permission ; but, finding the error of my way, I
have returned like a true vassal, to put myself in your power, that
you may do with my person as shall seem best to you. My people
will not obey me, nor do any thing that an uncle of mine does not
command : he governs this country, in my place, until I shall be of
mature age. If you would pursue and punish them for disobedience,
I will be your guide, since my fate at present forbids me doing more.

The Governor then, with thirty mounted men and as
many footmen, went in search of the people. Passing by
the towns of some of the chiefs who had gone off, he
cut down and destroyed the great maize-fields ; and going
along up the stream where the natives were, on an islet,
to which the cavalry could not go, he sent word to them,
by an Indian, that they should put away all their fears,
and, returning to their abodes, give him tamemes, as had
been done all the way along, since he did not wish to

have women, finding how very dear they were to them. The Indians judged it well to come and make their excuses to him, so they all went back to the town.

A Cacique of Acoste, who came to see the Governor, after tendering his services, and they had exchanged compliments and proffers of friendship, was asked if he had any information of a rich land; he answered yes: that towards the north there was a province called Chisca, and that a forge was there for copper, or other metal of that colour, though brighter, having a much finer hue, and was to appearances much better, but was not so much used, for being softer; which was the statement that had been given in Cutifachiqui, where we had seen some chopping-knives that were said to have a mixture of gold. As the country on the way was thinly peopled, and it was said there were mountains over which the beasts could not go, the Governor would not march directly thither, but judged that, keeping in an inhabited territory the men and animals would be in better condition, while he would be more exactly informed of what there was, until he should turn to it through the ridges and a region which he could more easily travel. He sent two Christians to the country of Chisca, by Indians who spoke the language, that they might view it, and were told that he would await their return at Chiaha for what they should have to say.

CHAPTER XVI.

How the Governor left Chiaha, and, having run a hazard of falling by the Hands of the Indians at Acoste, escaped by his Address : what occurred to him on the Route, and how he came to Coça.

When the Governor had determined to move from Chiaha towards Coste, he sent for the Cacique to come before him, and with kind words took his leave, receiving some slaves as a gift, which pleased him. In seven days the journey was concluded. On the seventh day of July, the camp being pitched among the trees, two crossbow-shot distant from the town, he went with eight men of his guard toward where the Cacique was, who received him evidently with great friendship. While they were conversing, some infantry went into the town after maize, and, not satisfied with what they got, they rummaged and searched the houses, taking what they would; at which conduct the owners began to rise and arm ; some of them, with clubs in their hands, going at five or six men who had given offence, beat them to their satisfaction. The Governor, discovering that they were all bent upon some mischief, and himself among them with but few Christians about him, turned to escape from the difficulty by a stratagem much against his nature, clear and reliable

as it was, and the more unwillingly as it grieved him that
an Indian should presume, either with or without cause,
to offer any indignity to a Christian : he seized a stave
and took part with the assailants against his own people,
which while it gave confidence, directly he sent a message
secretly to the camp, that armed men should approach
where he was ; then taking the Chief by the hand, speaking to him with kind words, drew him with some principal men away from the town, out into an open road in
sight of the encampment, where cautiously the Christians
issued and by degrees surrounded them. In this manner
they were conducted within the tents ; and when near his
marquee the Governor ordered them to be put under
guard. He told them that they could not go thence without giving him a guide and Indians for carrying loads,
nor until the sick men had arrived whom he had ordered
to come down by the river in canoes from Chiaha, and so
likewise those he had sent to the Province of Chisca. He
feared that both the one and the other had been killed by
the Indians. In three days they that went to Chisca got
back, and related that they had been taken through a
country so scant of maize, and with such high mountains,
that it was impossible the army should march in that
direction ; and finding the distance was becoming long,
and that they should be back late, upon consultation they
agreed to return, coming from a poor little town where
there was nothing of value, bringing a cow-hide as delicate as a calf-skin the people had given them, the hair
being like the soft wool on the cross of the merino with
the common sheep.

The Cacique having furnished the guide and tamemes, by permission of the Governor he went his way. The Christians left Coste the ninth day of July, and slept that night at Tali. The Cacique had come from the town to meet the Governor on the road, and made him this speech :—

EXCELLENT GREAT PRINCE :—

Worthy are you of being served and obeyed by all the princes of the world, for by the face can one judge far of the inner qualities. Who you are I knew, and also of your power, before your coming here. I wish not to draw attention to the lowliness in which I stand before you, to make my poor services acceptable and agreeable, since, where the strength fails, the will should instead be praised and taken. Hence, I dare to ask that you will only consider and attend to what you will command me to do here in your country.

The Governor answered, that his good-will and offer pleased him as much as though he had tendered him all the treasures of the earth : that he would always be treated by him as a true brother, favoured and esteemed. The Cacique ordered provision to be brought for two days' use, the time the Governor should be present ; and on his departure, gave him the use of two men and four women, who were wanted to carry burdens.

They travelled six days, passing by many towns subject to the Cacique of Coça ; and, as they entered those territories, numerous messengers came from him on the road every day to the Governor, some going, others coming, until they arrived at Coça, on Friday, the sixteenth of July. The Cacique came out to receive him at the distance of two crossbow-shot from the town, borne in a litter on the shoulders of his principal men, seated on a cushion, and covered with a mantle of marten-skins, of the size and shape of a woman's shawl: on his head he wore a diadem of plumes, and he was surrounded by many attendants playing upon flutes and singing. Coming to where the Governor was, he made his obeisance, and followed it by these words:—

POWERFUL LORD, SUPERIOR TO EVERY OTHER OF THE EARTH:—
Although I come but now to meet you, it is a long time since I have received you in my heart. That was done the first day I heard of you, with so great desire to serve, please, and give you contentment, that this, which I express, is nothing in comparison with that which is within me. Of this you may be sure, that to have received the dominion of the world would not have interested me so greatly as the sight of you, nor would I have held it for so great a felicity. Do not look for me to offer you that which is your own—this person, these lands, these vassals. My only desire is to employ myself in commanding these people, that, with all diligence and befitting respect, they conduct you hence to the town in festivity of voices and with flutes, where you will be lodged and waited upon by me and them, where all I possess you will do with as with your own, and in thus doing you will confer favour.

The Governor gave him thanks, and with mutual satisfaction they walked on toward the place conferring, the Indians giving up their habitations by order of their Cacique, and in which the General and his men took lodging. In the barbacoas was a great quantity of maize and beans: the country, thickly settled in numerous and large towns, with fields between, extending from one to another, was pleasant, and had a rich soil with fair river margins. In the woods were many anexeas, as well those of Spain as of the country; and wild grapes on vines growing up into the trees, near the streams; likewise a kind that grew on low vines elsewhere, the berry being large and sweet, but, for want of hoeing and dressing, had large stones.

It was the practice to keep watch over the Caciques that none should absent themselves, they being taken along by the Governor until coming out of their territories; for by thus having them the inhabitants would await their arrival in the towns, give a guide, and men to carry the loads, who before leaving their country would have liberty to return to their homes, as sometimes would the tamemes, so soon as they came to the domain of any chief where others could be got. The people of Coça, seeing their lord was detained, took it amiss, and, going off, hid themselves in the scrub, as well those of the town of the Cacique as those of the towns of the principal men his vassals. The Governor dispatched four captains in as many directions to search for them : many men and women were taken who were put in chains. Seeing how much harm they received, and how little they gained by going off, they came in, declaring that they desired to serve in all that it were possible. Of the prisoners, some of the chiefs, whom the Cacique interceded for, were let go ; of the rest, each one took away with him as slaves those he had in chains, none returning to their country save some whose fortune it was to escape, laboring diligently to file off their irons at night ; or, while on the march, could slip out of the way, observing the carelessness of those who had them in charge, sometimes taking off with them in their chains the burdens and the clothing with which they were laded.

11

CHAPTER XVII.

Of how the Governor went from Coça to Tastaluca.

The Governor rested in Coça twenty-five days. On Friday, the twentieth of August, he set out in quest of a province called Tastaluca, taking with him the Cacique of Coça. The first day he went through Tallimuchase, a great town without inhabitants, halting to sleep half a league beyond, near a river-bank. The following day he came to Ytaua, a town subject to Coça. He was detained six days, because of a river near by that was then swollen: so soon as it could be crossed he took up his march, and went towards Ullibahali. Ten or twelve chiefs came to him on the road, from the Cacique of that province, tendering his service, bearing bows and arrows and wearing bunches of feathers.

The Governor having arrived at the town with a dozen cavalry and several of his guard, he left them at the distance of a crossbow-shot and entered the town. He found all the Indians with their weapons, and, according to their ways, it appeared to him in readiness for action: he understood afterwards that they had determined to wrest the Cacique of Coça from his power, should that chief have called on them. The place was enclosed, and near by ran a small stream. The fence, which was like that seen afterwards to other towns, was of large timber sunk deep and firmly into the earth, having many long poles the size of the arm, placed crosswise to nearly the height of a lance, with embrasures, and coated with mud inside and out, having loop-holes for archery. The Governor ordered all his men to enter the town. The Cacique, who at the moment was at a town on the opposite shore, was sent for, and he came at once. After some words between him and the Governor, proffering mutual service, he gave the tamemes that were requisite and thirty women as slaves. Mançano, a native of Salamanca, of noble ancestry, having strayed off in search of the grapes, which are good here, and plenty, was lost.

The Christians left, and that day they arrived to sleep at a town subject to the lord of Ullibahali, and the next day they came to pass the night at the town of Toasi, where the inhabitants gave the Governor thirty women and the tamemes that were wanted. The amount of travel usually performed was five or six leagues a day, passing through settled country; and when through desert, all the haste possible was made, to avoid the want of maize. From Toasi, passing through some towns subject to the lord of the Province of Tallise, he journeyed five days, and arrived at the town the eighteenth day of September.

Tallise was large, situated by the side of a great river, other towns and many fields of maize being on the opposite shore, the country on both sides having the greatest abundance of grain. The inhabitants had gone off. The Governor sent to call the Cacique, who, having arrived,

after an interchange of kind words and good promises,
lent him forty men. A chief came to the Governor in
behalf of the Cacique of Tastaluca, and made the following address :—

VERY POWERFUL, VIRTUOUS, AND ESTEEMED LORD :—

The grand Cacique of Tastaluca, my master, sends me to salute
you. He bids me say, that he is told how all, not without reason,
are led captive by your perfections and power; that wheresoever
lies your path you receive gifts and obedience, which he knows are
all your due; and that he longs to see you as much as he could
desire for the continuance of life. Thus, he sends me to offer you
his person, his lands, his subjects; to say, that wheresoever it shall
please you to go through his territories, you will find service and
obedience, friendship and peace. In requital of this wish to serve
you, he asks that you so far favour him as to say when you will
come; for that the sooner you do so, the greater will be the obligation, and to him the earlier pleasure.

The Governor received and parted with the messenger graciously, giving him beads (which by the Indians
are not much esteemed), and other articles, that he should
take them to his lord. He dismissed the Cacique of
Coça, that he might return to his country: he of Tallise
gave him the tamemes that were needed; and, having
sojourned twenty days, the Governor set out for Tastaluca. He slept the night at a large town called Casiste,
and the next day, passing through another, arrived at a
village in the Province of Tastaluca; and the following
night he rested in a wood, two leagues from the town
where the Cacique resided, and where he was then
present. He sent the Field-Marshal, Luis de Moscoso,
with fifteen cavalry, to inform him of his approach.

The Cacique was at home, in a piazza. Before his

dwelling, on a high place, was spread a mat for him, upon which two cushions were placed, one above another, to which he went and sat down, his men placing themselves around, some way removed, so that an open circle was formed about him, the Indians of the highest rank being nearest to his person. One of them shaded him from the sun with a circular umbrella, spread wide, the size of a target, with a small stem, and having deer-skin extended over cross-sticks, quartered with red and white, which at a distance made it look of taffeta, the colours were so very perfect. It formed the standard of the Chief, which he carried into battle. His appearance was full of dignity: he was tall of person, muscular, lean, and symmetrical. He was the suzerain of many territories, and of a numerous people, being equally feared by his vassals and the neighbouring nations. The Field-Marshal, after he had spoken to him, advanced with his company, their steeds leaping from side to side, and at times towards the Chief, when he, with great gravity, and seemingly with indifference, now and then would raise his eyes, and look on as in contempt.

The Governor approached him, but he made no movement to rise; he took him by the hand, and they went together to seat themselves on the bench that was in the piazza. The Cacique addressed him these words :—

POWERFUL CHIEF :—

Your lordship is very welcome. With the sight of you I receive as great pleasure and comfort as though you were an own brother whom I dearly loved. It is idle to use many words here, as it is not well to speak at length where a few may suffice. The greater

the will the more estimable the deed ; and acts are the living witnesses of truth. You shall learn how strong and positive is my
will, and how disinterested my inclination to serve you. The gifts
you did me the favour to send I esteem in all their value, but most
because they were yours. See in what you will command me.

The Governor satisfied the Chief with a few brief
words of kindness. On leaving he determined, for certain
reasons, to take him along. The second day on the road
he came to a town called Piache : a great river ran near,
and the Governor asked for canoes. The Indians said
they had none, but that they could have rafts of cane and
dried wood, whereon they might readily enough go over,
which they diligently set about making, and soon com-
pleted. They managed them ; and the water being calm,
the Governor and his men easily crossed.

From the port of Espiritu Santo to Palache, a march
of about a hundred leagues, the course was west; from
Apalache to Cutifachiqui, which may be four hundred and
thirty leagues, it was northeast ; from thence to Xualla,
two hundred and fifty leagues, it was towards the north ;
and thence to Tastaluca, which may be some other two
hundred and fifty leagues, one hundred and ninety of
them were toward the west, going to the Province of
Coça, and the sixty southwardly, in going thence to Tastaluca.

After crossing the river of Piache, a Christian having
gone to look after a woman gotten away from him, he had
been either captured or killed by the natives, and the
Governor pressed the Chief to tell what had been done;
threatening, that should the man not appear, he would

never release him. The Cacique sent an Indian thence to Manilla, the town of a chief, his vassal, whither they were going, stating that he sent to give him notice that he should have provisions in readiness and Indians for loads; but which, as afterwards appeared, was a message for him to get together there all the warriors in his country.

The Governor marched three days, the last one of them continually through an inhabited region, arriving on Monday, the eighteenth day of October, at Manilla. He rode forward in the vanguard, with fifteen cavalry and thirty infantry, when a Christian he had sent with a message to the Cacique, three or four days before, with orders not to be gone long, and to discover the temper of the Indians, came out from the town and reported that they appeared to him to be making preparation; for that while he was present many weapons were brought, and many people came into the town, and work had gone on rapidly to strengthen the palisade. Luis de Moscoso said that, since the Indians were so evil disposed, it would be better to stop in the woods; to which the Governor answered, that he was impatient of sleeping out, and that he would lodge in the town.

Arriving near, the Chief came out to receive him, with many Indians singing and playing on flutes, and after tendering his services, gave him three cloaks of marten-skins. The Governor entered the town with the Caciques, seven or eight men of his guard, and three or four cavalry, who had dismounted to accompany them; and they seated themselves in a piazza. The Cacique of Tastaluca asked the Governor to allow him to remain there,

and not to weary him any more with walking; but, finding that was not to be permitted, he changed his plan,
and, under pretext of speaking with some of the chiefs,
he got up from where he sate, by the side of the Governor, and entered a house where were many Indians with
their bows and arrows. The Governor, finding that he
did not return, called to him; to which the Cacique
answered that he would not come out, nor would he
leave that town; that if the Governor wished to go in
peace, he should quit at once, and not persist in carrying
him away by force from his country and its dependencies.

CHAPTER XVIII.

How the Indians rose upon the Governor, and
what followed upon that Rising.

THE Governor, in view of the determination and furious answer of the Cacique, thought to soothe him with
soft words; to which he made no answer, but, with great
haughtiness and contempt, withdrew to where Soto could
not see nor speak to him. The Governor, that he might
send word to the Cacique for him to remain in the country at his will, and to be pleased to give him a guide,
and persons to carry burdens, that he might see if he
could pacify him with gentle words, called to a chief who
was passing by. The Indian replied, loftily, that he would
not listen to him. Baltasar de Gallegos, who was near,
seized him by the cloak of marten-skins that he had on,
drew it off over his head, and left it in his hands; whereupon, the Indians all beginning to rise, he gave him a
stroke with a cutlass, that laid open his back, when they,
with loud yells, came out of the houses, discharging
their bows.

The Governor, discovering that if he remained
there they could not escape, and if he should order his
men, who were outside of the town, to come in, the
horses might be killed by the Indians from the houses.

12

and great injury done, he ran out ; but before he could
get away he fell two or three times, and was helped to
rise by those with him. He and they were all badly
wounded: within the town five Christians were instantly
killed. Coming forth, he called out to all his men to get
farther off, because there was much harm doing from the
palisade. The natives discovering that the Christians
were retiring, and some, if not the greater number, at
more than a walk, the Indians followed with great boldness, shooting at them, or striking down such as they could
overtake. Those in chains having set down their burdens near the fence while the Christians were retiring,
the people of Mauilla lifted the loads on to their backs,
and, bringing them into the town, took off their irons,
putting bows and arms in their hands, with which to
fight. Thus did the foe come into possession of all the
clothing, pearls, and whatsoever else the Christians had
beside, which was what their Indians carried. Since
the natives had been at peace to that place, some of us,
putting our arms in the luggage, went without any ;
and two, who were in the town, had their swords and
halberds taken from them, and put to use.

The Governor, presently as he found himself in the
field, called for a horse, and, with some followers, returned and lanced two or three of the Indians; the rest,
going back into the town, shot arrows from the palisade.
Those who would venture on their nimbleness came out
a stone's throw from behind it, to fight, retiring from
time to time, when they were set upon.

At the time of the affray there was a friar, a clergy-

man, a servant of the Governor, and a female slave in the
town, who, having no time in which to get away, took to
a house, and there remained until after the Indians
became masters of the place. They closed the entrance
with a lattice door; and there being a sword among them,
which the servant had, he put himself behind the door,
striking at the Indians that would have come in; while,
on the other side, stood the friar and the priest, each with
a club in hand, to strike down the first that should enter.
The Indians, finding that they could not get in by the
door, began to unroof the house: at this moment the
cavalry were all arrived at Mauilla, with the infantry that
had been on the march, when a difference of opinion
arose as to whether the Indians should be attacked, in
order to enter the town; for the result was held doubtful, but finally it was concluded to make the assault.

CHAPTER XIX.

How the Governor set his Men in order of Battle and entered the Town of Mauilla.

So soon as the advance and the rear of the force were come up, the Governor commanded that all the best armed should dismount, of which he made four squadrons of footmen. The Indians, observing how he was going on arranging his men, urged the Cacique to leave, telling him, as was afterwards made known by some women who were taken in the town, that as he was but one man, and could fight but as one only, there being many chiefs present very skilful and experienced in matters of war, any one of whom was able to command the rest, and as things in war were so subject to fortune, that it was never certain which side would overcome the other, they wished him to put his person in safety; for if they should conclude their lives there, on which they had resolved rather than surrender, he would remain to govern the land : but for all that they said, he did not wish to go, until, from being continually urged, with fifteen or twenty of his own people he went out of the town, taking with him a scarlet cloak and other articles of the Christians' clothing, being whatever he could carry and that seemed best to him.

The Governor, informed that the Indians were leaving

the town, commanded the cavalry to surround it ; and
into each squadron of foot he put a soldier, with a brand,
to set fire to the houses, that the Indians might have no
shelter. His men being placed in full concert, he ordered
an arquebuse to be shot off : at the signal the four squadrons, at their proper points, commenced a furious onset,
and, both sides severely suffering, the Christians entered
the town. The friar, the priest, and the rest who were
with them in the house, were all saved, though at the cost
of the lives of two brave and very able men who went
thither to their rescue. The Indians fought with so great
spirit that they many times drove our people back out of
the town. The struggle lasted so long that many Christians, weary and very thirsty, went to drink at a pond near
by, tinged with the blood of the killed, and returned to the
combat. The Governor, witnessing this, with those who
followed him in the returning charge of the footmen,
entered the town on horseback, which gave opportunity
to fire the dwellings; then breaking in upon the Indians
and beating them down, they fled out of the place, the
cavalry and infantry driving them back through the gates,
where, losing the hope of escape, they fought valiantly ;
and the Christians getting among them with cutlasses,
they found themselves met on all sides by their strokes,
when many, dashing headlong into the flaming houses,
were smothered, and, heaped one upon another, burned to
death.

They who perished there were in all two thousand
five hundred, a few more or less : of the Christians there
fell two hundred, among whom was Don Carlos, brother-

in-law of the Governor; one Juan de Gamez, a nephew;
Men. Rodriguez, a Portugues; and Juan Vazquez, of Villanueva de Barcarota, men of condition and courage;
the rest were infantry. Of the living, one hundred and
fifty Christians had received seven hundred wounds from
the arrow; and God was pleased that they should be
healed in little time of very dangerous injuries. Twelve
horses died, and seventy were hurt. The clothing the
Christians carried with them, the ornaments for saying
mass, and the pearls, were all burned there; they having
set the fire themselves, because they considered the loss
less than the injury they might receive of the Indians
from within the houses, where they had brought the
things together.

The Governor learning in Manilla that Francisco Maldonado was waiting for him in the port of Ochuse, six
days' travel distant, he caused Juan Ortiz to keep the news
secret, that he might not be interrupted in his purpose;
because the pearls he wished to send to Cuba for show,
that their fame might raise the desire of coming to Florida, had been lost, and he feared that, hearing of him
without seeing either gold or silver, or other thing of
value from that land, it would come to have such
reputation that no one would be found to go there when
men should be wanted : so he determined to send no
news of himself until he should have discovered a rich
country.

CHAPTER XX.

How the Governor set out from Mauilla to go to Chicaça, and what befell him.

From the time the Governor arrived in Florida until he went from Manilla, there died one hundred and two Christians, some of sickness, others by the hand of the Indians. Because of the wounded, he stopped in that place twenty-eight days, all the time remaining out in the fields. The country was a rich soil, and well inhabited: some towns were very large, and were picketed about. The people were numerous everywhere; the dwellings standing a crossbow-shot or two apart.

On Sunday, the eighteenth of November, the sick being found to be getting on well, the Governor left Manilla, taking with him a supply of maize for two days. He marched five days through a wilderness, arriving in a province called Pafallaya, at the town Taliepatana; and thence he went to another, named Cabusto, near which was a large river, whence the Indians on the farther bank shouted to the Christians that they would kill them should they come over there. He ordered the building of a piragua within the town, that the natives might have no knowledge of it; which being finished in four days, and ready, he directed it to be taken on sleds half a league up stream, and in the morning thirty men entered it, well armed. The Indians discovering what was going on, they who were nearest went to oppose the landing, and did the best they could; but the Christians drawing near, and the piragua being about to reach the shore, they fled into some cane-brakes. The men on horses went up the river to secure a landing-place, to which the Governor passed over, with the others that remained. Some of the towns were well stored with maize and beans.

Thence towards Chicaça the Governor marched five days through a desert, and arrived at a river, on the farther side of which were Indians, who wished to arrest his passage. In two days another piragua was made, and when ready he sent an Indian in it to the Cacique, to say, that if he wished his friendship he should quietly wait for him; but they killed the messenger before his eyes, and with loud yells departed. He crossed the river the seventeenth of December, and arrived the same day at Chicaça, a small town of twenty houses. There the people underwent severe cold, for it was already winter, and snow fell: the greater number were then lying in the fields, it being before they had time to put up habitations. The land was thickly inhabited, the people living about over it as they do in Mauilla; and as it was fertile, the greater part being under cultivation, there was plenty of maize. So much grain was brought together as was needed for getting through with the season.

Some Indians were taken, among whom was one the Cacique greatly esteemed. The Governor sent an Indian to the Cacique to say, that he desired to see him and have his friendship. He came, and offered him the services of his person, territories, and subjects: he said that he would cause two chiefs to visit him in peace. In a few days he returned with them, they bringing their Indians. They presented the Governor one hundred and fifty conies, with clothing of the country, such as shawls and skins. The name of the one was Alimamu, of the other Niculasa.

The Cacique of Chicaça came to visit him many times: on some occasions he was sent for, and a horse taken, on which to bring and carry him back. He made complaint that a vassal of his had risen against him, withholding tribute; and he asked for assistance, desiring to seek him in his territory, and give him the chastisement he deserved. The whole was found to be feigned, to the end that, while the Governor should be absent with him, and the force divided, they would attack the parts separately—some the one under him, others the other, that remained in Chicaça. He went to the town where he lived, and came back with two hundred Indians, bearing bows and arrows.

The Governor, taking thirty cavalry and eighty infantry, marched to Saquechuma, the Province of the Chief whom the Cacique said had rebelled. The town was untenanted, and the Indians, for greater dissimulation, set fire to it; but the people with the Governor being very careful and vigilant, as were also those that had been left in Chicaça, no enemy dared to fall upon them. The Governor invited the caciques and some chiefs to dine with him, giving them pork to eat, which they so relished, although not used to it, that every night Indians would come up to some houses where the hogs slept, a crossbow-shot off from the camp, to kill and carry away what they could of them. Three were taken in the act: two the Governor commanded to be slain with arrows, and the remaining one, his hands having first been cut off, was sent to the Cacique, who appeared grieved that they had given offence, and glad that they were punished.

This Chief was half a league from where the Christians were, in an open country, whither wandered off four of the cavalry: Francisco Osorio, Reynoso, a servant of the Marquis of Astorga, and two servants of the Governor,—the one Ribera, his page, the other Fuentes, his chamberlain. They took some skins and shawls from the Indians, who made great outcry in consequence, and abandoned their houses. When the Governor heard of it, he ordered them to be apprehended, and condemned Osorio and Fuentes to death, as principals, and all of them to lose their goods. The friars, the priests, and other principal personages solicited him to let Osorio live, and moderate the sentence; but he would do so for no one. When about ordering them to be taken to the town-yard to be beheaded, some Indians arrived, sent by the Chief to complain of them. Juan Ortiz, at the entreaty of Baltasar de Gallegos and others, changed their words, telling the Governor, as from the Cacique, that he had understood those Christians had been arrested on his account; that they were in no fault, having offended him in nothing, and that if he would do him a favour, to let them go free: then Ortiz said to the Indians, that the Governor had the persons in custody, and would visit them with such punishment as should be an example to the rest. The prisoners were ordered to be released.

So soon as March had come, the Governor, having determined to leave Chicaça, asked two hundred tamemes of the Cacique, who told him that he would confer with his chiefs. Tuesday, the eighth, he went where the Cacique was, to ask for the carriers, and was told that he would send them the next day. When the Governor saw the Chief, he said to Luis de Moscoso that the Indians did not appear right to him; that a very careful watch should be kept that night, to which the Field Marshal paid little attention. At four o'clock in the morning the Indians fell upon them in four squadrons, from as many quarters, and directly as they were discovered, they beat a drum. With loud shouting, they came in such haste, that they entered the camp at the same moment with some scouts that had been out; of which, by the time those in the town were aware, half the houses were in flames. That night it had been the turn of three horsemen to be of the watch,—two of them men of low degree, the least value of any in the camp, and the third a nephew of the Governor, who had been deemed a brave man until now, when he showed himself as great a coward as either of the others; for they all fled, and the Indians, finding no resistance, came up and set fire to the place. They waited outside of the town for the Christians, behind the gates, as they should come out of the doors, having had no opportunity to put on their arms; and as they ran in all directions, bewildered by the noise, blinded by the smoke and the brightness of the flame, knowing not whither they were going, or were able to find their arms, or put saddles on their steeds, they saw not the Indians who shot arrows at them. Those of the horses that could break their halters got away, and many were burned to death in the stalls.

The confusion and rout were so great that each man fled by the way that first opened to him, there being none to oppose the Indians: but God, who chastiseth his own as he pleaseth, and in the greatest wants and perils hath them in his hand, shut the eyes of the Indians, so that they could not discern what they had done, and believed that the beasts running about loose were the cavalry gathering to fall upon them. The Governor, with a soldier named Tápia, alone got mounted, and, charging upon the Indians, he struck down the first of them he met with a blow of the lance, but went over with the saddle, because in the haste it had not been tightly drawn, and he fell. The men on foot, running to a thicket outside of the town, came together there: the Indians imagining, as it was dark, that the horses were cavalry coming upon them, as has been stated, they fled, leaving only one dead, which was he the Governor smote.

The town lay in cinders. A woman, with her husband, having left a house, went back to get some pearls that had remained there; and when she would have come out again the fire had reached the door, and she could not, neither could her husband assist her, so she was consumed. Three Christians came out of the fire in so bad plight, that one of them died in three days from that time, and the two others for a long while were carried in their pallets, on poles borne on the shoulders of Indians, for otherwise they could not have got along. There died in this affair eleven Christians, and fifty horses. One hundred of the swine remained, four hundred having been destroyed, from the conflagration of Manilla.

If, by good luck, any one had been able to save a garment until then, it was there destroyed. Many remained naked, not having had time to catch up their skin dresses. In that place they suffered greatly from cold, the only relief being in large fires, and they passed the night long in turning, without the power to sleep; for as one side of a man would warm, the other would freeze. Some contrived mats of dried grass sewed together, one to be placed below, and the other above them: many who laughed at this expedient were afterwards compelled to do the like. The Christians were left so broken up, that what with the want of the saddles and arms which had been destroyed, had the Indians returned the second night, they might, with little effort, have been overpowered. They removed from that town to the one where the Cacique was accustomed to live, because it was in the open field. In eight days' time they had constructed many saddles from the ash, and likewise lances, as good as those made in Biscay.

CHAPTER XXI.

How the Indians returned to attack the Christians. and how the Governor went to Alimamu, and they tarried to give him Battle in the Way.

On Wednesday, the fifteenth day of March, in the year 1541, eight days having passed since the Governor had been living on a plain, half a league from the place where he wintered, after he had set up a forge, and tempered the swords which in Chicaça had been burned, and already had made many targets, saddles, and lances, [on Tuesday night,] at four o'clock in the morning, while it was still dark, there came many Indians, formed in three squadrons, each from a different direction, to attack the camp, when those who watched beat to arms. In all haste he drew up his men in three squadrons also, and leaving some for the defence of the camp, he went out to meet them. The Indians were overthrown and put to flight. The ground was plain, and in a condition advantageous to the Christians. It was now daybreak; and but for some disorder, thirty or forty more enemies might have been slain. It was caused by a friar raising great shouts in the camp, without any reason, crying, "To the camp! To the camp!" In consequence the

Governor and the rest went thither, and the Indians had time to get away in safety.

From some prisoners taken, the Governor informed himself of the region in advance. On the twenty-fifth day of April he left Chicaça and went to sleep at a small town called Alimamu. Very little maize was found; and as it became necessary to attempt thence to pass a desert, seven days' journey in extent, the next day the Governor ordered that three captains, each with cavalry and foot, should take a different direction, to get provision for the way. Juan de Añasco, the Comptroller, went with fifteen horse and forty foot on the course the Governor would have to march, and found a staked fort where the Indians were awaiting them. Many were armed, walking upon it, with their bodies, legs, and arms painted and ochred, red, black, white, yellow, and vermilion in stripes, so that they appeared to have on stockings and doublet. Some wore feathers, and others horns on the head, the face blackened, and the eyes encircled with vermilion, to heighten their fierce aspect. So soon as they saw the Christians draw nigh they beat drums, and, with loud yells, in great fury came forth to meet them. As to Juan de Añasco and others it appeared well to avoid them, and to inform the Governor, they retired, over an even ground in sight, the distance of a crossbow-shot from the enclosure, the footmen, the crossbow-men, and targeteers putting themselves before those on horseback, that the beasts might not be wounded by the Indians, who came forth by sevens and eights to discharge their bows at them and retire. In sight of the Christians they made a fire, and, taking an Indian by the head and feet, pretended to give him many blows on the head and cast him into the flames, signifying in this way what they would do with the Christians.

A message being sent with three of the cavalry to the Governor, informing him of this, he came directly. It was his opinion that they should be driven from the place. He said that if this was not done they would be emboldened to make an attack at some other time, when they might do him more harm: those on horseback were commanded to dismount, and, being set in four squadrons, at the signal charged the Indians. They resisted until the Christians came up to the stakes; then, seeing that they could not defend themselves, they fled through that part near which passed a stream, sending back some arrows from the other bank; and because, at the moment, no place was found where the horses might ford, they had time to make their escape. Three Indians were killed and many Christians wounded, of whom, after a few days, fifteen died on the march. Every one thought the Governor committed a great fault in not sending to examine the state of the ground on the opposite shore, and discover the crossing-place before making the attack; because, with the hope the Indians had of escaping unseen in that direction, they fought until they were broken; and it was the cause of their holding out so long to assail the Christians, as they could, with safety to themselves.

CHAPTER XXII.

How the Governor went from Quizquiz, and thence to the River Grande.

THREE days having gone by since some maize had been sought after, and but little found in comparison with the great want there was of it, the Governor became obliged to move at once, notwithstanding the wounded had need of repose, to where there should be abundance. He accordingly set out for Quizquiz, and marched seven days through a wilderness, having many pondy places, with thick forests, fordable, however, on horseback, all to some basins or lakes that were swum. He arrived at a town of Quizquiz without being descried, and seized all the people before they could come out of their houses. Among them was the mother of the Cacique; and the Governor sent word to him, by one of the captives, to come and receive her, with the rest he had taken. The answer he returned was, that if his lordship would order them to be loosed and sent, he would come to visit and do him service.

The Governor, since his men arrived weary, and likewise weak, for want of maize, and the horses were also lean, determined to yield to the requirement and try to have peace; so the mother and the rest were ordered to

14

be set free, and with words of kindness were dismissed. The next day, while he was hoping to see the Chief, many Indians came, with bows and arrows, to set upon the Christians, when he commanded that all the armed horsemen should be mounted and in readiness. Finding them prepared, the Indians stopped at the distance of a crossbow-shot from where the Governor was, near a river-bank, where, after remaining quietly half an hour, six chiefs arrived at the camp, stating that they had come to find out what people it might be; for that they had knowledge from their ancestors that they were to be subdued by a white race; they consequently desired to return to the Cacique, to tell him that he should come presently to obey and serve the Governor. After presenting six or seven skins and shawls brought with them, they took their leave, and returned with the others who were waiting for them by the shore. The Cacique came not, nor sent another message.

There was little maize in the place, and the Governor moved to another town, half a league from the great river, where it was found in sufficiency. He went to look at the river, and saw that near it there was much timber of which piraguas might be made, and a good situation in which the camp might be placed. He directly moved, built houses, and settled on a plain a crossbow-shot from the water, bringing together there all the maize of the towns behind, that at once they might go to work and cut down trees for sawing out planks to build barges. The Indians soon came from up the stream, jumped on shore, and told the Governor that they were the vassals of a great lord, named Aquixo, who was the suzerain of many towns and people on the other shore; and they made known from him, that he would come the day after, with all his people, to hear what his lordship would command him.

The next day the Cacique arrived, with two hundred canoes filled with men, having weapons. They were painted with ochre, wearing great bunches of white and other plumes of many colours, having feathered shields in their hands, with which they sheltered the oarsmen on either side, the warriors standing erect from bow to stern, holding bows and arrows. The barge in which the Cacique came had an awning at the poop, under which he sate; and the like had the barges of the other chiefs: and there, from under the canopy, where the chief man was, the course was directed and orders issued to the rest. All came down together, and arrived within a stone's cast of the ravine, whence the Cacique said to the Governor, who was walking along the river-bank, with others who bore him company, that he had come to visit, serve, and obey him; for he had heard that he was the greatest of lords, the most powerful on all the earth, and that he must see what he would have him do. The Governor expressed his pleasure, and besought him to land, that they might the better confer; but the Chief gave no reply, ordering three barges to draw near, wherein was great quantity of fish, and loaves like bricks, made of the pulp of ameixas, which Soto receiving, gave him thanks and again entreated him to land.

Making the gift had been a pretext, to discover if any

harm might be done; but, finding the Governor and his people on their guard, the Cacique began to draw off from the shore, when the crossbow-men, who were in readiness, with loud cries shot at the Indians, and struck down five or six of them. They retired with great order, not one leaving the oar, even though the one next to him might have fallen, and covering themselves, they withdrew. Afterward they came many times and landed: when approached, they would go back to their barges. These were fine-looking men, very large and well formed; and what with the awnings, the plumes, and the shields, the pennons, and the number of people in the fleet, it appeared like a famous armada of galleys.

During the thirty days that were passed there, four piraguas were built, into three of which, one morning, three hours before daybreak, the Governor ordered twelve cavalry to enter, four in each, men in whom he had confidence that they would gain the land, notwithstanding the Indians, and secure the passage, or die: he also sent some crossbow-men of foot with them, and in the other piragua, oarsmen, to take them to the opposite shore. He ordered Juan de Guzman to cross with the infantry, of which he had remained Captain in the place of Francisco Maldonado: and because the current was stiff, they went up along the side of the river a quarter of a league, and in passing over they were carried down, so as to land opposite the camp; but, before arriving there, at twice the distance of a stone's cast, the horsemen rode out from the piraguas to an open area of hard and even ground, where they all reached without accident.

So soon as they had come to shore the piraguas returned; and when the sun was up two hours high, the people had all got over. The distance was near half a league: a man standing on the shore could not be told, whether he were a man or something else, from the other side. The stream was swift, and very deep; the water, always flowing turbidly, brought along from above many trees and much timber, driven onward by its force. There were many fish of several sorts, the greater part differing from those of the fresh waters of Spain, as will be told hereafter.

CHAPTER XXIII.

How the Governor went from Aquixo to Casqui, and thence to Pacaha; and how this Country differs from the other.

The Rio Grande being crossed, the Governor marched a league and a half, to a large town of Aquixo, which was abandoned before his arrival. Over a plain thirty Indians were seen to draw nigh, sent by the Cacique, to discover what the Christians intended to do, but who fled directly as they saw them. The cavalry pursued, killed ten, and captured fifteen. As the town toward which the Governor marched was near the river, he sent a captain, with the force he thought sufficient, to take the piraguas up the stream. These, as they frequently wound about through the country, having to go round the bays that swell out of the river,, the Indians had opportunity to attack those in the piraguas, placing them in great peril, being shot at with bows from the ravines, while they dared not leave the shore, because of the swiftness of the current; so that, as soon as the Governor got to the town, he directly sent cross-bow-men to them down the stream, for their protection. When the piraguas arrived, he ordered them to be taken to pieces, and the spikes kept for making others, when they should be needed.

The Governor slept at the town one night, and the day following he went in quest of a province called Pacaha, which he had been informed was nigh Chisca, where the Indians said there was gold. He passed through large towns in Aquixo, which the people had left for fear of the Christians. From some Indians that were taken, he heard that three days' journey thence resided a great Cacique, called Casqui. He came to a small river, over which a bridge was made, whereby he crossed. All that day, until sunset, he marched through water, in places coming to the knees; in others, as high as the waist. They were greatly rejoiced on reaching the dry land; because it had appeared to them that they should travel about, lost, all night in the water. At midday they came to the first town of Casqui, where they found the Indians off their guard, never having heard of them. Many men and women were taken, much clothing, blankets, and skins; such they likewise took in another town in sight of the first, half a league off in the field, whither the horsemen had run.

This land is higher, drier, and more level than any other along the river that had been seen until then. In the fields were many walnut-trees, bearing tender-shelled nuts in the shape of acorns, many being found stored in the houses. The tree did not differ in any thing from that of Spain, nor from the one seen before, except the leaf was smaller. There were many mulberry-trees, and trees of amexeas, having fruit of vermilion hue, like one of Spain, while others were gray, differing, but far better. All the trees, the year round, were as green as if they stood in orchards, and the woods were open.

The Governor marched two days through the country of Casqui, before coming to the town where the Cacique was, the greater part of the way lying through fields thickly set with great towns, two or three of them to be seen from one. He sent word by an Indian to the Cacique, that he was coming to obtain his friendship and to consider him as a brother; to which he received for answer, that he would be welcomed; that he would be received with special good-will, and all that his lordship required of him should be done; and the Chief sent him on the road a present of skins, shawls, and fish. After these gifts were made, all the towns into which the Governor came were found occupied; and the inhabitants awaited him in peace, offering him skins, shawls, and fish.

Accompanied by many persons, the Cacique came half a league on the road from the town where he dwelt to receive the Governor, and, drawing nigh to him, thus spoke :—

VERY HIGH, POWERFUL, AND RENOWNED MASTER :—
    I greet your coming. So soon as I had notice of you, your power and perfections, although you entered my territory capturing and killing the dwellers upon it, who are my vassals, I determined to conform my wishes to your will, and hold as right all that you might do, believing that it should be so for a good reason, providing against some future event, to you perceptible but from me concealed; since an evil may well be permitted to avoid another greater, that good can arise, which I trust will be so; for from so excellent a prince, no bad motive is to be suspected. My ability is so small to serve you, according to your great merit, that though you should

consider even my abundant will and humility in proffering you all
manner of services, I must still deserve little in your sight. If this
ability can with reason be valued, I pray you receive it, and with it
my country and my vassals, of me and them disposing at your pleasure; for though you were lord of the earth, with no more good-
will would you be received, served, and obeyed.

The Governor responded appropriately in a few words
which satisfied the Chief. Directly they fell to making
each other great proffers, using much courtesy, the Cacique inviting the Governor to go and take lodging in his
houses. He excused himself, the better to preserve peace,
saying that he wished to lie in the field; and, because the
heat was excessive, he pitched the camp among some
trees, quarter of a league from the town. The Cacique
went to his town, and returned with many Indians singing, who, when they had come to where the Governor was,
all prostrated themselves. Among them were two blind
men. The Cacique made an address, of which, as it was
long, I will give the substance in a few words. He said,
that inasmuch as the Governor was son of the Sun, he
begged him to restore sight to those Indians: whereupon
the blind men arose, and they very earnestly entreated
him to do so. Soto answered them, that in the heavens
above there was One who had the power to make them
whole, and do whatever they could ask of Him, whose
servant he was; that this great Lord made the sky
and the earth, and man after His image; that He had
suffered on the tree of the true cross to save the human
race, and risen from the grave on the third day,—what of
man there was of Him dying, what of divinity being immortal; and that, having ascended into heaven He was

there with open arms to receive all that would be con-
verted to Him. He then directed a lofty cross of wood to
be made and set up in the highest part of the town,
declaring to the Cacique that the Christians worshipped
that, in the form and memory of the one on which Christ
suffered. He placed himself with his people before it, on
their knees, which the Indians did likewise; and he told
them that from that time thenceforth they should thus
worship the Lord, of whom he had spoken to them, that
was in the skies, asking Him for whatsoever they stood in
need.

The Chief being asked what was the distance to
Pacaha, he answered that it was one day's journey, and
said that on the extreme of his territory there was a lake,
like an estuary, that entered into the Rio Grande, to which
he would send persons in advance to build a bridge, whereby they might pass over it. The night of the day the
Governor left, he slept at a town of Casqui; and the next
day he passed in sight of two other towns, and arrived
at the lake, which was half a crossbow-shot over, of great
depth and swiftness of current. The Indians had just
got done the bridge as he came up. It was built of wood,
in the manner of timber thrown across from tree to tree;
on one side there being a rail of poles, higher than the
rest, as a support for those who should pass. The Cacique of Casqui having come with his people, the Governor sent word by an Indian to the Cacique of Pacaha,
that though he might be at enmity with him of Casqui,
and that Chief be present, he should receive neither
injury nor insult, provided that he attended in peace

and desired his friendship, for as a brother would he treat him. The Indian went as he was bi.l, and returned, stating that the Cacique took no notice of the message, but that he fled out of the town, from the back part, with all his people. Then the Governor entered there, and with the cavalry charged in the direction the Indians were running, and at another town, a quarter of a league off, many were taken. As fast as they were captured, the horsemen delivered them to the Indians of Casqui, who, from being their enemies, brought them with great heed and pleasure to the town where the Christians were, greatly regretting that they had not the liberty to kill them. Many shawls, deer-skins, lion and bear skins, and many cat-skins were found in the town. Numbers who had been a long time badly covered, there clothed themselves. Of the shawls they made mantles and cassocks; some made gowns and lined them with cat-skins, as they also did the cassocks. Of the deer-skins were made jerkins, shirts, stockings, and shoes; and from the bear-skins they made very good cloaks, such as no water could get through. They found shields of raw cow-hide out of which armour was made for the horses.

CHAPTER ..XIII.

On Wednesday, the nineteenth day of June, the
Governor entered Pacaha, and took quarters in the town
where the Cacique was accustomed to reside. It was
enclosed and very large. In the towers and the palisade
were many loopholes. There was much dry maize, and
the new was in great quantity, throughout the fields.
At the distance of half a league to a league off were
large towns, all of them surrounded with stockades.

Where the Governor stayed was a great lake, near to
the enclosure; and the water entered a ditch that well-
nigh went round the town. From the River Grande to
the lake was a canal, through which the fish came into
it, and where the Chief kept them for his eating and
pastime. With nets that were found in the place, as
many were taken as need required; and however much
might be the casting, there was never any lack of them.
In the many other lakes about were also many fish,
though the flesh was soft, and none of it so good as that
which came from the river. The greater number differ
from those in the fresh water of Spain. There was a fish

called bagre, the third part of which was head, with gills
from end to end, and along the sides were great spines,
like very sharp awls. Those of this sort that lived in the
lake were as big as pike; in the river were some that
weighed from one hundred to one hundred and fifty
pounds. Many were taken with the hook. There was
one in the shape of barbel; another like bream, with the
head of a hake, having a colour between red and brown,
and was the most esteemed. There was likewise a kind
called peel-fish, the snout a cubit in length, the upper
lip being shaped like a shovel. Another fish was like a
shad. Except the bagres and the peel, they were all
of scale. There was one, called perco, the Indians sometimes brought, the size of a hog, and had rows of teeth
above and below.

The Cacique of Casqui many times sent large presents
of fish, shawls, and skins. Having told the Governor
that he would deliver into his hands the Cacique of
Pacaha, he went to Casqui, and ordered many canoes to
ascend the river, while he should march by land, taking
many of his warriors. The Governor, with forty cavalry
and sixty infantry, was conducted by him up stream; and
the Indians who were in the canoes discovered the
Cacique of Pacaha on an islet between two arms of the
river. Five Christians entered a canoe, of whom was
Don Antonio Osorio, to go in advance and see what
number of people the Cacique had with him. There
were five or six thousand souls, who, directly as they saw
the people, taking the Indians who went in the canoes to
be Christians also, the Cacique, and as many as could

get into three canoes that were there, fled to the opposite
bank; the greater part of the rest, in terror and confusion, plunging into the river to swim, many, mostly
women and infants, got drowned. Then the Governor,
who was on land, without knowing what was passing
with Don Antonio and those who accompanied him,
ordered the Christians, in all haste, to enter the canoes
with the Indians of Casqui, and they directly joining
Don Antonio on the islet, many men and women were
taken, and much clothing.

Many clothes, which the Indians had in cane hurdles
and on rafts to carry over, floated down stream, the people
of Casqui filling their canoes with them; and, in fear
that the Christians might take these away, their Chief
went off with them down the river to his territory, without taking leave. At this the Governor became indignant,
and directly returning to Pacaha, two leagues on the road,
he overran the country of Casqui, capturing twenty or
thirty of its men. The horses being tired, and there remaining no time that day to go farther, he went on to
Pacaha, with the intention of marching in three or four
days upon Casqui, directly letting loose a man of Pacaha,
sending word by him to its Chief, that should he desire
his friendship to come to him, and together they would
go to carry war upon Casqui: and immediately there
arrived many people of Pacaha, bringing as the chief an
Indian, who was exposed by a prisoner, brother of the
Cacique. The Governor told them that their lord must
come; that he well knew that Indian was not he; for that
nothing could be done without its being known to him

before they so much as thought of it. The Cacique came the next day, followed by many Indians, with a large gift of fish, skins, and shawls. He made a speech, that all were glad to hear, and concluded by saying, that although his lordship had causelessly inflicted injury on his country and his subjects, he did not any the less cease to be his, and was always at his command. The Governor ordered his brother to be let go, and some principal men he held captives. That day a messenger arrived from Casqui, saying that his master would come early on the morrow to excuse the error he had committed in going away without his license; to which the Governor bade him say, in return, to the Cacique, that if he did not come himself in person he would go after him, and inflict the punishment he deserved.

The Chief of Casqui came the next day, and after presenting many shawls, skins, and fish, he gave the Governor a daughter, saying that his greatest desire was to unite his blood with that of so great a lord as he was, begging that he would take her to wife. He made a long and discreet oration, full of praise of Soto; and concluded by asking his forgiveness, for the love of that cross he had left, for having gone off without his permission; that he had done so because of the shame he felt for what his people had done without his consent. The Governor said that he had taken a good sponsor; that he had himself determined, if the Cacique had not come to apologize, to go after him and burn his towns, kill him and his people, and lay waste his country. To this the Chief replied :—

Master:—

I and mine belong to you; and my territory is yours, so that you will destroy it, if you will, as your own, and your people you will slay. All that falls from your hand I shall receive as from my lord's, and as merited chastisement. Know, that the service you have done me in leaving that cross has been signal, and more than I have deserved; for, you know, of great droughts the maize in our fields was perishing, and no sooner had I and mine thrown ourselves on our knees before it, asking for water, than the want was supplied.

The Governor made friendship between the Chiefs of Casqui and Pacaha, and placed them at the table, that they should eat with him. They had a difficulty as to who should sit at his right hand, which the Governor quieted by telling them that among the Christians the one seat was as good as the other; that they should so consider it, and while with him no one should understand otherwise, each taking the seat he first came to. Thence he sent thirty horsemen and fifty footmen to the Province of Caluça, to see if in that direction they could turn back towards Chisca, where the Indians said there was a foundry of gold and copper. They travelled seven days through desert, and returned in great extremity, eating green amexeas and maize-stalks, which they had found in a poor town of seven or eight houses. The Indians stated that thence towards the north, the country, being very cold, was very thinly populated; that cattle were in such plenty, no maize-field could be protected from them, and the inhabitants lived upon the meat. Seeing that the country was so poor off for maize that there could be no support, the Governor asked the Indians in what direction there were most inhabitants; and they said that they had knowledge of a large province and a country of great abundance, called Quiguate, that lay in the southern direction.

10

CHAPTER XXV.

How the Governor went from Pacaha to Aquiguate
and to Coligoa, and came to Cayas.

The Governor rested in Pacaha forty days, during
which time the two Caciques made him presents of fish,
shawls, and skins, in great quantity, each striving to
outdo the other in the magnitude of the gifts. At the
time of his departure, the Chief of Pacaha bestowed on
him two of his sisters, telling him that they were tokens
of love, for his remembrance, to be his wives. The
name of one was Macanoche, that of the other Mochila.
They were symmetrical, tall, and full: Macanoche bore
a pleasant expression; in her manners and features
appeared the lady; the other was robust. The Cacique
of Casqui ordered the bridge to be repaired; and the
Governor, returning through his territory, lodged in the
field near his town. He brought there much fish,
exchanged two women for as many shirts with two of
the Christians, and furnished a guide and tamemes. The
Governor marched to one of his towns, and slept, and
the next night came to another that was near a river,
where he ordered him to bring canoes, that he might
cross over. There taking his leave, the Chief went back.

The Governor travelled towards Aquiguate, and on

the fourth day of August came to the residence of the
Cacique, who, although he had sent him a present, on
the road, of many shawls and skins, abandoned the
place through fear on his arrival. That town was the
largest seen in Florida: one-half of it was occupied by
the Governor and his people; and, after a few days,
discovering that the Indians were dealing in falsehoods,
he ordered the other part to be burned, that it might
not afford them cover should they attack him at night,
nor be an embarrassment to his cavalry in a movement
to repel them. An Indian having come, attended by a
multitude, declaring himself to be the Cacique, the
Governor delivered him over to be looked after by his
body-guard. Many of the Indians went off, and returned
with shawls and skins; but, finding small opportunity
for carrying out their evil plan, one day the pretended
Cacique, walking out of the house with the Governor,
ran away with such swiftness that not one of the Christians could overtake him ; and plunging into the river, at
the distance of a crossbow-shot from the town, he made
for the other shore, where many Indians, giving loud
shouts, began to make use of their arrows. The Governor directly crossed over to attack them with horse and
foot; but they dared not await him : following them up,
he came to a town that was abandoned, before which
there was a lake the horses could not pass over, and on
the other side were many females. The footmen having
crossed, capturing many of them, took much clothing.
Returning to the camp early in the night, the sentinels
seized a spy, who assenting to the request to lead to

where the Cacique was, the Governor directly set out
with twenty cavalry and fifty infantry in quest of him.
After travelling a day and a half, they found him in a
thick wood; and a soldier, ignorant of who he was, having struck him on the head with a cutlass, he called
out not to kill him, that he was the Chief; so he was
captured, and with him one hundred and forty of his
people.

The Governor, returning to Quiguate, directed him
to tell his people to come and serve the Christians; but,
after waiting some days, in the hope of their arrival, and
finding that they did not come, he sent two captains,
each on an opposite side of the river, with infantry and
cavalry, whereby many of both sexes were made prisoners. The Indians, seeing the harm that they received
for their rebellious conduct, waited on the Governor to
take his commands, coming and going often, bringing
with them presents of fish. The Cacique and two of his
wives being at their liberty in the quarters of the Governor, which were guarded by his halberdiers, he asked
them what part of the country was most inhabited; to
which they replied, that to the south, or down the river,
where were large towns, and the Caciques governed wide
territories, with numerous people; and that to the northwest was a province, near some mountains, called
Coligoa. He, with the others, deemed it well to go
thither first; saying that the mountains, perhaps, would
make a difference in the soil, and that silver and gold
might afterward follow.

The country of Aquiguate, like that of Casqui and

Pacaha, was level and fertile, having rich river margins, on which the Indians made extensive fields. From Tascaluça to the River Grande may be three hundred leagues; a region very low, having many lakes: from Pacaha to Quiguate there may be one hundred and ten leagues. There he left the Cacique in his own town; and an Indian guided them through an immense pathless thicket of desert for seven days, where they slept continually in ponds and shallow puddles. Fish were so plentiful in them that they were killed with blows of cudgels; and as the Indians travelled in chains, they disturbed the mud at the bottom, by which the fish, becoming stupefied, would swim to the surface, when as many were taken as were desired.

The inhabitants of Coligoa had never heard of the Christians, and when these got so near their town as to be seen, they fled up stream along a river that passed near by there; some throwing themselves into the water, whence they were taken by their pursuers, who, on either bank, captured many of both sexes, and the Cacique with the rest. Three days from that time came many Indians, by his order, with offerings of shawls, deer-skins, and two cowhides: they stated that at the distance of five or six leagues towards the north were many cattle, where the country, being cold, was thinly inhabited; and that, to the best of their knowledge, the province that was better provisioned than any other, and more populous, was one to the south, called Cayas.

About forty leagues from Quiguate stood Coligoa, at the foot of a mountain, in the vale of a river of medium

size, like the Caya, a stream that passes through Estremadura. The soil was rich, yielding maize in such pro-
fusion that the old was thrown out of store to make room
for the new grain. Beans and pumpkins were likewise
in great plenty; both were larger and better than those
of Spain: the pumpkins, when roasted, have nearly the
taste of chestnuts. The Cacique continued behind in his
own town, having given a guide for the way to Cayas.

We travelled five days, and came to the Province of
Paliscma. The house of the Cacique was canopied with
coloured deer-skins, having designs drawn on them, and
the ground was likewise covered in the same manner, as
if with carpets. He had left it in that state for the use
of the Governor, a token of peace, and of a desire for
friendship, though still he did not dare to await his
coming. The Governor, finding that he had gone away,
sent a captain with horse and foot to look after him; and
though many persons were seen, because of the roughness
of the country, only a few men and boys were secured.
The houses were few and scattered: only a little maize
was found.

Directly the Governor set forward and came to Tata-
licoya, whence he took the Cacique, who guided him to
Cayas, a distance of four days' journey from that town.
When he arrived and saw the scattered houses, he
thought, from the information he had received of the
great populousness of the country, that the Cacique was
lying to him—that it was not the province; and he menaced him, bidding him tell where he was. The Chief, as
likewise the other Indians taken near by, declared that to

be in Cayas, the best town in all the province; and that although the houses were far apart, the country occupied being extensive, it had numerous people and many maize-fields. The town was called Tanico. The camp was placed in the best part of it, nigh a river. On the day of arrival, the Governor, with some mounted men, went a league farther, but found no one, and only some skins, which the Cacique had put on the road to be taken, a sign of peace, by the usage of the country.

CHAPTER XXVI.

How the Governor went to visit the Province of
Tulla, and what happened to him.

The Governor tarried a month in the Province of
Cayas. In this time the horses fattened and throve more
than they had done at other places in a longer time, in
consequence of the large quantity of maize there. The
blade of it, I think, is the best fodder that grows. The
beasts drank so copiously from the very warm and brack-
ish lake, that they came having their bellies swollen with
the leaf when they were brought back from watering. To
that spot the Christians had wanted salt: they now made
a quantity and took it with them. The Indians carry it
into other parts, to exchange for skins and shawls.

The salt is made along by a river, which, when the
water goes down, leaves it upon the sand. As they cannot gather the salt without a large mixture of sand, it is
thrown together into certain baskets they have for their
purpose, made large at the mouth and small at the bottom. These are set in the air on a ridge-pole ; and water
being thrown on, vessels are placed under them wherein
it may fall ; then, being strained and placed on the fire, it
is boiled away, leaving salt at the bottom.

The lands on the shores of the river were fields, and

maize was in plenty. The Indians dared not cross the river to where we were. Some appearing, were called to by the soldiers who saw them, and having come over were conducted by them before the Governor. On being asked for the Cacique, they said that he was peaceful but afraid to show himself. The Governor directly sent them back to tell him to come, and, if he desired his friendship, to bring an interpreter and a guide for the travel before them; that if he did not do so he would go in pursuit, when it would be the worse for him. The Governor waited three days, and finding that the Cacique did not come, he went in pursuit and brought him there a captive, with one hundred and fifty of his people. He asked him if he had knowledge of any great cacique, and in what direction the country was most inhabited. The Indian stated, that the largest population about there was that of a province lying to the southward, thence a day and a half's travel, called Tulla; that he could give him a guide, but no interpreter; that the tongue of that country was different from his, and that he and his ancestors had ever been at war with its chiefs, so that they neither conversed together nor understood each other.

Then the Governor, with cavalry and fifty infantry, directly set out for Tulla, to see if it were such a land as he might pass through with his troops. So soon as it became known that he had reached there, the inhabitants were summoned; and as they gathered by fifteen and twenty at a time, they would come to attack the Christians. Finding that they were sharply handled, and that in running the horses would overtake them, they got

17

upon the house-tops, where they endeavoured to defend themselves with their bows and arrows. When beaten off from one roof, they would get up on to another; and the Christians while going after some, others would attack them from an opposite direction. The struggle lasted so long that the steeds, becoming tired, could not be made to run. One horse was killed and others were wounded. Of the Indians fifteen were slain, and forty women and boys made prisoners; for to no one who could draw a bow and could be reached was his life spared him.

The Governor determined at once to go back, before the inhabitants should have time to come together. That afternoon he set out, and travelling into the night, he slept on the road to avoid Tulla, and arrived the next day at Cayas. Three days later he marched to Tulla, bringing with him the Cacique, among whose Indians he was unable to find one who spoke the language of that place. He was three days on the way, and at his arrival found the town abandoned, the inhabitants not venturing to remain for him. But no sooner did they know that he was in the town, than, at four o'clock on the morning of the first night, they came upon him in two squadrons, from different directions, with bows and arrows and with long staves like pikes. So soon as they were felt, both cavalry and infantry turned out. Some Christians and some horses were injured. Many of the Indians were killed.

Of those made captive, the Governor sent six to the Cacique, their right hands and their noses cut off, with the message, that, if he did not come to him to apologize and render obedience, he would go in pursuit, and to him,

and as many of his as he might find, would he do as he
had done to those he sent. He allowed him three days
in which to appear. making himself understood by signs,
in the best manner possible, for want of an interpreter.
At the end of that time an Indian, bearing a back-load of
cow-skins from the Cacique, arrived, weeping with great
sobs, and coming to where the Governor was, threw himself at his feet. Soto raised him up, and the man made a
speech, but there was none to understand him. The Governor, by signs, told him to return and say to the Cacique,
that he must send him some one who could speak with the
people of Cayas. Three Indians came the next day with
loads of cow-skins, and three days afterward came twenty
others. Among them was one who understood those of
Cayas. After a long oration from him, of apologies for
the Cacique and in praise of the Governor, he concluded
by saying, that he with the others had come, in behalf of
the Chief, to inquire what his lordship would command,
for that he was ready to serve him.

At hearing these words the Governor and the rest
were all rejoiced; for in no way could they go on without
a guide. He ordered the man to be safely kept, and told
him to tell the Indians who came with him to go back
to the Cacique and say, that he forgave him the past and
greatly thanked him for the interpreter and the presents;
that he should be pleased to see him, and to come the
next day, that they might talk together. He came at the
end of three days, and with him eighty Indians. As he
and his men entered the camp they wept,—the token of
obedience and the repentance of a past error, according

to the usage of that country. He brought a present of
many cow-skins, which were found very useful; the country being cold, they were taken for bed-covers, as they
were very soft and the wool like that of sheep. Near by,
to the northward, are many cattle. The Christians did
not see them, nor go where they were, because it was a
country thinly populated, having little maize. The Cacique of Tulla made an address to the Governor, in which
he apologized and offered him his country, his vassals, and
his person. The speech of this Cacique—like those of
the other chiefs, and all the messengers in their behalf
who came before the Governor—no orator could more
elegantly phrase.

CHAPTER XXVII.

How the Governor went from Tulla to Autiamque, where he passed the Winter.

The Governor informed himself of the country in every direction. He ascertained that toward the west there was a thin population, and to the southeast were great towns, principally in a province, abundant of maize, called Autiamque, at the distance of about eighty leagues, ten days' journey from Tulla. The winter was already come. The cold, rain, and snow did not permit the people to travel for two or three months in the year, and the Governor feared to remain among that sparse population, lest his force could not be subsisted for that length of time. Moreover, the Indians said that near Autiamque was a great water, which, from their account, appeared to him to be an arm of the sea. Hence, he determined to winter in that province, and in the following summer to go to the sea-side, where he would build two brigantines,—one to send to Cuba, the other to New Spain, that the arrival of either might bear tidings of him. Three years had elapsed since he had been heard of by Doña Ysabel, or by any person in a civilized community. Two hundred and fifty of his men were dead, likewise one hundred and fifty horses. He desired to recruit from Cuba of man and beast, calculating, out of his property there, to refit and again go back to advance, to discover and to conquer farther on towards the west, where he had not reached, and whither Cabeça de Vaca had wandered.

Having dismissed the Caciques of Tulla and Cayas, the Governor took up his course, marching five days over very sharp mountains, and arrived in a peopled district called Quipana. Not a native could be captured, because of the roughness of the country, and the town was among ridges. At night an ambuscade was set, in which two men were taken, who said that Antiamque was six days' journey distant, and that there was another province toward the south, eight days' travel off, called Guahate, very abundant in maize and very populous. However, as Autiamque was nearer, and most of the Indians spoke of it, the Governor continued on his journey thither.

At the end of three days he came to a town called Anoixi. Having sent a captain in advance, with thirty horse and fifty foot, they came suddenly upon the inhabitants, taking many of both sexes. On the second day afterwards, the Governor arrived at another town, called Catamaya, and slept in the adjacent fields. Two Indians coming to him from the Cacique, with the pretext of a message, in order to ascertain his business, he told them to say to their master, that he wished to speak with him; but they came no more, nor was other word returned. The next day the Christians went to the town, which was without people, and having taken what maize they needed, that night they reached a wood to rest, and the day following arrived at Antiamque.

They found in store much maize, also beans, walnuts, and dried ameixas in large quantities. Some Indians were taken while gathering up their clothing, having already carried away their wives. The country was level and very populous. The Governor lodged in the best portion of the town, and ordered a fence immediately to be put up about the encampment, away from the houses, that the Indians without might do no injury with fire. Measuring off the ground by pacing, he allotted to each his part to build, according to the Indians he possessed; and the timber being soon brought by them, in three days it was finished, made of very high trees sunk deep in the ground, and traversed by many pieces.

Near by passed a river of Cayas, the shores of it well peopled, both above and below the town. Indians appeared on the part of the Cacique with a present of shawls and skins, and a lame Chief, the lord of a town called Tietiquaquo, subject to the Cacique of Antiamque, came frequently to visit the Governor, and brought him gifts of the things he possessed. The Cacique sent to the Governor to inquire what length of time he would remain in his territory; and hearing that he was to be there more than three days, he sent no more messages nor Indians, but treated with the lame Chief to insurge. Numerous inroads were made, in which many persons of both sexes were taken, and among the rest that Chief, whom the Governor, having reprehended and admonished, set at liberty, in consideration of the presents he had made, giving him two Indians to bear him away on their shoulders.

The Cacique of Autiamque, desiring to drive the strangers out of his territory, ordered spies to be set about them. An Indian, coming at night to the entrance of the palisade, was noticed by a soldier on guard, who, putting himself behind the door as he entered, struck him down with a cutlass. When taken before the Governor, he was asked why he came, but fell dead without utterance. The next night the Governor sent a soldier to beat the alarm, and cry out that he saw Indians, in order to ascertain how fast the men would hasten to the call. This was done also in other places, at times when it appeared to him they were careless, that he might reprove those who were late in coming; so that for danger, as well as for doing his duty, each one on such occasion would strive to be the first.

The Christians stayed three months in Autiamque, enjoying the greatest plenty of maize, beans, walnuts, and dried ameixas; also conies, which they had never had ingenuity enough to ensnare until the Indians there taught them. The contrivance is a strong spring, that lifts the animal off its feet, a noose being made of a stiff cord to run about the neck, passing through rings of cane, that it may not be gnawed. Many of them were taken in the maize-fields, usually when it was freezing or snowing. The Christians were there a month in snow, when they did not go out of town, save to a wood, at the distance of two crossbow-shots, to which, whenever fuel was wanted, a road was opened, the Governor and others, on horseback, going to and returning from it many times, when it was brought from there by those of foot. In this time many conies were killed with arrows by the Indians, who were now allowed to go at large in their shackles. The animal is of two sorts; one of them like that of Spain, the other of the colour, form, and size of the great hare, though longer even, and having bigger loins.

18

CHAPTER XXVIII.

How the Governor went from Autiamque to Nilco,
and thence to Guachoya.

On Monday, the sixth day of March, of the year
1542 of the Christian era, the Governor set out from
Autiamque to seek Nilco, which the Indians said was
nigh the River Grande, with the purpose, by going to
the sea, to recruit his forces. He had not over three
hundred efficient men, nor more than forty horses. Some
of the beasts were lame, and useful only in making out
the show of a troop of cavalry; and, from the lack of
iron, they had all gone a year without shoes, though,
from the circumstance of travelling in a smooth country,
they had little need of them.

Juan Ortiz died in Autiamque, a loss the Governor
greatly regretted; for, without an interpreter, not knowing whither he was travelling, Soto feared to enter the
country, lest he might get lost. Thenceforth a lad, taken
in Cutifachiqui, who had learned somewhat of the language of the Christians, served as the interpreter. The
death was so great a hindrance to our going, whether on
discovery or out of the country, that to learn of the
Indians what would have been rendered in four words,
it became necessary now to have the whole day: and

oftener than otherwise the very opposite was understood
of what was asked; so that many times it happened the
road that we travelled one day, or sometimes two or
three days, would have to be returned over, wandering
up and down, lost in thickets.

The Governor went to a province called Ayays,
arriving at a town near the river that passed by Cayas,
and by Autiamque, from which he had been ten days in
coming. He ordered a piragua to be built, in which he
crossed; and, having arrived on the other shore, there set
in such weather that marching was impossible for four
days, because of snow. When that ceased to fall, he
travelled three days through desert, a region so low, so
full of lakes and bad passages, that at one time, for the
whole day, the travel lay through water up to the knees
at places, in others to the stirrups; and occasionally, for
the distance of a few paces, there was swimming. And
he came to Tutelpinco, a town untenanted, and found to
be without maize, seated near a lake that flowed copiously into the river, with a violent current. Five Christians, in charge of a captain, in attempting to cross, by
order of the Governor, were upset; when some seized
hold of the canoe they had employed, others of trees that
grew in the water, while one, a worthy man, Francisco
Bastian, a native of Villanueva de Barcarota, became
drowned. The Governor travelled all one day along the
margin of the lake, seeking for a ford, but could discover
none, nor any way to get over.

Returning to Tutelpinco at night, the Governor
found two friendly natives, who were willing to show

him the crossing, and the road he was to take. From the reeds and timber of the houses, rafts and causeways were made, on which the river was crossed. After three days' marching, at Tianto, in the territory of Nilco, thirty Indians were taken, among whom were two Chiefs of the town. A captain, with infantry and cavalry, was directly dispatched to Nilco, that the inhabitants might not have time to carry off their provisions. In going through three or four large towns, at the one where the Cacique resided, two leagues from where the Governor stayed, many Indians were found to be in readiness, with bows and arrows, who, surrounding the place, appeared to invite an onset; but so soon as they saw the Christians drawing nigh to them without faltering, they approached the dwelling of the Cacique, setting fire to it, and, by a pond near the town, through which the horses could not go, they fled.

The following day, Wednesday, the twenty-ninth of March, the Governor arrived at Nilco, making his quarters, and those of his people, in the town of the Cacique, which was in an open field, that for a quarter of a league over was all inhabited; and at the distance of from half a league to a league off were many other large towns, in which was a good quantity of maize, beans, walnuts, and dried ameixas. This was the most populous of any country that was seen in Florida, and the most abundant in maize, excepting Coça and Apalache. An Indian, attended by a party, arrived at the camp, and, presenting the Governor with a cloak of marten-skins and a string of pearls, he received some

margaridetas (a kind of bead much esteemed in Peru),
and other trinkets, with which he was well pleased. At
leaving, he promised to be back in two days, but did not
return. In the night-time, however, the Indians came in
canoes, and carrying away all the maize they could take,
set up their huts on the other side of the river, among
the thickest bushes. The Governor, finding that the
Indian did not arrive within the time promised, ordered
an ambuscade to be placed at some cribs, near the lake,
to which the Indians came for maize. Two of them
were taken, who told him that the person who had come
to visit him was not the Cacique, but one sent by him,
pretending to be he, in order to observe what might be
the vigilance of the Christians, and whether it was
their purpose to remain in that country, or to go farther.
Directly a captain, with men on horseback and foot, were
sent over to the other shore; but, as their crossing was
observed, only ten or a dozen Indians, of both sexes,
could be taken; and with these the Christians returned
to camp.

This river, passing by Anilco, is the same that
flows by Cayas and Autiamque, and falls into the
River Grande, which flows by Pacaha and Aquixo,
near the Province of Guachoya, the lord of which
ascended in canoes to carry war upon him of Nilco.
In his behalf a messenger came to the Governor, saying
that the Cacique was his servant, desiring to be so considered, and that in two days from that time he would
come to make his salutation. He arrived in season,
accompanied by some of his principal men, and with

great proffers and courtesy, he presented many shawls
and deer-skins. The Governor gave him some articles of
barter, showing him much attention, and inquired what
towns there might be on the river below. He replied
that he knew of none other than his own; that opposite
was the Province of a Cacique called Quigaltam; then,
taking his leave, returned to his town.

The Governor determined to go to Guachoya within
a few days, to learn if the sea were near, or if there were
any inhabited territory nigh it, where he might find subsistence whilst those brigantines were building, that he
desired to send to a country of Christians. As he crossed
the River of Nilco, there came up Indians in canoes
from Guachoya, who, when they saw him, thinking that
he was in their pursuit, to do them harm, they returned
down the river, and informed the Cacique, when he took
away from the town whatsoever his people could carry,
and passed over with them, all that night, to the other
bank of the River Grande. The Governor sent a captain with fifty men, in six canoes, down the river to
Guachoya; while he, with the rest, marched by land,
arriving there on Sunday, the seventeenth day of April.
He took up his quarters in the town of the Cacique,
which was palisaded, seated a crossbow-shot from the
stream, that is there called the River Tamalisen, Tapatu
at Nilco, Mico at Coça, and at its entrance is known as
The River.

CHAPTER XXIX.

The Message sent to Quigaltam, and the Answer
brought back to the Governor, and what occurred
the while.

So soon as the Governor arrived in Guachoya, he
ordered Juan de Añasco, with as many people as could
go in the canoes, to ascend the river; for while they were
coming from Anilco they saw some cabins newly built on
the opposite shore. The Comptroller went, and brought
back the boats laded with maize, beans, dried ameixas,
and the pulp of them made into many loaves. The same
day an Indian arrived from Guachoya, and said that the
Cacique would come on the morrow. The next day,
many canoes were seen ascending the river; and the
people in them remained for an hour on the opposite side
of the River Grande, in consultation, as to whether they
should come to us or not; but finally they concluded to
come, and crossed the river, among them being the Cacique of Guachoya with many Indians, bringing much
fish, many dogs, skins, and blankets. So soon as they
had landed, they went to the lodging of the Governor in
the town, and having presented him with the offerings,
the Cacique thus spoke :—

POTENT AND EXCELLENT MASTER:—

I entreat you to forgive me the error I committed in going away from this town, and not waiting to greet and to obey you; since the occasion should have been for me, and is, one of pride: but I dreaded what I should not have feared, and did consequently what was out of reason; for error comes of haste, and I left without proper thought. So soon as I had reflected, I resolved not to follow the inclination of the foolish, which is to persist in his course, but to take that of the discreet and the wise: thus have I changed my purpose, coming to see in what it is you will bid me serve you, within the farthermost limits of my control.

The Governor received him with much pleasure, thanking him for the proffers and gift. Being asked if he had any information of the sea, he said, none, nor of any other inhabited country below on that side of the river, except a town two leagues distant, belonging to a chief subject to him; nor on the other shore, save three leagues down, the Province of Quigaltam, the lord of which was the greatest of that country. The Governor, suspecting that the Cacique spoke untruthfully, to rid his towns of him, sent Juan de Añasco with eight of cavalry down the river, to discover what population might be there, and get what knowledge there was of the sea. He was gone eight days, and stated, when he got back, that in all that time he could not travel more than fourteen or fifteen leagues, on account of the great bogs that came out of the river, the cane-brakes and thick scrubs there were along the margin, and that he had found no inhabited spot.

The Governor sank into a deep despondency at sight of the difficulties that presented themselves to his reaching the sea; and, what was worse, from the way in which the men and horses were diminishing in numbers, he could not sustain himself in the country without succour. Of that reflection he pined: but, before he took to his pallet, he sent a messenger to the Cacique of Quigaltam, to say that he was the child of the Sun, and whence he came all obeyed him, rendering their tribute; that he besought him to value his friendship, and to come where he was; that he would be rejoiced to see him; and in token of love and his obedience, he must bring him something from his country that was in most esteem there. By the same Indian the Chief returned this answer:—

As to what you say of your being the son of the Sun, if you will cause him to dry up the great river, I will believe you: as to the rest, it is not my custom to visit any one, but rather all, of whom I have ever heard, have come to visit me, to serve and obey me, and pay me tribute, either voluntarily or by force: if you desire to see me, come where I am; if for peace, I will receive you with special good-will; if for war, I will await you in my town; but neither for you, nor for any man, will I set back one foot.

When the messenger returned, the Governor was already low, being very ill of fevers. He grieved that he was not in a state to cross the river at once, and go in quest of the Cacique, to see if he could not abate that pride; though the stream was already flowing very powerfully, was nearly half a league broad, sixteen fathoms in height, rushing by in furious torrent, and on either shore were many Indians; nor was his power any longer so great that he might disregard advantages, relying on his strength alone.

Every day the Indians of Guachoya brought fish, until they came to be in such plenty that the town was covered with them.

19

The Governor having been told by the Cacique, that
on a certain night the Chief of Quigaltam would come
to give him battle, he suspected it to be a fiction of his
devising to get him out of his country, and he ordered
him to be put under guard, and from that night forth the
watch to be well kept. When asked why the Chief
did not come, he said that he had, but that, finding the
Governor in readiness, he dared not adventure; and he
greatly importuned him to send the captains over
the river, offering to supply many men to go upon
Quigaltam; to which the Governor said, that so soon as
he got well he would himself go to seek that Cacique.
Observing how many Indians came every day to the town,
and how populous was that country, the Governor fearing
that they would plot together, and practise on him some
perfidy, he permitted the gates in use, and some gaps in
the palisade that had not yet been closed up, to remain
open, that the Indians might not suppose he stood in fear,
ordering the cavalry to be distributed there; and the
night long they made the round, from each squadron
going mounted men in couples to visit the scouts, outside
the town, at points in the roads, and to the crossbow-men
that guarded the canoes in the river.

That the Indians might stand in terror of them, the
Governor determined to send a captain to Nilco, which
the people of Guachoya had told him was inhabited, and,
treating the inhabitants there severely, neither town
would dare to attack him: so he commanded Captain
Nuño de Tobar to march thither with fifteen horsemen,
and Captain Juan de Guzman, with his company of foot,

to ascend the river by water in canoes. The Cacique of
Guachoya ordered canoes to be brought, and many warriors to come, who went with the Christians. Two
leagues from Nilco, the cavalry, having first arrived,
waited for the foot, and thence together they crossed the
river in the night. At dawn, in sight of the town, they
came upon a scout, who, directly as he saw the Christians, set up loud yells, and fled to carry the news to those
in the place. Nuño de Tobar, and those with him, hastened on so rapidly, that they were upon the inhabitants
before they could all get out of the town. The ground
was open field; the part of it covered by the houses,
which might be a quarter of a league in extent, contained five or six thousand souls. Coming out of them,
the Indians ran from one to another habitation, numbers
collecting in all parts, so that there was not a man on
horseback who did not find himself amidst many; and
when the Captain ordered that the life of no male should
be spared, the surprise was such, that there was not a
man among them in readiness to draw a bow. The cries
of the women and children were such as to deafen those
who pursued them. About one hundred men were slain;
many were allowed to get away badly wounded, that
they might strike terror into those who were absent.

Some persons were so cruel and butcher-like that
they killed all before them, young and old, not one having
resisted little nor much; while those who felt it their
duty to be wherever there might be resistance, and were
esteemed brave, broke through the crowds of Indians,
bearing down many with their stirrups and the breasts

of their horses, giving some a thrust and letting them
go, but encountering a child or a woman would take and
deliver it over to the footmen. To the ferocious and the
bloodthirsty, God permitted that their sin should rise up
against them in the presence of all—when there was occasion for fighting showing extreme cowardice, and in the
end paying for it with their lives.

Eighty women and children were captured at Nilco,
and much clothing. The Indians of Guachoya, before
arriving at the town, had come to a stop, and from without watched the success of the Christians over the inhabitants; and when they saw that these were scattered,
that the cavalry were following and lancing them, they
went to the houses for plunder, filling the canoes with
clothing; and lest the Christians might take away what
they got, they returned to Guachoya, where they came
greatly astonished at what they had seen done to the
people of Nilco, which they, in great fear, recounted cir-
cumstantially to their Cacique.

CHAPTER XXX.

The Death of the Adelantado, Don Hernando de
Soto, and how Luys Moscoso de Alvarado was
chosen Governor.

The Governor, conscious that the hour approached
in which he should depart this life, commanded that
all the King's officers should be called before him, the
captains and the principal personages, to whom he
made a speech. He said that he was about to go into
the presence of God, to give account of all his past life;
and since He had been pleased to take him away at such
a time, and when he could recognize the moment of his
death, he, His most unworthy servant, rendered Him
hearty thanks. He confessed his deep obligations to
them all, whether present or absent, for their great
qualities, their love and loyalty to his person, well tried
in the sufferance of hardship, which he ever wished to
honour, and had designed to reward, when the Almighty should be pleased to give him repose from labour
with greater prosperity to his fortune. He begged that
they would pray for him, that through mercy he might
be pardoned his sins, and his soul be received in glory:
he asked that they would relieve him of the charge
he held over them, as well of the indebtedness he was

under to them all, as to forgive him any wrongs they
might have received at his hands.   To prevent any
divisions that might arise, as to who should command,
he asked that they would be pleased to elect a principal
and able person to be governor, one with whom they
should all be satisfied, and, being chosen, they would
swear before him to obey: that this would greatly satisfy
him, abate somewhat the pains he suffered, and moderate the anxiety of leaving them in a country, they knew
not where.

Baltasar de Gallegos responded in behalf of all,
consoling him with remarks on the shortness of the
life of this world, attended as it was by so many toils
and afflictions, saying that whom God earliest called
away, He showed particular favour; with many other
things appropriate to such an occasion: And finally,
since it pleased the Almighty to take him to Himself,
amid the deep sorrow they not unreasonably felt, it was
necessary and becoming in him, as in them, to conform
to the Divine Will: that as respected the election of a
governor, which he ordered, whomsoever his Excellency
should name to the command, him would they obey.
Thereupon the Governor nominated Luys Moscoso de
Alvarado to be his Captain-General; when by all those
present was he straightway chosen and sworn Governor.

The next day, the twenty-first of May, departed this
life the magnanimous, the virtuous, the intrepid Captain,
Don Hernando de Soto, Governor of Cuba and Adelantado of Florida.   He was advanced by fortune, in the
way she is wont to lead others, that he might fall the

greater depth: he died in a land, and at a time, that
could afford him little comfort in his illness, when the
danger of being no more heard from stared his companions in the face, each one himself having need of sympathy, which was the cause why they neither gave him
their companionship nor visited him, as otherwise they
would have done.

Luys de Moscoso determined to conceal what had
happened from the Indians; for Soto had given them to
understand that the Christians were immortal; besides,
they held him to be vigilant, sagacious, brave; and,
although they were at peace, should they know him to
be dead, they, being of their nature inconstant, might
venture on making an attack; and they were credulous
of all that he had told them, who made them believe
that some things which went on among them privately,
and he had come at without their being able to see how,
or by what means, that the figure which appeared in a
mirror he showed, told him whatsoever they might be
about, or desired to do; whence neither by word nor
deed did they dare undertake any thing to his injury.

So soon as the death had taken place, Luys de Moscoso
directed the body to be put secretly into a house, where
it remained three days; and thence it was taken at night,
by his order, to a gate of the town, and buried within.
The Indians, who had seen him ill, finding him no
longer, suspected the reason; and passing by where he
lay, they observed the ground loose, and, looking about,
talked among themselves. This coming to the knowledge
of Luys de Moscoso, he ordered the corpse to be taken

up at night, and among the shawls that enshrouded it
having cast abundance of sand, it was taken out in a
canoe and committed to the middle of the stream. The
Cacique of Guachoya asked for him, saying: "What
has been done with my brother and lord, the Governor?"
Luys de Moscoso told him that he had ascended into
the skies, as he had done on other many occasions; but
as he would have to be detained there some time, he had
left him in his stead. The Chief, thinking within himself
that he was dead, ordered two well-proportioned young
men to be brought, saying, that it was the usage of the
country, when any lord died, to kill some persons, who
should accompany and serve him on the way, on which
account they were brought; and he told him to command
their heads to be struck off, that they might go accordingly to attend his friend and master. Luys de Moscoso
replied to him, that the Governor was not dead, but only
gone into the heavens, having taken with him of his soldiers sufficient number for his need, and he besought him
to let those Indians go, and from that time forward not
to follow so evil a practice. They were presently ordered
to be let loose, that they might return to their houses;
but one of them refused to leave, alleging that he did
not wish to remain in the power of one who, without
cause, condemned him to die, and that he who had saved
his life he desired to serve so long as he should live.

Luys de Moscoso ordered the property of the Governor
to be sold at public outcry. It consisted of two male and
three female slaves, three horses, and seven hundred
swine. For each slave, or horse, was given two or three

hundred cruzados, to be paid at the first melting up of
gold or silver, or division of vassals and territory, with
the obligation that should there be nothing found in the
country, the payment should be made at the end of a
year, those having no property to pledge to give their
bond. A hog brought in the same way, trusted, two
hundred cruzados. Those who had left any thing at
home bought more sparingly, and took less than others.
From that time forward most of the people owned and
raised hogs; they lived on pork, observed Fridays and
Saturdays, and the vespers of holidays, which they had
not done before; for, at times, they had passed two or
three months without tasting any meat, and on the day
they got any, it had been their custom to eat it.

20

CHAPTER XXXI.

How the Governor Luys de Moscoso left Guachoya and went to Chaguate, and from thence
to Aguacay.

Some were glad of the death of Don Hernando de
Soto, holding it certain that Luys de Moscoso, who was
given to leading a gay life, preferred to see himself at
ease in a land of Christians, rather than continue the
toils of war, discovering and subduing, which the people had come to hate, finding the little recompense that
followed. The Governor ordered that the captains and
principal personages should come together, to consult
and determine upon what they would do; and, informed
of the population there was on all sides, he found that
towards the west the country was most inhabited, and
that descending the stream, after passing Quigaltam, it
was desert and had little subsistence. He besought them
all to give him their opinion in writing, signed with
their names, that, having the views of every one, he
might determine whether to follow down the river or
enter the land.

To every one it appeared well to march westwardly,
because in that direction was New Spain, the voyage by
sea being held more hazardous and of doubtful accom-

plishment, as a vessel of sufficient strength to weather a storm could not be built, nor was there captain nor pilot, needle nor chart, nor was it known how distant might be the sea; neither had they any tidings of it, or if the river did not take some great turn through the land, or might not have some fall over rocks where they might be lost. Some, who had seen the sea-card, found that by the shore, from the place where they were to New Spain, there should be about five hundred leagues; and they said that by land, though they might have to go round-about sometimes, in looking for a peopled country, unless some great impassable wilderness should intervene, they could not be hindered from going forward that summer; and, finding provision for support in some peopled country where they might stop, the following summer they should arrive in a land of Christians; and that, going by land, it might be they should discover some rich country which would avail them. Moscoso, although it was his desire to get out of the land of Florida in the shortest time, seeing the difficulties that lay before him in a voyage by sea, determined to undertake that which should appear to be the best to all.

Monday, the fifth of June, the Governor left Guachoya, receiving a guide from the Cacique who remained in his town. They passed through a province called Catalte; and, going through a desert six days' journey in extent, on the twentieth of the month they came to Chaguate. The Cacique of the province had been to visit the Governor, Don Hernando de Soto, at Antiamque, where he took him presents of shawls, skins, and

salt. The day before Luys de Moscoso arrived, a sick
Christian becoming missed, whom the Indians were suspected to have killed, he sent word to the Cacique to
look for and return him—that in so doing he would continue to be his friend; if otherwise, the Cacique should
not hide from him anywhere, nor he nor his, and that he
would leave his country in ashes. The Chief directly
came, and, bringing the Christian, with a large gift of
shawls and skins, he made this speech :—

EXCELLENT MASTER :—

    I would not deserve that opinion you have of me for all the
wealth of the world. Who impelled me to visit and serve that excellent lord, the Governor, your father, in Autiamque, which you
should have remembered, where I offered myself, with all loyalty,
truth, and love, to serve and obey his lifetime: or what could have
been my purpose, having received favours of him, and without
either of you having done me any injury, that I should be moved to
do that which I should not? Believe me, no outrage, nor worldly
interest, could have been equal to making me act thus, or could
have so blinded me. Since, however, in this life, the natural course
is, after one pleasure should succeed many pains, fortune has been
pleased with your indignation to moderate the joy I felt in my heart
at your coming, and have failed where I aimed to hit, in pleasing
this Christian, who remained behind lost, treating him in a manner
of which he shall himself speak, thinking that in this I should do
you service, and intending to come with and deliver him to you at
Chaguate, serving you in all things, to the extent possible in my
power. If for this I deserve punishment from your hand, I shall
receive it, as coming from my master's, as though it were favour.

The Governor answered, that because he had not
found him in Chaguate he was incensed, supposing that he
had kept away, as others had done; but that, as he now
knew his loyalty and love, he would ever consider him a
brother, and would favour him in all matters. The Ca-

cique went with him to the town where he resided, the distance of a day's journey. They passed through a small town where was a lake, and the Indians made salt: the Christians made some on the day they rested there, from water that rose near by from springs in pools. The Governor was six days in Chaguate, where he informed himself of the people there were to the west. He heard that three days' journey distant, was a province called Aguacay.

On leaving Chaguate, a Christian remained behind, named Francisco de Guzman, bastard son of a gentleman of Sevilla, who, in fear of being made to pay for gaming debts in the person of an Indian girl, his concubine, he took her away with him; and the Governor, having marched two days before he was missed, sent word to the Cacique to seek for and send him to Aguacay, whither he was marching, but the Chief never did. Before arriving at this province they received five Indians, coming with a gift of skins, fish, and roasted venison, sent on the part of the Cacique. The Governor reached his town on Wednesday, the fourth day of July, and finding it unoccupied, lodged there. He remained in it a while, making some inroads, in which many Indians of both sexes were captured. There they heard of the South Sea. Much salt was got out of the sand, gathered in a vein of earth like slate, and was made as they make it in Cayas.

CHAPTER XXXII.

How the Governor went from Aguacay to Naguatex,
and what happened to him.

THE day the Governor left Aguacay he went to sleep
near a small town, subject to the lord of that province.
He set the encampment very nigh a salt lake, and that
afternoon some salt was made. He marched the next
day, and slept between two mountains, in an open grove;
the next after, he arrived at a small town called Pato;
and on the fourth day of his departure from Aguacay he
came to the first inhabited place, in a province called
Amaye. There they took an Indian, who said that
thence to Naguatex was a day and a half's journey, all
the way lying through an inhabited region.

Having passed out of Amaye, on Saturday, the twentieth of July, between that place and Naguatex, at mid-day,
along a clump of luxuriant woods, the camp was seated.
From thence Indians being seen, who had come to espy
them, those on horseback went in their pursuit, killed six,
and captured two. The prisoners being asked by the
Governor why they had come, they said, to discover the
numbers he had, and their condition, having been sent by
their lord, the Chief of Naguatex; and that he, with other

caciques, who came in his company and his cause, had
determined on giving him battle that day.

While thus conferring, many Indians advanced, formed
in two squadrons, who, so soon as they saw that they
were descried, giving whoops, they assailed the Christians
with great fury, each on a different quarter; but finding
how firm was the resistance, they turned, and fleeing,
many lost their lives; the greater part of the cavalry
pursuing them, forgetful of the camp, when those that
remained were attacked by other two squadrons, that had
lain in concealment, who, in their turn, having been with-
stood, paid the penalty that the first had done.

When the Christians came together, after the Indians
fled, they heard loud shouting, at the distance of a crossbow-shot from where they were; and the Governor sent
twelve cavalry to see what might be the cause.   Six
Christians were found amidst numerous Indians, two,
that were mounted, defending four on foot, with great
difficulty; and they, as well as those who went to their
succour, finally ended by killing many.   They had got
lost from those who followed after the first squadrons,
and, in returning to the camp, fell among them with
whom they were found fighting.   One Indian, brought
back alive, being asked by the Governor who they were
that had come to give him battle, said the Cacique of
Naguatex, the one of Maye, and another of a province
called Hacanac, lord of great territories and numerous
vassals, he of Naguatex being in command.   The Governor, having ordered his right arm to be cut off, and his
nose, sent him to the Cacique, with word that he would

march the next day into his territory to destroy it, and that if he wished to dispute his entrance to await him.

The Governor stopped there that night, and the following day he came to the habitations of Naguatex, which were much scattered, and having asked for the town of the Cacique, he was told that it stood on the opposite side of a river near by. He marched thitherward; and coming to the river, on the other bank he saw many Indians awaiting him, set in order to defend the passage; but, as he did not know whether it might be forded or not, nor whereabouts it could be crossed, and having some wounded men and horses, he determined to repose for some time in the town where he was, until they should be healed.

In consequence of the great heats that prevailed, he pitched his camp a quarter of a league from the river, in a fine open grove of high trees, near a brook, close to the town. Some Indians taken there, having been asked if the river were fordable, said yes, at times it was, in certain places; on the tenth day he sent two captains, each with fifteen cavalry, one up and the other down the stream, with guides to show where they might get over, to see what towns were to be found on the opposite side. They were both opposed by the Indians, who defended the passages the best they could; but these being taken notwithstanding, on the other shore they found many habitations, with much subsistence; and having seen this, the detachments went back to the camp.

CHAPTER XXXIII.

How the Cacique of Naguatex came to visit the Governor, and how the Governor went thence, and arrived at Nondacao.

From Naguatex, where the Governor was, he sent a message to the Cacique, that, should he come to serve and obey him, he would pardon the past; and if he did not, he would go to look after him, and would inflict the chastisement he deserved for what he had done. At the end of two days the Indian got back, bringing word that to-morrow the Cacique would come. The day before his arrival, the Chief sent many Indians in advance of him, among whom were some principal men, to discover in what mood the Governor was, and determine whether he would himself come or not. They went back directly as they had announced his approach, the Cacique arriving in a couple of hours afterward, well attended by his people. They came one before another, in double file, leaving an opening through the midst, where he walked. They arrived in the Governor's presence weeping, after the usage of Tula (thence to the eastward not very distant), when the Chief, making his proper obeisance, thus spoke :—

Very High and Powerful Lord, whom all the Earth should serve and obey:—

I venture to appear before you, after having been guilty of so

21

great and bad an act, that, for only having thought of it, I merit
punishment. Trusting in your greatness, although I do not deserve
pardon, yet for your own dignity you will show me mercy, having
regard to my inferiority in comparison with you, forgetting my
weakness, which to my sorrow, and for my greater good, I have
come to know.

I believe that you and yours must be immortal; that you are
master of the things of nature; since you subject them all, and
they obey you, even the very hearts of men. Witnessing the
slaughter and destruction of my men in battle, which came of
my ignorance, and the counsel of a brother of mine, who fell in
the action, from my heart did I repent the error that I committed,
and directly I desired to serve and obey you: wherefore have I
come, that you may chastise and command me as your own.

The Governor replied, that the past would be for-
given; and that, should he thenceforward do his duty, he
would be his friend, favouring him in all matters.

At the end of four days Luys de Moscoso set forward,
and arrived at a river he could not pass, it ran so full,
which to him appeared wonderful at the time, more
than a month having gone by since there had been rain.
The Indians said, that it often increased in that manner,
without there being rain anywhere, in all the country.
It was supposed to be caused by the sea entering in; but
he learned that the water always flowed from above,
and that the Indians nowhere had any information of
the sea.

The Governor returned back to where he had been
the last days; and, at the end of eight more, understanding that the river might then be crossed, he left, and
passed over to the other bank, where he found houses,
but no people. He lodged out in the fields, and sent word
to the Cacique to come where he was, and to give him

a guide to go on with. After some days, finding that the Cacique did not come, nor send any one, he dispatched two captains, each of them in a different direction, to set fire to the towns, and seize the people that might be found. They burned much provision, and captured many Indians. The Cacique, seeing the damage his territories, were receiving, sent five principal men to Moscoso, with three guides, who understood the language farther on, whither he would go.

Directly the Governor set out from Naguatex, arriving, on the third day, at a hamlet of four or five houses, belonging to the Cacique of the poor province named Nissohone, a thinly peopled country, having little maize. Two days' journey on the way, the Indians who guided the Governor, in place of taking him to the west, would lead him to the east, and at times they went through heavy thickets, out of the road: in consequence, he ordered that they should be hanged upon a tree. A woman, taken in Nissohone, served as the guide, who went back to find the road.

In two days' time the Governor came to another miserable country, called Lacane. An Indian was taken, who said the land of Nondacao was very populous, the houses much scattered, as in mountainous regions, and there was plenty of maize. The Cacique came with his Indians, weeping, as those of Naguatex had done, which is, according to their custom, significant of obedience; and he made a present of much fish, offering to do whatsoever might be required of him. He took his departure, leaving a guide for the Province of Soacatino.

CHAPTER XXXIIII.

How the Governor marched from Nondacao to Soacatino and Guasco, passing through a Wilderness,
whence, for want of a Guide and Interpreter, he
retired to Nilco.

The Governor set out from Nondacao for Soacatino,
and on the fifth day came to a province called Aays.
The inhabitants had never heard of the Christians. So
soon as they observed them entering the territory the
people were called out, who, as fast as they could get
together, came by fifties and hundreds on the road, to
give battle. While some encountered us, others fell
upon our rear; and when we followed up those, these
pursued us. The attack continued during the greater
part of the day, until we arrived at their town. Some
men were injured, and some horses, but nothing so as to
hinder travel, there being not one dangerous wound
among all. The Indians suffered great slaughter.

The day on which the Governor departed, the guide
told him he had heard it said in Nondacao, that the
Indians of Soacatino had seen other Christians; at which
we were all delighted, thinking it might be true, and that
they could have come by way of New Spain; for if it
were so, finding nothing in Florida of value, we should
be able to go out of it, there being fear we might perish

in some wilderness. The Governor, having been led for
two days out of the way, ordered the Indian to be put to
the torture, when he confessed that his master, the Cacique of Nondacao, had ordered him to take them in
that manner, we being his enemies, and he, as his vassal,
was bound to obey him. He was commanded to be cast
to the dogs, and another Indian guided us to Soacatino,
where we came the following day.

The country was very poor, and the want of maize
was greatly felt. The natives being asked if they had
any knowledge of other Christians, said they had heard
that near there, towards the south, such men were moving
about. For twenty days the march was through a very
thinly peopled country, where great privation and toil
were endured; the little maize there was, the Indians
having buried in the scrub, where the Christians, at the
close of the day's march, when they were well weary,
went trailing, to seek for what they had need of it to eat.

Arrived at a province called Guasco, they found
maize, with which they loaded the horses and the Indians; thence they went to another settlement, called
Naquiscoça, the inhabitants of which said that they had
no knowledge of any other Christians. The Governor ordered them put to torture, when they stated that farther
on, in the territories of another chief, called Naçacahoz,
the Christians had arrived, and gone back toward the
west, whence they came. He reached there in two days,
and took some women, among whom was one who said
that she had seen Christians, and, having been in their
hands, had made her escape from them. The Governor

sent a captain with fifteen cavalry to where she said they
were seen, to discover if there were any marks of horses,
or signs of any Christians having been there; and after
travelling three or four leagues, she who was the guide
declared that all she had said was false; and so it was
deemed of every thing else the Indians had told of having seen Christians in Florida.

As the region thereabout was scarce of maize, and no
information could be got of any inhabited country to the
west, the Governor went back to Guasco. The residents
stated, that ten days' journey from there, toward the
sunset, was a river called Daycao, whither they sometimes
went to drive and kill deer, and whence they had seen
persons on the other bank, but without knowing what
people they were. The Christians took as much maize
as they could find, to carry with them; and journeying
ten days through a wilderness, they arrived at the river
of which the Indians had spoken. Ten horsemen sent in
advance by the Governor had crossed; and, following a
road leading up from the bank, they came upon an encampment of Indians living in very small huts, who,
directly as they saw the Christians, took to flight, leaving
what they had, indications only of poverty and misery.
So wretched was the country, that what was found everywhere, put together, was not half an alqueire of maize.
Taking two natives, they went back to the river, where
the Governor waited; and on coming to question the
captives, to ascertain what towns there might be to the
west, no Indian was found in the camp who knew their
language.

The Governor commanded the captains and principal personages to be called together, that he might determine now by their opinions what was best to do. The majority declared it their judgment to return to the River Grande of Guachoya, because in Anilco and thereabout was much maize; that during the winter they would build brigantines, and the following spring go down the river in them in quest of the sea, where having arrived, they would follow the coast thence along to New Spain,—an enterprise which, although it appeared to be one difficult to accomplish, yet from their experience it offered the only course to be pursued. They could not travel by land, for want of an interpreter; and they considered the country farther on, beyond the River Daycao, on which they were, to be that which Cabeça de Vaca had said in his narrative should have to be traversed, where the Indians wandered like Arabs, having no settled place of residence, living on prickly pears, the roots of plants, and game; and that if this should be so, and they, entering upon that tract, found no provision for sustenance during winter, they must inevitably perish, it being already the beginning of October; and if they remained any longer where they were, what with rains and snow, they should neither be able to fall back, nor, in a land so poor as that, to subsist.

The Governor, who longed to be again where he could get his full measure of sleep, rather than govern and go conquering a country so beset for him with hardships, directly returned, getting back from whence he came.

CHAPTER XXXV.

How the Christians returned to Nilco, and thence went to Minoya, where they prepared to build Vessels in which to leave Florida.

When what had been determined on was proclaimed in the camp, many were greatly disheartened. They considered the voyage by sea to be very hazardous, because of their poor subsistence, and as perilous as was the journey by land, whereon they had looked to find a rich country, before coming to the soil of Christians. This was according to what Cabeça de Vaca told the Emperor, that after seeing cotton cloth, would be found gold, silver, and stones of much value, and they were not yet come to where he had wandered; for before arriving there, he had always travelled along the coast, and they were marching far within the land; hence by keeping toward the west they must unavoidably come to where he had been, as he said that he had gone about in a certain region a long time, and marched northward into the interior. Now, in Guasco, they had already found some turkoises, and shawls of cotton, which the Indians gave them to understand, by signs, were brought from the direction of the sunset; so that they who should take that course must approach the country of Christians.

There was likewise much other discontent. Many grieved to go back, and would rather have continued to run the peril of their lives than leave Florida poor. They were not equal, however, to changing what was resolved on, as the persons of importance agreed with the Governor. There was one, nevertheless, who said afterwards that he would willingly pluck out an eye, to put out another for Luys de Moscoso, so greatly would he grieve to see him prosper; with such bitterness did he inveigh against him and some of his friends, which he would not have dared to do, only he knew that in a couple of days from that time the government would have to be relinquished.

From Daycao, where they were, to the Rio Grande, was a distance of one hundred and fifty leagues, towards which they had marched always westwardly; and, as they returned over the way, with great difficulty could they find maize to eat; for, wheresoever they had passed, the country lay devastated, and the little that was left, the Indians had now hidden. The towns they had burned in Naguatex, of which they had repented, they found already rebuilt, and the houses full of maize. That country is populous and abundant. Pottery is made there of clay, little differing from that of Estremoz or Montemor.

To Chaguete, by command of the Cacique, the Indians came in peace, and said, that the Christian who had remained there would not come. The Governor wrote to him, sending ink and paper, that he might answer. The purport of the letter stated his determination to leave Florida, reminded him of his being a Christian,

22

and that he was unwilling to leave him among heathen; that he would pardon the error he had committed in going to the Indians, should he return; and that if they should wish to detain him, to let the Governor know by writing. The Indian who took the letter came back, bringing no other response than the name and rubric of the person written on the back, to signify that he was alive. The Governor sent twelve mounted men after him; but, having his watchers, he so hid himself that he could not be found. For want of maize the Governor could not tarry longer to look for him; so he left Chaguete, crossed the river at Aays, and following it down, he discovered a town which they had not seen before, called Chilano.

They came to Nilco, where the Governor found so little maize, that there was not enough to last while they made the vessels; for during seed-time, while the Christians were in Guachoya, the Indians, in fear of them, had not dared to come and plant the grounds; and no other land about there was known to have maize, that being the most fertile region of the vicinity, and where they had the most hope of finding sustenance. Everybody was confounded.

Many thought it bad counsel to have come back from the Daycao, and not to have taken the risk of continuing in the way they were going by land; as it seemed impossible they should escape by sea, unless a miracle might be wrought for them; for there was neither pilot nor sea-chart; they knew not where the river entered the sea, nor of the sea could they get any information; they had

nothing out of which to make sails, nor for rope a sufficiency of enequen (a grass growing there, which is like
hemp), and what they did find was saved for calk;
nor was there wherewith to pitch them. Neither could
they build vessels of such strength that any accident
might not put them in jeopardy of life; and they greatly
feared what befell Narvaez, who was lost on the coast,
might happen to them also. But the most of all they
feared was the want of maize; for without that they
could not support themselves, or do any thing they would.
All were in great dismay.

The Christians chose to commend themselves to God
for relief, and beseech Him to point them out a way by
which they might be saved. By His goodness He was
pleased that the people of Anilco should come peacefully, and state that two days' journey thence, near the
River Grande, were two towns of which the Christians
had not heard, in a fertile country named Aminoya; but
whether it then contained maize or not, they were unable
to tell, as they were at war with those places; they would
nevertheless be greatly pleased to go and destroy them, with
the aid of the Christians. The Governor sent a captain
thither, with horsemen and footmen, and the Indians
of Anilco. Arriving at Aminoya, he found two large
towns in a level, open field, half a league apart, in sight
of each other, where he captured many persons, and
found a large quantity of maize. He took lodging in
one of the towns, and directly sent a message to the Governor concerning what he had found, with which all were
well content. They set out from Anilco in the beginning

of December, and on that march, as well as before coming there from Chilano, they underwent great exposure;
for they passed through much water, and rain fell many
times, bringing a north wind, with severe cold, so that
when in the field they had the water both above and
below them; and if at the end of a day's journey they
found dry ground to lie upon, they had occasion to be
thankful. In these hardships nearly all the Indians in
service died, and also many Christians, after coming to
Aminoya; the greater number being sick of severe and
dangerous diseases, marked with inclination to lethargy.
André de Vasconcelos died there, and two Portuguese
brothers of Elvas, near of kin to him, by the name of
Soti.

The Christians chose for their quarters what appeared
to be the best town: it was stockaded, and stood a quarter of a league distant from the Rio Grande. The maize
that lay in the other town was brought there, and when
together the quantity was estimated to be six thousand
fanegas. For the building of ships better timber was
found than had been seen elsewhere in all Florida; on
which account, all rendered many thanks to God for so
signal mercy, encouraging the hope in them, that they
should be successful in their wish to reach a shore of
Christians.

CHAPTER XXXVI.

How Seven Brigantines were built, and the Christians took their Departure from Aminoya.

So soon as the Christians arrived in Aminoya, the Governor commanded the chains to be collected which every one brought along for Indians, the iron in shot, and what was in the camp. He ordered a furnace to be set up for making spikes, and likewise timber to be cut down for the brigantines. A Portuguese, of Ceuta, had learned to saw lumber while a captive in Fez; and saws had been brought for that purpose, with which he taught others, who assisted him. A Genoese, whom God had been pleased to spare (as without him we could not have gone away, there being not another person who knew how to construct vessels), built the brigantines with the help of four or five Biscayan carpenters, who hewed the plank and ribs for him; and two calkers, one a Genoese, the other a Sardinian, closed them up with the oakum, got from a plant like hemp, called enequen, of which I have before spoken; but from its scarcity the flax of the country was likewise used, as well as the ravellings of shawls. The cooper sickened to the point of death, and there was not another workman; but God was pleased to give him health, and notwith-

standing he was very thin, and unfit to labour, fifteen
days before the vessels sailed, he had made for each of
them two of the half-hogsheads sailors call quartos, four
of them holding a pipe of water.

The Indians of a province called Tagoanate, two
days' journey up the river, likewise those of Anilco and
Guachoya, and other neighbouring people, seeing the
vessels were building, thought, as their places of concealment were by the water's side, that it was the purpose to
come in quest of them; and because the Governor had
asked for shawls, as necessary out of which to make sails,
they came often, and brought many, as likewise a great
deal of fish.

Of a verity, it did appear that God chose to favour the
Christians in their extreme need, disposing the Indians
to bring the garments; otherwise, there had been no way
but to go and fetch them. Then the town where they
were, as soon as the winter should set in, would become
so surrounded by water, and isolated, that no one could
travel from it by land farther than a league, or a league
and a half, when the horses could no longer be used.
Without them we were unable to contend, the Indians
being so numerous; besides, man to man on foot, whether
in the water or on dry ground, they were superior, being
more skilful and active, and the conditions of the country
more favourable to the practice of their warfare.

They also brought us ropes; and the cables needed
were made from the bark of mulberry-trees. Anchors
were made of stirrups, for which others of wood were
substituted. In March, more than a month having

passed since rain fell, the river became so enlarged that it
reached Nilco, nine leagues off; and the Indians said,
that on the opposite side it also extended an equal
distance over the country.

The ground whereon the town stood was higher, and
where the going was best, the water reached to the
stirrups. Rafts were made of trees, upon which were
placed many boughs, whereon the horses stood; and in
the houses were like arrangements; yet, even this not
proving sufficient, the people ascended into the lofts; and
when they went out of the houses it was in canoes, or, if
on horseback, they went in places where the earth was
highest.

Such was our situation for two months, in which time
the river did not fall, and no work could be done.   The
natives, coming in canoes, did not cease to visit the brigantines.   The Governor, fearing they would attack him
in that time, ordered one of those coming to the town to
be secretly seized, and kept until the rest were gone;
which being done, he directed that the prisoner should
be tortured, in order to draw out from him any plotting
of treason that might exist.   The captive said, that the
Caciques of Nilco, Guachoya, Taguanate, and others,
in all some twenty, had determined to come upon him,
with a great body of people.   Three days before they
should do so, the better to veil their evil purpose and
perfidy, they were to send a present of fish; and on the
day itself, another present was to be sent in advance of
them, by some Indians, who, with others in the conspi-
racy, that were serving, should set fire to the houses,

after getting possession of the lances placed near the doors of the dwellings, when the Caciques, with all their people, being concealed in the thicket nigh the town, on seeing the flame, should hasten to make an end of them.

The Governor ordered the Indian to be put in a chain; and on the day that was stated, thirty men having come with fish, he commanded their right hands to be cut off, sending word by them to the Cacique of Guachoya, whose they were, that he and his might come when they pleased, he desired nothing better, but they should learn that they could not think of a thing that he did not know their thought before them. At this they were all greatly terrified; the Caciques of Nilco and Taguanate came to make excuses, and a few days after came the Cacique of Guachoya, with a principal Indian, his vassal, stating that he had certain information of an agreement between the Caciques of Nilco and Taguanate to come and give the Christians battle.

So soon as some Indians arrived from Nilco, the Governor questioned them, and they confirming what was said, he delivered them at once to the principal Indian of Guachoya, who took them out of the town and killed them. The next day came others from Taguanate, who likewise having confessed, the Governor commanded that their right hands and their noses should be cut off, and he sent them to the Cacique. With this procedure the people of Guachoya were well satisfied, and often came with presents of shawls and fish, and of hogs, which were the breeding of some sows lost there the year

before. Having persuaded the Governor to send people
to Taguanate, so soon as the waters fell, they brought
canoes, in which infantry went down the river, and a
captain proceeded by land with cavalry; and having
guided them until they came to Taguanate, the Christians assaulted the town, took many men and women,
and shawls, which, with what they had already, sufficed
for their want.

In the month of June the brigantines were finished,
and the Indians having stated that the river rose but
once in the year, which was with the melting of snow,
that had already passed, it being now summer, and a
long time since rain had fallen, God was pleased that the
water should come up to the town, where the vessels
were, whence they floated into the river; for had they
been taken over ground, there would have been danger of
tearing open the bottoms, thereby entirely wrecking
them, the planks being thin, and the spikes made short
for the lack of iron.

In the time that the Christians were there, the people
of Aminoya came to offer their service, being compelled
by hunger to beg some ears of that corn which had been
taken from them. As the country was fertile, they were
accustomed to subsist on maize; and as all that they
possessed had been seized, and the population was
numerous, they could not exist. Those who came to the
town were weak, and so lean that they had not flesh on
their bones, and many died near by, of clear hunger and
debility. The Governor ordered, under pain of heavy
punishments, that maize should not be given to them;

23

still, when it was seen that they were willing to work, and that the hogs had a plenty, the men, pitying their misery and destitution, would share their grain with them; so that when the time arrived for departure, there was not enough left to answer for what was needed. That which remained was put into the brigantines and the great canoes, which were tied together in couples. Twenty-two horses were taken on board, being the best there were in the camp; the flesh of the rest was jerked, as was also that of the hogs that remained. On the second day of July, of the year one thonsand five hundred and forty-three, we took our departure from Aminoya.

CHAPTER XXXVII.

How the Christians, on their Voyage, were attacked in the River, by the Indians of Quigualtam, and what happened.

The day before the Christians left Aminoya, it was
determined to dismiss the men and women that were
serving, with the exception of some hundred slaves, more
or less, put on board by the Governor, and by those he
favoured. As there were many persons of condition,
whom he could not refuse what he allowed to others, he
made use of an artifice, saying, that while they should be
going down the river they might have the use of them;
but on coming to the sea they would have to be left,
because of the necessity for water, and there were but few
casks; while he secretly told his friends to take the slaves,
that they would carry them to New Spain. All those
to whom he bore ill-will, the greater number, not suspecting his concealment from them, which after a while
appeared, thought it inhuman for so short service, in
return for so much as the natives had done, to take them
away, to be left captives out of their territories, in the
hands of other Indians, abandoning five hundred males
and females, among whom were many boys and girls
who understood and spoke Spanish. The most of

them wept, which caused great compassion, as they were all Christians of their own free will, and were now to remain lost.

In seven brigantines went three hundred and twenty-two Spaniards from Aminoya. The vessels were of good build, except that the planks were thin, on account of the shortness of the spikes; and they were not pitched, nor had they decks to shed the water that might enter them, but planks were placed instead, upon which the mariners might run to fasten the sails, and the people accommodate themselves above and below.

The Governor appointed his captains, giving to each of them his brigantine, taking their word and oath to obey him until they should come to the land of Christians. He chose for himself the brigantine he liked best. On the day of his departure they passed by Guachoya, where the Indians, in canoes, were waiting for them in the river, having made a great arbour on the shore, to which they invited him, but he made excuse, and passed along. They accompanied him until arriving where an arm of the river extends to the right, near which they said was Quigualtam; and they importuned him to go and make war upon it, offering their assistance. As they had told him there were three days' journey down the river to that province, suspecting they had arranged some perfidy, he dismissed them there; then, submitting himself to where lay the full strength of the stream, went his voyage, driven on rapidly by the power of the current and aid of oars.

On the first day they came to land in a clump of trees,

by the left bank, and at dark they retired to the vessels.
The following day they came to a town, where they went
on shore, but the occupants dared not tarry for them.
A woman who was captured, being questioned, said the
town was that of a chief named Iluhasene, a subject of
Quignaltam, who, with a great many people, was waiting
for them. Mounted men went down the river, and finding some houses, in which was much maize, immediately
the rest followed. They tarried there a day, in which
they shelled and got ready as much maize as was needed.
In this time many Indians came up the river in canoes;
and, on the opposite side, in front, somewhat carelessly
put themselves in order of battle. The Governor sent
after them the crossbow-men he had with him, in two
canoes, and as many other persons as they could hold,
when the Indians fled; but, seeing the Spaniards were
unable to overtake them, returning, they took courage,
and, coming nearer, menaced them with loud yells. So
soon as the Christians retired, they were followed by
some in canoes, and others on land, along the river;
and, getting before them, arrived at a town near the
river's bluff, where they united, as if to make a stand.
Into each canoe, for every brigantine was towing one at
the stern for its service, directly entered some men, who,
causing the Indians to take flight, burned the town.
Soon after, on the same day, they went on shore in a
large open field, where the Indians dared not await their
arrival.

The next day a hundred canoes came together, having
from sixty to seventy persons in them, those of the

principal men having awnings, and themselves wearing
white and coloured plumes, for distinction. They came
within two crossbow-shot of the brigantines, and sent a
message in a small canoe, by three Indians, to the intent
of learning the character of the vessels, and the weapons
that we use. Arriving at the brigantine of the Governor,
one of the messengers got in, and said that he had been
sent by the Cacique of Quigaltam, their lord, to commend
him, and to make known that whatever the Indians of
Guachoya had spoken of him was falsely said, they being
his enemies; that the Chief was his servant, and wished
to be so considered. The Governor told him that he believed all that he had stated to be true; to say so to
him, and that he greatly esteemed him for his friendship.

With this the messengers went to where the others,
in the canoes, were waiting for them; and thence they all
came down yelling, and approached the Spaniards with
threats. The Governor sent Juan de Guzman, captain of
foot, in the canoes, with twenty-five men in armour, to
drive them out of the way. So soon as they were seen
coming, the Indians, formed in two parts, remained
quietly until they were come up with, when, closing, they
took Juan de Guzman, and those who came ahead with
him, in their midst, and, with great fury, closed hand to
hand with them. Their canoes were larger than his, and
many leaped into the water—some to support them, others
to lay hold of the canoes of the Spaniards, to cause them
to capsize; which was presently accomplished, the Christians falling into the water, and, by the weight of their
armour, going to the bottom; or when one by swimming,

or clinging to a canoe, could sustain himself, they with paddles and clubs, striking him on the head, would send him below.

When those in the brigantines who witnessed the defeat desired to render succour, the force of the stream would not allow them to return. One brigantine, which was that nighest to the canoes, saved four men, who were all of those that went after the Indians who escaped. Eleven lost their lives; among whom was Juan de Guzman and a son of Don Carlos, named Juan de Vargas. The greater number of the others were also men of consideration and of courage. Those who escaped by swimming said, that they saw the Indians get into the stern of one of their canoes with Juan de Guzman, but whether he was carried away dead or alive, no one could state.

CHAPTER XXXVIII.

How the Christians were Pursued by the Indians.

The natives, finding they had gained a victory, took so great encouragement that they proceeded to attack the brigantines, which they had not dared to do before. They first came up with one in the rear-guard, commanded by Calderon, and at the first volley of arrows twenty-five men were wounded. There were only four on board in armour, who went to the side of the vessel for its defence. Those unprotected, finding how they were getting hurt, left the oars, placing themselves below under the cover; and the brigantine, beginning to swing about, was going where the current of water chanced to take her, when one of the men in armour, seeing this, without waiting the Captain's order, made one of the infantry take the oar and steer, while he stood before to cover him with his shield. The Indians afterwards came no nearer than bow-shot, whence they could assail without being assaulted, or receiving injury, there being in each brigantine only a single crossbow much out of order; so that the Christians had little else to do than to stand as objects to be shot at, watching for the shafts. The natives, having left this brigantine, went to another, against which they fought for half an hour: and, one after another, in this way they ran through with them all.

The Christians had mats with them to lie upon of two thicknesses, very close and strong, so that no arrow could pierce them, that, when safety required, were hung up; and the Indians, finding that these could not be traversed, directed their shafts upward, that, exhausted, fell on board, inflicting some wounds. Not satisfied with this, they strove to get at the men with the horses; but the brigantines were brought about the canoes in which they were, to give them protection, and in this position conducted them along. The Christians, finding themselves thus severely tried, and so worn out that they could bear up no longer, determined to continue their journey in the dark, thinking that they should be left alone on getting through the region of Quigualtam. While they proceeded and were least watchful, supposing themselves to be left, they would be roused with deafening yells near by: and thus were they annoyed through the night and until noon, when they got into another country, to the people of which they were recommended for a like treatment, and received it.

Those Indians having gone back to their country, these followed the Christians in fifty canoes, fighting them all one day and night. They sprang on board a brigantine of the rear-guard, by the canoe that floated at the stern, whence they took out an Indian woman, and wounded from thence some men in the brigantines. The men with the horses in the canoes, becoming weary with rowing day and night, at times got left behind, when

the Indians would directly set upon them, and those in
the brigantines would wait until they should come up:
so that in consequence of the slow way that was made,
because of the beasts, the Governor determined to go on
shore and slaughter them. So soon as any befitting
ground for it was seen, a landing was made, the animals
were butchered, and the meat cured and brought on board.
Four or five horses having been let go alive, the Indians,
after the Spaniards had embarked, went up to them, to
whom being unused, they were alarmed, running up and
down, neighing in such way that the Indians took fright,
plunging into the water; and thence entering their
canoes, they went after the brigantines, shooting at the
people without mercy, following them that evening and
the night ensuing, until ten o'clock the next day, when
they returned up stream.

From a small town near the bank, there came out
seven canoes that pursued the Christians a short distance,
shooting at them; but finding, as they were few, that
little harm was done, they went back. From that time
forth the voyage, until near the end, was unattended by
any misadventure; the Christians in seventeen days going
down a distance of two hundred and fifty leagues, a little
more or less, by the river. When near the sea, it becomes divided into two arms, each of which may be a
league and a half broad.

CHAPTER XXXIX.

How the Christians came to the Sea, what occurred then, and what befell them on the
Voyage.

Half a league before coming to the sea, the Christians cast anchor, in order to take rest for a time, as they
were weary from rowing. They were disheartened also,
many days having gone by since they had eaten other
thing than maize, parched and then boiled, given out in
daily rations of a casque by strake to a mess of three.

While riding at anchor, seven canoes of natives came
to attack those we had brought in the canoes along with
us. The Governor ordered men to enter ours in armour,
to go after the Indians and drive them away. There
also came some by land, through thicket and bog, with
staves, having very sharp heads of fish-bone, who fought
valiantly those of us who went out to meet them. Such
as were in the canoes, awaited with their arrows the
approach of those sent against them; and presently,
on the engaging of these, as well as those on land, they
wounded some on our side in both contests. When we
on shore drew nigh to them they would turn their backs,
running like fleet steeds before infantry, making some
turns without ever getting much beyond the flight of an

arrow, and, returning again, they would shoot without
receiving any injury from us, who, though we had some
bows, were not skilled to use them; while the Indians on
the water, finding their pursuers unable to do them harm,
though straining at the oars to overtake them, leisurely
kept within a circle, their canoes pausing and returning, as in a skirmish. The men discovered that the
more successful their effort to approach, the greater was
their own injury; so, when they succeeded simply in
driving them off, they went back to the brigantines.

After remaining two days, the Christians went to
where that branch of the river enters the sea; and having sounded there, they found forty fathoms depth of
water. Pausing then, the Governor required that each
should give his opinion respecting the voyage, whether
they should sail to New Spain direct, by the high sea, or
go thither keeping along from shore to shore. There
were different opinions upon this, in which Juan de
Añasco, who was very presumptuous, valuing himself
much upon his knowledge of navigation, with other
matters of the sea of which he had little experience,
influenced the Governor; and his opinion, like that of
some others, was, that it would be much better to put
out to sea, and cross the Gulf by a passage three-fourths
less far, than going from shore to shore, which was very
circuitous, because of the bend made by the land. He
said that he had seen the sea-chart; that whence they
were the coast ran west to the River of Palmas, and
thence south to New Spain; consequently, that keeping in sight of land, there would be wide compassing,

with long detention, and risk of being overtaken by
the winter before coming to the country of Christians;
while, with a fair wind, in ten or twelve days' time
they should arrive there, by keeping a straight course.

The majority were not of that way of thinking, and
said there was more safety in going along the coast,
though it might take longer; the vessels being frail, and
without decks, a light storm might suffice to wreck them;
and in consequence of the little room they had for water,
if calm or head wind should occur, or adverse weather,
they would also run great hazard; but even were the
vessels so substantial that they might venture in them,
there being neither pilot nor sea-card to show the way, it
was not wise to traverse the sea. This, the opinion of
the greater number, was approved; and it was decided
to go along from one to another shore.

When they were about to depart, the brigantine of
the Governor parted her cable, the anchor attached to it
remaining in the river; and, notwithstanding she was
near the shore, the depth was so great that, although it
was industriously sought for by divers, it could not be
found. This gave much anxiety to the Governor and
the others on board. With a stone for crushing maize,
and the bridles that remained, belonging to some of the
fidalgos and gentlemen who rode, they made a weight
that took the place of the anchor.

On the eighteenth day of July the vessels got under
weigh, with fair weather, and wind favourable for the
voyage. The Governor, with Juan de Añasco, put to
sea in their brigantines, and were followed by all the

rest, who, at two or three leagues out, having come
up with the two, the Captains asked the Governor why
he did not keep the land; and told him that if he
meant to leave it he should say so, though he ought not
to do that without having the consent of the rest,
otherwise they would not follow his lead, but each would
do as he thought best.   The Governor replied that he
would do nothing without consulting them; he desired
to get away from the shore to sail the better, and with the
greater safety at night; that in the morning, when time
served, he would return.   With a favourable wind they
sailed all that day in fresh water, the next night, and the
day following until vespers, at which they were greatly
amazed; for they were very distant from the shore, and
so great was the strength of the current of the river, the
coast so shallow and gentle, that the fresh water entered
far into the sea.

    That afternoon, on the starboard bow, they saw
some kays, whither they went, and where they reposed at
night.   There Juan de Añasco, with his reasoning, concluded by getting all to consent, and deem it good, that
they should go to sea, declaring, as he had before said,
that it would be a great gain, and shorten their voyage.
They navigated two days, and when they desired to get
back in sight of land they could not, because the wind
came off from it: and on the fourth day, finding that the
water was giving out, fearing extremity and peril, they
all complained of Juan de Añasco, and of the Governor,
who had listened to his advice: and all the Captains

declared they would run no farther out, and that the
Governor might go as he chose.

It pleased God that the wind should change a little;
and, at the end of four days from the time of their having gone out to sea, by strength of arm they arrived, in
want of fresh water, in sight of the coast, and with great
labour gained it on an open beach. That afternoon the
wind came round from the south, which on that coast is
a side wind, and so stiff that it threw the brigantines
on to the land, the anchors bending of their slenderness,
and dragging. The Governor ordered all to leap into the
water, on the larboard side, to hold them, and when each
wave had passed they would launch the brigantines to
seaward, sustaining them in this manner until the wind
went down.

CHAPTER XL.

How the Brigantines lost Sight of each other in a
Storm, and afterwards came together at a Kay.

The tempest having passed off from the beach where
the brigantines were riding, the people went on shore.
With mattocks they dug holes there, into which the water
having flowed, they thence filled their pipkins. The
next day they left; and sailing two days, they entered a
basin, like a cove, which afforded shelter against a high
wind that blew from the south. There they tarried, unable to leave, until the fourth day, when the sea subsided
and they went out by rowing. They sailed until near
evening; the wind then freshened, driving them in such
manner upon the land, that they regretted having left the
harbour; for no sooner was it nightfall than the storm
began to rise on the sea, and with its approach the wind
gradually increased. The brigantines separated. The
two that were farthest out entered an arm of the sea, a
couple of leagues beyond the place where the others
found themselves at dark. The five that were astern
remained from half a league to a league apart, along an
exposed beach, upon which the winds and waves were
casting them, without one vessel's knowing the fate of
another. The anchors having yielded, the vessels were

dragging them: the oars, at each of which seven and
eight were pulling seaward, could not hold the vessels;
the rest of the men, leaping into the water, with the
utmost diligence, after the wave had passed that drove
them to the shore, would launch the brigantine; while
those on board, before another wave could come, baled
out with bowls the water that came in upon them.

While thus engaged, in great fear of being lost, from
midnight forward they suffered the intolerable torment
of a myriad of mosquitos. The flesh is directly inflamed
from their sting, as though it had received venom. Towards morning the wind lulled, and the sea went down;
but the insects continued none the less. The sails, which
were white, appeared black with them at daylight; while
the men could not pull at the oars without assistance to
drive away the insects. Fear having passed off with the
danger of the storm, the people observing the swollen
condition of each other's faces, and the marks of the
blows they had given and received to rid them of the
mosquitos, they could but laugh. The vessels came together in a creek, where lay the two brigantines that
preceded them. Finding a scum the sea casts up, called
copee, which is like pitch, and used instead on shipping,
where that is not to be had, they payed the bottoms of
their vessels with it.

After remaining two days they resumed their voyage;
and having run likewise two days, they entered an arm
of the sea and landed. Spending there a couple of days,
they left; six men on the last day having gone up the
bay in a canoe without finding its head. The brigantines

25

went out in a head-wind blowing from the south, which being light, and the people having a strong desire to hasten the voyage, they pulled out by strength of arm to sea with great toil, and making little headway for two days, they entered by an arm of the sea behind an islet which it encircles, where followed such bad weather, that they were not unmindful to give thanks for that good shelter. Fish abounded there. They were taken in nets and with the line. A man having thrown out a cord made fast to his arm, a fish caught at the hook and drew him into the water up to the neck, when, remembering a knife that he had providentially kept, he cut himself loose.

At the close of the fourteenth day of their stay, the Almighty having thought proper to send fair weather, the Christians very devoutly formed a procession for the return of thanks, in which, moving along the beach, they supplicated Him that He would take them to a land in which they might better do Him service.

CHAPTER XLI.

How the Christians arrived at the River Panico.

WHERESOEVER the people dug along the shore they found fresh water. The jars being filled, and the procession concluded, they embarked; and, going ever in sight of land, they navigated for six days. Juan de Añasco said it would be well to stand directly out to sea; for that he had seen the card, and remembered that, from the Rio de Palmas onward, the coast ran south, and up to that time they had gone westwardly. According to his opinion, by the reckoning he kept, the river could not be distant from where they were.

That night they ran out, and in the morning they saw palm-trees rising above the water, the coast trending southwardly; and from midday forward great mountains appeared, which had nowhere been seen until then; for to that place, from the port of Espiritu Santo, where they had entered Florida, was a low, level shore, not discoverable at sea until very near. From what they observed, they thought that during the night they had passed the Rio de Palmas, sixty leagues distant from Panico, in New Spain. So they consulted together.

Some were of opinion that it would not be well to sail in the dark, lest they should overrun the Rio de

Panico; others, that they could not be so near as to run
by it that night, and that it would not be well to lose a
favourable wind: so they agreed to spread half the sails
and keep on their way. Two of the brigantines, which
ran with all sail up, at daylight passed the river without
seeing it: of the five that remained behind, the first that
arrived was the one Calderon commanded, from which,
when a quarter of a league off, and before the entrance
had been discovered, the water was observed to be thick
and found to be fresh. Coming opposite the river, they
saw where the waves broke upon a shoal, at the entrance
into the sea; and, not any one knowing the place, they
were in doubt whether they should go in there or pass
by; but finally, having agreed to enter, they approached
the shore without getting into the current, and went in
the port, where no sooner had they come, than they saw
Indians of both sexes in the apparel of Spain. Asking in
what country they were, they received the answer in their
own language, that it was the Rio de Panico, and that
the town of the Christians was fifteen leagues inland.
The pleasure that all received at this news cannot be sufficiently expressed: they felt as though a life had been
newly given them. Many, leaping on shore, kissed the
ground; and all, on bended knees, with hands raised
above them, and their eyes to heaven, remained untiring
in giving thanks to God.

Those who were coming astern, when they saw that
Calderon with his brigantine had anchored in the river,
directly steered to enter the port. The other two, which
had gone by, tried to run to sea, that they might put

about to join the rest, but could not, the wind being adverse and the sea fretful; so, fearing that they might be lost, they came nigh the land and cast anchor. A storm came up, and finding that they could not sustain themselves there, much less at sea, they determined to run on shore; and as the brigantines were small, drawing but little water, and the beach sandy, the force of the wind on the sails carried them up dry, without injury to any one.

If those who gained the haven at that time were made happy, these were oppressed by a double weight of gloom, not knowing what had happened to their companions, nor in what country they were, fearing likewise that it might be one of a hostile people. They had come upon the coast two leagues below the port. So soon as they found themselves clear of the sea, each took on the back what he could carry of his things, and, travelling inland, they found Indians, who told whence they were, and changed what was sorrow into joy. The Christians rendered many thanks to God for having rescued them from those numberless perils.

CHAPTER XLII.

How the Christians came to Panico, and of their Reception by the Inhabitants.

From the time the Christians left the River Grande, to come by sea from Florida to the River of Panico, were fifty-two days. On the tenth day of September, of the year 1543, they entered the Panico, going up with the brigantines. In the many windings taken by the stream, the light wind was often unfavourable, and the vessels in many places made slow headway, having to be towed with much labour against a strong current; so that, after having sailed four days, the people, discovering themselves greatly retarded in the desire to get among Christians, and of taking part in the divine offices, which for a long season had not been listened to by them, they gave up the brigantines to the sailors, and went on by land to Panico.

Just as the Christians arrived at the town, in their clothing of deer-skin, dressed and dyed black, consisting of frock, hose, and shoes, they all went directly to the church, to pray and return thanks for their miraculous preservation. The townspeople, having already been informed of their coming by the Indians, and now knew of the arrival, invited some to their houses, and enter-

tained them for acquaintance' sake, or for having heard
of them, or because they came from the same parts of
country with themselves. The Alcalde-Mayor took the
Governor home with him: the rest, as they came up, he
directed to be lodged by sixes and tens, according to the
means of individuals, who provided their guests with
abundance of fowls and maizen-bread, and with the
fruits of the country, which are like those of Cuba,
already described.

The town of Panico might contain some seventy
housekeepers. The dwellings were chiefly of stone and
mortar; some were of poles, and all of them thatched
with grass. The country is poor. No gold or silver is
to be found. Residents have the fullest supply both of
food and servants. The most wealthy have not an income above five hundred cruzados annually, which is
tribute paid by their Indian vassals, in cotton clothing,
fowls, and maize.

Of the persons who got back from Florida, there
landed at that port three hundred and eleven Christians.
The Alcalde-Mayor directly sent a townsman by post to
inform the Viceroy, who resided in Mexico, of the arrival
of three hundred of the men who had gone with Don
Hernando de Soto in the discovery and conquest of
Florida; and, for their being in the service of the King,
that he would make provision for their support. Don
Antonio de Mendoza was greatly amazed at this news, as
were all others of that city; for the people having entered far into Florida, they had been considered lost,
nothing being heard from them in a long while; and it

appeared to him to be a thing impossible, that without a fortress to which they might betake themselves, or support of any sort, they should have sustained themselves for such a length of time among the heathen. He immediately gave an order, directing that subsistence should be given them wheresoever it might be needed, and the Indians found requisite for carrying their burdens; and, should there be refusal, to take by force, without incurring any penalty, whatsoever should be necessary. The mandate was so well obeyed, that on the road, before the people had arrived at the towns, the inhabitants went out to receive them, bringing fowls and provisions.

CHAPTER XLIII.

The Favour the People found in the Viceroy and Residents of Mexico.

From Panico to the great city of Mestitam, Mexico, there are sixty leagues, and as many leagues from each to the port of Vera Cruz, which is where the embarkations take place for Spain, and where those who go hence to New Spain arrive. These three towns, equidistant, are inhabited by Spaniards, and form a triangle: Vera Cruz on the south, Panico on the east, and Mexico, which is inland, on the west. The country is so populous, that the Indian towns farthest apart are not more than half a league to a league from each other.

Some of the people who came from Florida remained in Panico, reposing a month, others fifteen days, or such time as each pleased; for no one turned a grudging face to his guest, but, on the contrary, gave him of every thing he had, and appeared sad at his leave-taking; which may well enough be believed, for the provisions the natives brought in payment of their tribute more than sufficed for consumption, so that there was no one in that town to buy or to sell, and few Spaniards being there, the inhabitants were glad of company. All the clothing in the custody of the Alcalde-Mayor, paid to

26

him there as the Emperor's tax, he divided among those
that would go to receive any.

He who had a coat of mail was happy, since for it a
horse might be had in exchange. Some got mounted,
and those not able to get beasts, who were the greater
number, took up the journey on foot. They were well
received by the Indians, and better served than they
could have been at their own homes, particularly in
respect of every thing to eat; for, if an Indian was asked
for a fowl, he would bring four; and if for any sort of
fruit, though it might be a league off, some one would
run to fetch it; and were a Christian ill, the people
would carry him, in a chair, from their own to the next
town. Wheresoever they came, the Cacique of the place,
through an Indian who bears a rod of justice in his hand
they call tapile (which is equivalent to saying meirinho),
ordered provisions to be brought, and men for the loads
of such things as there were, and the others necessary to
carry the invalids.

The Viceroy sent a Portuguese to them, twenty
leagues from Mexico, with quantity of confections, rai-
sins, pomegranates, and other matters proper for the sick,
should they need them; and, in advance, ordered that all
should be clothed at the royal charge. The news of
their approach being known to the citizens, they went
out on the highway to receive them, and with great
courtesy entreated for their companionship as favour, each
one taking to his house as many as he dared, giving
them for raiment all the best he could, the least well
dressed wearing clothes worth thirty cruzados and up-

ward. Clothing was given to those who chose to go for it to the residence of the Viceroy, and the persons of condition ate at his board: at his house was a table for all those of less rank that would eat there. Directly he informed himself of the quality of each one, that he might show him the consideration that was his due. Some of the Conquistadores placed them all down to table together, fidalgos and boors, oftentimes seating the servant and his master shoulder to shoulder; which was done mostly by artisans and men of mean condition, those better bred asking who each one was, and making a difference in persons.

Nevertheless, all did the best they could with good will, telling those they had under their roofs that they could bring no impoverishment, nor should they hesitate to receive whatsoever they offered; since they had found themselves in like condition when others had assisted them, such being the fortunes of the country. God reward them: and those whom He saw fit should escape, coming out of Florida to tread the soil of Christians, be He pleased that they live to serve Him; and to the dead, and to all those who believe in Him, and confess that in Him is their faith, grant, through His compassion, the glory of paradise. Amen.

CHAPTER XLIIII.

WHICH SETS FORTH SOME OF THE DIVERSITIES AND PECU-
LIARITIES OF FLORIDA; AND THE FRUIT, BIRDS, AND
BEASTS OF THE COUNTRY.

FROM the port of Espiritu Santo, where the Christians
went on shore, to the Province of Ocute, which may be a
distance of four hundred leagues, a little more or less, the
country is very level, having many ponds, dense thickets,
and, in places, tall pine-trees: the soil is light, and there
is not in it a mountain nor a hill.

The land of Ocute is more strong and fertile than the
rest, the forest more open; and it has very good fields
along the margins of the rivers. From there to Cutifachiqui are about one hundred and thirty leagues, of
which eighty leagues are of desert and pine forests,
through which run great rivers. From Cutifachiqui to
Xuala there may be two hundred and fifty leagues, and
all a country of mountains: the places themselves are
on high level ground, and have good fields upon the
streams.

Thence onward, through Chiaha, Coça, and Talise,
the country of which is flat, dry, and strong, yielding
abundance of maize, to Tascaluça, may be two hundred
and fifty leagues; and thence to Rio Grande, a distance of

about three hundred leagues, the land is low, abounding
in lakes. The country afterward is higher, more open,
and more populous than any other in Florida; and along
the River Grande, from Aquixo to Pacaha and Coligoa,
a distance of one hundred and fifty leagues, the land is
level, the forest open, and in places the fields very fertile
and inviting.

From Coligoa to Autiamque may be two hundred
and fifty leagues of mountainous country; thence to
Guacay may be two hundred and thirty leagues of level
ground; and the region to Daycao, a distance of one
hundred and twenty leagues, is continuously of mountainous lands.

From the port of Espiritu Santo to Apalache they
marched west and northeast; from Cutifachiqui to Xuala,
north; to Coça, westwardly; and thence to Tascaluça
and the River Grande, as far as the Provinces of Quizquiz and Aquixo, to the westward; from thence to Pacaha northwardly, to Tula westwardly, to Autiamque
southwardly, as far as the Province of Guachoya and
Daycao.

The bread that is eaten all through Florida is made
of maize, which is like coarse millet; and in all the
islands and Indias belonging to Castilla, beginning with
the Antillas, grows this grain. There are in the country
many walnuts likewise, and amexeas, mulberries, and
grapes. The maize is planted and picked in, each person having his own field; fruit is common for all, because
it grows abundantly in the woods, without any necessity
of setting out trees or pruning them. Where there are

mountains the chestnut is found, the fruit of which is somewhat smaller than the one of Spain. Westward of the Rio Grande the walnut differs from that which is found before coming there, being of tenderer shell, and in form like an acorn; while that behind, from the river back to the port of Espiritu Santo, is generally rather hard, the tree and the nut being in their appearance like those of Spain. There is everywhere in the country a fruit, the produce of a plant like ligoacam, that is propagated by the Indians, having the appearance of the royal pear, with an agreeable smell and taste; and likewise another plant, to be seen in the fields, bearing a fruit like strawberry, near to the ground, and is very agreeable. The amexeas are of two sorts, vermilion and gray, of the form and size of walnuts, having three or four stones in them. They are better than any plums that are raised in Spain, and make much better prunes. The grapes appear only to need dressing; for, although large, they have great stones: the other fruits are all in great perfection, and are less unhealthy than those of Spain.

There are many lions and bears in Florida, wolves, deer, jackals, cats, and conies; numerous wild fowl, as large as pea-fowl; small partridges, like those of Africa, and cranes, ducks, pigeons, thrushes, and sparrows. There are blackbirds larger than sparrows and smaller than stares; hawks, goss-hawks, falcons, and all the birds of rapine to be found in Spain.

The Indians are well proportioned: those of the level country are taller and better shaped of form than those of the mountains; those of the interior enjoy a greater abundance of maize and clothing than those of the coast, where the land is poor and thin, and the people along it more warlike.

The direction from the port of Espiritu Santo to Apalache, and thence to Rio de las Palmas, is from east to west; from that river towards New Spain, it is south-wardly; the sea-coast being gentle, having many shoals and high sand-hills.

Deo Gratias.

This Relation of the Discovery of Florida was impressed in the house of Andree de Burgos, Printer and Cavalleiro of the house of Senhor Cardinal iñante.

It was finished the tenth day of February, of the year one thousand five hundred and fifty-seven, in the noble and ever loyal city of Evora.

INDEX

27

CHAPTER VI.

CHAPTER VII.

CHAPTER VIII.

CHAPTER IX.

CHAPTER X.

CHAPTER XI.

CHAPTER XII.

CHAPTER XIII.

ANNOTATIONS

MADE BY THE TRANSLATOR TO MATTERS IN THE RELAÇAM.

ERRATA.—A gentleman who has carefully scrutinized the text makes some suggestions of error. Where the difference of time is but a day—and the instances of such in the original are many—it has not been annotated. It may be well to name, for the purposes of investigation, the days of the week on which several years begin: Wednesday in 1539, Thursday, leap year, in 1540, Saturday in 1541, Sunday in 1542, and Monday in 1543.

The following are the more important errors:—at page 39, the year 1540 should be 1539; at page 52, line 8, the 21st of the month was on *Sunday*, not Wednesday; at page 69, the 5th day of July should be that day in *June;* at page 75, the 16th of July should be the 26th; at page 91, Sunday, the 18th of November, came on Thursday, and, as the stay at Manvilla was twenty-eight days from the 18th of October, probably *Sunday* the 14th is the right date; at page 98, there is a typographical blunder, one or more, also error in the date on the first line of the section, which might correctly read *Tuesday* the 15th; at page 112, the 19th day of June came on *Sunday*—the 29th was Wednesday. At page 154, the 22d of July came on *Saturday.*

At page 73, the 7th day of July is a misprint for the 2d; and at page 56, Tuesday the 12th should be *Monday*—both errors in the translation.

CHAPTER I.

THESE items of accounts, selected from two early manuscripts, to show the value of moneys mentioned in different parts of the text, give some idea, likewise, of the decreased value of the precious metals from their dates to the present time. In an appraisement made "in the usual money of Castilla," at Cadiz, of personal property given in dower, by Catalina de Prado, with

her daughter, Maria Gomez, to Alonso Velez, in the year 1529,
are these among other estimates :—

	Maravedis.	
One negress slave, named Ynés, sixteen years of age, little more or less, valued at fifty ducados . .	XVIIIM	DIIL
One jewel with three pearls and a garnet, at six thousand mrs.	VIM	
One cross ✝ of lignum vitæ of Indias, set in gold with three pearls, at two castellanos . . .	MDIIII	LXX
One pair house table-cloths, at six reales	MII	IIII

Items of ship's expenses, presented in a suit between the
Oidores Matienzo and Villalobos, in the Island of Española, before
the *escribano* Pedro Ledesma, in the year 1526, concerning the
right to a discovery, made in 1520, of a shore and river on the
eastern coast of North America, in latitude 33° 30′.

First—four arrobas of olive oil, cost eighteen reales and a half, come to four pesos and five tomines in gold	IIIIpᵒ	Vtᵉ	
Also—bought in Baracoa three hundred and forty-two cargas of bread, at four and a half reales each, come to ninety-six pesos one tomine and six granos	XCVIpᵒ	Itᵉ	VIgₒ
Two linen shirts, one ducado . . .	pᵒ	VIIᵉ	

These show the *grano* to have been one 96th in the 100 parts
of the *peso;* the *tomine,* one 8th of the *peso;* the *real,* one 16th;
the *maravedi,* one 544th part, or 34 parts to the real; the *caste-
llano,* 89 parts of the *peso;* and the *ducado,* 69 parts, although in
Cuba it appears to have been rated at 75 parts. The *cruzado,* a
Portuguese coin, according to numerous authorities, is the same
as the *ducado.* It is so stated in the "Florida of the Inca;" and
Garibay, in treating of the events of the year 1521, says: "The
cruzado is of equal value with the Castilian ducado." The *peso*
is considered to be an ounce of pure silver, of the weight of
sixteen ounces to the Castilian pound.

IN the apportionment of treasure arising from spoil and the
ransom of Atahualpa, which took place at Caxamalca, the 17th
day of June, 1533, the name of Soto stands third in importance

on the roll, with the share of $23,000. The gross sum of metal amounted to 1,326,539 pesos in gold and 408,952 pesos of silver, the *peso* being the value of an ounce of silver—sixteen to the pound. The statement is made from the official records.

	Marks of silver.	Pesos in gold.
To the Church	90	2,220
The Adelantado Francisco Pizarro, himself, interpreters, and a horse	2,350	57,220
Hernando Pizarro	1,267	31,080
Hernando de Soto	724	17,740
Father Ino. de Sosa, Vicar of the Army .	310—6	7,770
Juan Pizarro	407—2	11,100
Pedro de Candia . . .	407—2	9,909
Gonzalo Pizarro	384—5	9,909

Then follow the names of fifty-seven others of cavalry and one hundred and five of infantry.

AMONG the papers in the noted suit brought by Doña Ysabel de Bobadilla against Hernan Ponçe de Leon, existing in the *Archivo Real de Indias*, at Sevilla, is an instrument of writing made at Cuzco, the 27th day of June, in the year 1535, which shows that Soto and Ponçe held their property in common, each with the other, in whatsoever either might possess, or should in any way acquire, or of whatsoever nature; and that they had been thus associated for eighteen or nineteen years. Directly upon its execution, as appears from testimony, Soto went to Nombre de Dios, where he embarked for Spain.

Another instrument, made by the same parties at Havana, the 13th day of May, 1539, ratifying the first, declares the amount taken by the Adelantado to Spain, and registered, to be fifty thousand dollars in gold and three thousand marks of silver; and it further states, that he had received seven thousand castellanos as the dower of his wife, although this, from the relinquishment of a paternal bequest by the mother of Ysabel, printed in the Appendix, appears to have been specifically a stock-farm in Panamá, with the breeding mares, cattle, and the slaves tending them. Besides these amounts, from the evidence afforded by a letter of instructions, preserved in the *Biblioteca Nacional* of Madrid,

28

addressed probably by Soto while in Spain, seemingly to his agent at Court, the property of the partners in lands, houses, and Indians, in Peru, appears likewise to have been large.

YSABEL DE BOBADILLA was the third daughter of Pedro Árias Dávila, *el Galán*, conqueror of Nicaragua, the second of the house and estate of Puñonrostro, by Ysabel de Bobadilla, granddaughter of Francisco Fernandez de Bobadilla and Maria Peñalosa, residents of Segovia. Doña Maria Peñalosa, the second daughter, named after her maternal grandmother, became the wife of Rodrigo de Contreras, Governor of Nicaragua, by the appointment of his father-in-law; and the eldest daughter, Doña Elvira, became the wife of Urban de Arellano. A son, Árias Gonçalo Dávila, succeeded to the name and estates.

The marriage of Ysabel and Soto was childless; the descendants of her sister Elvira continue in Spain; those of Maria are perpetuated in America in the name of Contreras.

The title of Count of Puñonrostro began with Juan, brother of Pedro Árias, or Pedrárias, as he was usually called, who, having served Fernando and Ysabel in their wars, and afterwards Felipe, the husband of Juana, their daughter, held Toledo successfully against the *Comuneros* for the grandson, afterward the Emperor Charles V.; and, among other noted military actions of the time, relieved the fortress at Madrid. For his well-tried loyalty the Emperor conferred on him a title—the name of his town—of which a grandchild, Juan Portocarrero, became the next possessor, and whose son married Francisca, granddaughter of the first Marquis of Charcas, Francisco Pizarro, Conqueror of Peru; the title thence went to the line of Pedrárias, through his son Árias Gonzalo, to Pedro Árias de Bobadilla, who became the third count of Puñonrostro. The title has continued in the family to the Count, in the present Marquis of Casasola, by the name Árias Dávila Mathieu, who, in the year 1858, was Chief Equerry of Her Majesty Queen Ysabel II.

Pedrárias Dávila had the seigniory of Puñonrostro, but was never count: he was a great military disciplinarian, and in the year 1514 became governor of Tierra-firme.

The Patent issued to Hernando de Soto, dated at Valladolid, the 20th day of April, in the year 1537, a translation of which is given in the Appendix, confers on him military and political authority, the position of governor and captain-general over two hundred leagues of the coast he should select from that he shall discover, conquer, quiet, and colonize, within the Province of Rio de las Palmas, that of Florida, and those farther on, of Tierra Nueva, in the country given aforetime to Lucas Vazquez de Ayllón, with the office of alguazil-mayor in perpetuity over a dozen leagues square of land, in fee, to be apportioned to him, not to include any seaport or chief town of a Province, "with the jurisdiction and title that we shall designate at the time we direct the bestowal." The portion of the instrument quoted is probably to be understood as a promise to confer a title of nobility, and of the grade doubtless the Relaçam states, which had precedents in the fortunate career of American adventure. That all the important aids attending the enterprise might be the better held in hand for success, the government of the Island of Cuba was also bestowed on him, to continue during the royal pleasure.

* * *

CHAPTER II.

The fortunes attending the army of Pánfilo de Narvaez, in its attempt to conquer Florida, are told by Alvar Nuñez Cabeça de Vaca, one of four survivors of that enterprise. In 1557, the time at which the *Relaçam* came from the press, his narrative had already been made public many years, having been printed in 1542, at Zamora, with the title: *La relaciom que dio Aluar nuñez cabeça de vaca de lo acaescido en las Indias en la armada donde yua por gouernador Pãphilo de narbaez, desde el uño de reynte y siete hasta el año de treynta y seys que boluio a Seuilla con tres de su compañia.* Of this edition, only one copy—that in the possession of James Lenox, in this country—is known to be extant. In 1555 it was printed at Valladolid with the production styled *Commentarios*, after the return of Cabeça de Vaca from the government of the Province of La Plata, written by his secretary, Pero Hernandez, the works together bearing the title: *La relacion y comentarios del governador Aluar nuñez cabeça de vaca de lo acaescido en las dos jornadas que hizo a las Yndias*, the first book bearing the running title of *Naufragios*.

The *Relacion* of Cabeça de Vaca is a story of wild misadventure, from the Bay of Tampa to Yee'ora, or Village of Corazones, at the junction of the Mulatos with the eastern branch of the River Yakee, in Sonora, made in the long period of nearly eight years, from 1528 to 1536, during the early part of which the army was wasted and lost by privation, accidents, shipwreck, in conflicts with the natives, and civil broils. In this time, near the close of the journey, he saw traces of the precious metals, and cotton clothing worn by the Indians, who told him of the great houses towards the north—in Cíbola. The host of Soto, it will be seen in the twenty-seventh and thirty-fifth chapters, marked well the position the narrator indicated, and the reasons why he believed the country to have wealth.

GEIRA, in Portuguese, the quantity of arable land a pair of oxen may ordinarily plough in a day.

AMONG the records belonging to the marquisate of Astorga, which * * * * * Osorio, Count of Altamira, Duke of Montemar, represents, is the will of Don Pedro Alvarez Osorio, second Marquis of Astorga, father of the nobleman referred to in the text, dated at Astorga, the 7th day of July, in the year 1505, some passages of which doubtless refer to members of the family afterward in the army of Soto.

"Again: inasmuch as Don Diego and Doña Teresa, my legitimate children, and Don Alonso, and Don Juan, and Don Antonio, and Doña Ysabel, and Doña Catalina, my children, are not of age, it is my wish, and I desire, that they remain under tutelage and government until they are of an age to know how to take the management of their estates."

"Again: I order what I have taken from the Jews against their will, when they went out of the kingdom, movable as well as real, to be ascertained and returned to the owners or to their heirs."

"Again: I order that there be annually given to Don Antonio, my son, for his subsistence, one hundred thousand maravedises, until such time as the income of fifty thousand maravedises shall be given to him from the Church, to be paid in the best manner and form possible, with which duty I charge my son Don Alvaro, under pain of forfeiture of my benediction; and should that sum not be coming from the Church, let the hundred thousand be paid during lifetime."

"Again: to Galaor Osorio, other twenty thousand maravedis; and I strongly charge it upon Don Alvaro, my son, so to aid and favour him, that he may receive income from the Church, and to assist him with some benefices that may become vacant, to which he may have the presentation."

"Again: I order that there be given to his brother, Garcia Osorio, forty thousand maravedis: And likewise I order that they strive to bring back Villagomez, my servant (*criado*), to this House, and return to strive, for he is servant and kinsman, and that they give him what shall be proper."

Some particulars in the life of Garcia Osorio appear in one of the official papers printed in the Appendix.

THE BIEDMA spoken of is Luys, not Antonio. He wrote the account of the march of the army, *Relacion de la Isla de la Florida*, given in this volume. His title as *factor*, and that of Añasco as *contador*, of Gaytan as treasurer, and Gallegos as *alcaide-mayor*, are also added in translations made from the book of entries at Sevilla.

CHAPTER V.

THE person mentioned as Governor of one of the Canary Islands was Guillén Peraza de Ayala, proprietor of Hierro and Gomera. His mother, Doña Beatriz de Bobadilla, was first cousin to the mother of Doña Ysabel, and a sister of the Marquesa de Moya, the associate of the Queen of Castilla from childhood, and her honored intimate through life. The father of these celebrated women was Mosen Pedro de Bobadilla, castellan of the Alcázares of Segovia.

Some highly interesting particulars in the life of Doña Beatriz are given in the "History of the Canaries," by Glas, translated, according to Viera y Clavijo, from a work on the subject of those Islands, in manuscript, by the Franciscan Juan de Galindo. Hernan Peraza, Conde de la Gomera, having been sent to Spain, on the complaint of the widow of Juan Rejon, charged with the murder of her husband, a pardon was granted him by Ysabel, through the intercession of influential friends, in consideration of his returning to serve, with some companies of troops, in the conquest of the Great Canary. At the same time, as the King was supposed to have a passion for one of the Ladies of Honour, Beatriz, and an opportunity for removing her creditably from Court presented itself, she was given in marriage by the Queen, with great ceremonial, to Hernan Peraza, who returned with her to the Islands.

In the course of time, the Count, becoming enamoured with a female of the country, was killed by one of the natives—a deed for which he, with many others, supposed accomplices, was punished with great cruelty by Pedro de Vera, the final subjugator of the people of that Group, after a protracted war of seventy-seven years. This is the grandsire of that Vera, the very opposite in character, who, with the maternal name of Cabeça de Vaca, wrote the story of the disasters he shared with Narvaez in attempting the conquest of Florida.

The widow of Peraza soon after married Alonso de Lugo, though not before she had, by arbitrary acts, caused two Spaniards to be hanged—one for treason to her government, the other for expressions cast on the purity of her womanly conduct. Coming to Spain afterward, against the advice of her husband, to answer for her administration, she was received with the most friendly feelings at Court. One morning, however, the beauteous Beatriz was found lying in her bed lifeless. The funeral, by order of the Queen, was one of magnificence.

Alonso de Lugo continued to administer the affairs of Gomera, until the youthful Count, assisted by his friends, obliged him to relinquish the station; and the step-father being taken from the Island, Guillén governed for the public content and welfare.

Garcilasso names the daughter of the Count of Gomera, Doña Leonor, and describes her as a beauty of seventeen summers, whom the Adelantado earnestly solicited of her father, that he might marry her to some one of high position in his prospective conquest. The lady, it may be seen, is mentioned in the will of Soto, with substantial remembrance both of her and her husband.

CHAPTER VI.

THE RIVER CÁUTO, misspelled Tanto in the text, is the largest river of Cuba, and runs its entire course westwardly a distance of sixty leagues.

ASASCO, called Daubusco in the text, bore the royal license of exclusive privilege to trade with the inhabitants of Florida. The record of it exists in the archives of Indias at Seville, in the volume entitled *Libro de la Florida de Capitulaciones y Asientos desde el año 1517, hasta el de 1578*, a translation of which into English is given in the Appendix to this volume.

CHAPTER IX.

The *ano paracusi* (according to the friar Francisco Pareja, in his Catechism in Spanish of the Timuquana tongue), with *holata yco*, or *olata aco*, or *utinama*, are principal caciques, having other chiefs subject to them. From this stock comes a counsellor, *ynihama*, "who leads the cacique by the hand," and from him descend other lines or stages in society. Perhaps the XIIII. plate in the *Brevis Narratio* of De Bry, Second Part, illustrates the rank and relation of these personages to each other.

CHAPTER XI.

Villa harta (in the Portuguese, *Villa-farta*) is a small town of Spain, in the Province of Córdova, six leagues from the city, and twenty-eight from Sevilla, situated in a healthy climate, on the side of the elevated mountain of La Solana, having an uneven, stony, and fertile soil. It is strictly agricultural, and only commercial to the extent of sending away its superfluous productions of grain and wine, pork, and a little honey. The district is also very plentiful in game. Its insignificance could scarcely have permitted it to rise to the casualty of giving its name to another town; and the meaning of the word "harta," abundant, will be thought perhaps sufficient reason alone for its use, without seeking other explanation.

The name of the Chief Uzachil is spelled, in Oviedo, *Uçahile;* by Garcilasso, *Ochile;* by Captain Biedma, *Veachile;* in Herrera, *Osachile;* and is perhaps that of the personage or dignitary spoken of by Cabeça de Vaca as met by the army of Narvaez, in about the same region of country, in the year 1528, whom he calls Dulchanchellin.

"Having learned this much, we left the next day, going ever in quest of that country which the Indians had told us of as Apalache, carrying for guides those of them we had taken. We travelled until the seventeenth day of June, without seeing any natives who would venture to await our coming up with them, when a chief approached, carried on the back of another Indian, and covered with a painted deer-skin, having a great many people walking in advance of him, playing on flutes of cane. In this manner he came up to where the Governor stood, and was with him an hour. By signs we gave him to understand that we were going to Apalache; and it appeared to us, by those he made, that he was an enemy to its people, and would go to assist us against them. We gave him beads and hawk-bells, with other articles of traffic, and he presented the Governor with the skin he wore, and then returned, we following him in the road he took.

"That night we came to a very wide and deep river, with current very rapid. As we could not venture to cross with rafts, we made a canoe for the purpose, and spent a day in getting over. If the Indians had desired to dispute our passage, they could well have done so; for, even with their help, we had great difficulty in effecting it. One of the horsemen, Juan Vazquez by name, a native of Cuellar, impatient of detention, having entered the river, the violence of the current cast him from his horse, when he grasped the reins of the bridle, and both were drowned. The people of that chief, whose name was Dulchanchellin, found the body of the beast, and told us where we should find the corpse in the river below. This death gave us much pain, for until then, not one had been missing."—NAUFRAGIOS.

29

CHAPTER XV.

In the account given of the march of Soto by his private secretary (see Oviedo), Guazule or Guazulle is spelled Guasili; and the writer says, because of the good fortune that attended the soldiers there, the Chief having given them many tamemes, much maize, and many little dogs, they would say at a favourable throw of dice, " The house of Guasuli !" in recollection of the luck that there befell them. The word is spelled, in all the other narratives, nearly in the same way as that more familiar to Spanish ears, Guazul or Gazul, the name borne by a tribe of *Berberiscos* of the coast of Africa, who had given it to a town of the Peninsula they once guarded—Alcalá de los Guazules (*ul*, the ; *calat*, castle), whence has come the word there *gandul*, vagabond, as a term of reproach, from the Arabic into the familiar language of the country.

Barbacoa, Maiz, Tameme, Petaca, are words used in this narrative derived from Indian tongues, and recognized in the Spanish. " Barbacoa," of which we have not the elements, is from the Yucayo, and in its simplest signification appears to mean scaffolding raised on posts, such an arrangement as was made for burning Ortiz, mentioned in Chapter IX.; or a crib, such as was used for storing the crop ; or a staging put up in the fields, whereon the natives watched, that birds should not take the grain. From it, through the Spanish, comes the word into the English " barbacue," and, perhaps, the word " bucanier," through the French. " Maiz " belongs also to the same language, the one spoken by the natives of Cuba and Hayti. " Tameme," used by the descendants of the Spaniards in Mexico, is from *tlamama* or *tlameme* in the Mexican language proper, signifying porter, or carrier of loads on the back. " Petaca " is likewise from the Mexican, a corruption of *petla calli*, cane house, a word in general use all over Spanish America for cigar-case, or other box made of grass.

CHAPTER XVII.

THE AMEIJOA is the green gage, the Claudia of Spain, where it is produced in perfection and abundance. The shape of the plum is precisely that of the persimmon, the fruit undoubtedly that is referred to as growing without being planted, and wild in the woods. Moreover, as will be seen in the concluding chapter, which treats of the soil of Florida, its animal and vegetable life, this fruit is spoken of as of two kinds, the red and gray, and as being the size of a walnut, with three or four pits, and also as making a far better prune than the plum of Spain. They are the *Diospyros Virginiana* and the *D. Texana*.

CHAPTER XXIV.

WITH reference to the fishes that are mentioned in this chapter, we are indebted for the following observations to Professor Theodore Gill, of the Smithsonian Institution.

"I have carefully perused the account, and although there is little on which to base the identification of the species, I am disposed to believe that the following conjectures will at least closely approximate the truth. The historian enumerates five species, of which three have scales, while the others are naked. The scaleless species are the 'bagre' and the 'peel-fish.'

"The 'bagre' is undoubtedly the large 'cat-fish' of the West, known as *Ictalurus cærulescens*, that being the only species that attains a weight of 'one hundred to one hundred and fifty pounds.' The head is large, as in all its congeners, but not as big as would be inferred from the text; the 'great spines, like very sharp awls,' along the side, are the spines of the pectoral fins. The species is very generally distributed in the hydrographical basin of the Mississippi. The 'peel-fish,' with 'the snout a cubit in length, the upper lip being shaped like a shovel,' is very clearly the singular fish universally known throughout the West as the 'spoonbill-cat' or sturgeon, and 'paddle-fish.' It is related to the ordinary sturgeons, but is distinguished by the peculiar leaf-like expansion of the snout, the extension of the gill covers, and the presence of minute teeth on the jaws in the young. The species observed was the *Polyodon spatula*, occurring in the Mississippi River and all its larger tributaries. The only other species of the genus, besides the American, inhabit the rivers of China and Japan.

"The scaly fishes are not so easily determinable. The one shaped like a barbel was probably the *Cycleptus elongatus*, a member of the family of 'suckers,' or *Catastomidæ*. That species would probably be recognized by most or all casual observers as having a greater superficial resemblance to the barbel of Europe than any other of our fishes. The fish 'like a shad' was perhaps the species which has been introduced into the ichthyological system as *Pomolobus chrysochloris*, and which is very closely related to the 'fall herring' or 'shad' of the Eastern fishermen. The bream-like fish cannot be identified with any approach to certainty; but it is possible that it may have been the fish now known in Louisiana and Mississippi as 'tarpon' or 'big scale,' and called by naturalists *Megalops cyprinoides*. That species more nearly fulfils the requisites as to form of head and excellence as food than any of the species of the lower Mississippi basin known to me. The 'perco' is probably referable to the genus *Haploidonotus*, the species of which are generally called 'white perch' or 'drum' by the inhabitants of the west. That type, at least, is the only one that possesses the combination of scaly body, teeth in the jaws, and size, referred to in the notice." RAFINESQUE writes: "A remarkable peculiarity of this fish consists in the strange grunting noise which it produces, and from which is derived its specific name, *H. grunniens*. It is intermediate between the dumb grunt of a hog, and the single croaking noise of the bullfrog: that grunt is only repeated at intervals, and not in quick succession."—*Ichthyologia Ohienis*, 1820, p. 25.

POLYODON SPATULA.

HEAD AND SNOUT FROM ABOVE.

Drawn from specimens in the Smithsonian Institution, for The Bradford Club.

"I will merely add that all the fishes mentioned, save the *Megalops*, ascend high up the Mississippi River and its larger tributary streams, while the *Megalops* enters the rivers of the Southern coast generally, and does not ascend far above tide-water."

In a note to the translation made by Hakluyt of this work, republished in London by the Hakluyt Society, and edited by William B. Rye, with good discretion and research, is this curious conjecture:—

" The words *pexe pereo*, in the original Portuguese, are in all probability a misprint for *pexe*, or *peyxe*, fish, and *porco*, hog, the two words together meaning a porpoise, which English word, indeed, is derived from the corresponding Latin words, *porcus piscis.*"

CHAPTER XXV.

THE RIVER CAYA, a western limit of Spain, takes its rise in the adjoining kingdom of Portugal, among the mountains of San Manuel and La Rabona, flowing through the Province of Badajóz, and, at about a league from the city of the same name, empties itself into the River Guadiana. The stream, unspanned by bridges, is crossed during the season of floods in little boats.

CHAPTER XXXI.

THE ocean, as surveyed from Biscay, was the North Sea, and that name, for the maritime people there, extended over the Atlantic: the discovery of another ocean, the Pacific, as seen from Panamá, became, in contradistinction for Spaniards, the South Sea.

CHAPTER XLI.

THE RIVER PÁNUCO, in the text misspelled Panico, has for its outlet the bar of Puerto Escondido. The town of Pánuco is about nine leagues distant from that entrance, situate on the south bank of the river, in 22° 4' of northern latitude.

CHAPTER XLIII.

THE *topile* was an officer that the conquerors, *conquistadores*, found in the civil government of Mexico, with powers judicial and ministerial similar to those exercised by the *marino* or *alguazil* among themselves, and by the sheriff in England.

ORDER OF ST. JAGO.

SOTO.

ÁRIAS.

RELATION

OF THE

CONQUEST OF FLORIDA,

PRESENTED BY

LUYS HERNANDEZ DE BIEDMA

IN THE YEAR 1544

TO THE

KING OF SPAIN IN COUNCIL.

TRANSLATED FROM THE ORIGINAL DOCUMENT.

30

ACCOUNT

OF

THE ISLAND OF FLORIDA.

WE arrived at the port of Baya Honda, where we landed six hundred and twenty men and two hundred and twenty-three horses. As soon as we went on shore, we found out, from some Indians taken, that there was a Christian in the country, one of the people who had come into it with Pánfilo de Narvaez, and we started in search of him. He was in the possession of a chief, some eight leagues distant from the harbour. We met him on the way, for the Cacique, hearing that we had left the ships, asked the Christian if it was his desire to go where we were; who answered that it was, and he sent him off with nine Indians. He came naked like them, with a bow and some arrows in his hands, his body wrought over like theirs. They who discovered the natives thought they were come to spy out the condition of our people, and dashed after them. The Indians fled towards a little wood near by, but the horsemen coming up with them, one Indian received a thrust from a lance, and the Christian, having nearly forgotten our language, himself would

have been slain, had he not remembered to call upon the
name of Our Lady, whereby he was recognized.   We
brought him with great rejoicing before the Governor.

Twelve years had passed since the Christian had come
among the Indians.   He knew their tongue, and, from
the long habit of speaking that only, he was more than
four days among us before he could connect an idea without putting to every word of Spanish four or five words
of Indian, though he came after a while to recover our
speech entirely.   His knowledge of the country was so
limited that he could tell us of nothing twenty leagues
off, neither from having seen it nor by hearsay ; however, from first seeing us, he said there was no place at
which to find gold.

We left Baya Honda to explore inland, taking with
us all the people that had come on shore excepting
twenty-six cavalry and sixty infantry, left in charge of
the port until the Governor should be heard from, or
should send orders for them to join him.   We took our
way towards the west, then turned to the northwest,
having information of a Cacique named Hurripacuxi,
who lived about twenty leagues from the coast, to whom
the Indians said they all paid tribute.   Thence we went,
through swamps and over rivers, fifteen or twenty
leagues, to a town which the Indians represented to
us as very wonderful, and where the inhabitants, by
shouting, caused birds on the wing to drop.   On arrival
there we found it to be a small town, called Etocale.
We got some maize, beans, and little dogs, which were no
small relief to people who came perishing with hunger.

We remained seven or eight days, and in that time
made several forays, to catch Indians for guides to the
Province of Apalache, which had great fame wheresoever we went.   Three or four men were taken, of
whom the best informed knew nothing of the country
two leagues in advance.   We went on still in the direction of New Spain, keeping some ten or twelve leagues
from the coast.

   In four or five days' march we passed through several
towns, and came to a moderately large one, called Agua-
caleeuen.   The inhabitants were all found to have gone
off affrighted into the woods.   We remained six or seven
days, to hunt some Indians for guides, and while engaged
in the search we caught ten or twelve women, one of
whom was declared to be the daughter of the Cacique.
The consequence was, that her father came to us in peace.
He promised we should have interpreters and guides;
but, as he did not give them, we had to take him along
with us.   With the intent of wresting him from us, at
the close of six or seven days' march there came upon us
about three hundred and fifty warriors, with bows and
arrows, of whom we killed some and captured the
remainder.   Among them were Indians who had knowledge of the country farther inland, yet they told us
very false stories.

   We crossed another river, in a Province called
Veachile, and found towns on the farther bank which
the inhabitants had left, though we did not fail, in
consequence, to find some food in them, which we
needed.   We set out for another town, named Aguile,

which is on the confines of Apalache, a river dividing
the one from the other province. Across this stream we
made a bridge, by lashing many pines together, upon
which we went over with much danger, as there were
Indians on the opposite side who disputed our passage;
when they found, however, that we had landed, they
went to the nearest town, called Ivitachuco, and there
remained until we came in sight, when as we appeared
they set all the place on fire and took to flight.

There are many towns in this Province of Apalache,
and it is a land abundant in subsistence. They call all
that other country we were travelling through, the Province of Yustaga.

We went to another town, called Iniahico. There it
appeared to us to be time we should know of those who
remained at the port, and that they should hear from us;
for we proposed to travel so far inland that we might not
be able to hear of them again. The distance we had
now marched from them was one hundred and ten
leagues, and the Governor gave orders that they should
come to where we then were.

From that town we went to look for the sea, which
was about nine leagues off, and we found, on the shore,
where Pánfilo de Narvaez had built his boats. We found
the spot whereon the forge had stood, and many bones of
horses. The Indians told us, through the interpreter,
what others like us there had done. Juan de Añasco put
signals on some trees standing near the water, because he
was commanded to return to the port, and bid the people
there come on by the way we had marched, while he

should sail in the two brigantines and the boat that were left, and we would await his arrival, at the Province of Apalache.

Juan de Añasco sent the people on by land, while he came by sea, as the Governor had ordered, encountering much fatigue and danger; for he could not find the coast he had observed from the land before leaving, discovering no marks whatsoever from the sea, as these were in shallow inlets, that with the rise of tide had water in them, and with the ebb were bare. We made a piragua, which went out every day two leagues to sea, looking for the brigantines, to show them where to stop. I was thankful when the people arrived, not less for those that came by land than those by water.

On the arrival of the brigantines, the Governor directed that they should sail westwardly to discover a harbour, if one were near, whence to ascertain, by exploring the coast, if any thing could be found inland. Francisco Maldonado, a gentleman of Salamanca, had the command. He coasted along the country, and entered all the coves, creeks, and rivers he discovered, until he arrived at a river having a good entrance and harbour, with an Indian town on the seaboard. Some inhabitants approaching to traffic, he took one of them, and directly turned back with him to join us. On this voyage he was absent two months, which appeared to us all to be a thousand years, inasmuch as it detained us so long from advancing to what we understood was to be found in the interior.

After Maldonado got back, the Governor told him,

that, as we were about to set off in quest of the country
which that Indian stated to be on another sea, he must
return with the brigantines to Cuba, where the Doña
Ysabel de Bobadilla, his wife, remained; and if within
six months' time he should hear nothing of us, to come
with the brigantines, and run the shore as far as the
River Espiritu Santo, to which we should have to resort.
The vessels went to the Island, and we took our way
again northward, going to seek after what the Indian
had told us of.

We marched five days through an uninhabited country, when, coming to a great river, as we could not
build a bridge over it, because of the stiffness of the
current, we made a piragua. With this we reached the
opposite shore, where we found a Province called Acapa-
chiqui, very abundant in the food to which the Indians
are accustomed. We saw some towns, and others there
were we did not visit, because the country was one of
very large swamps. There was a change in the habitations, which were now in the earth, like caves: heretofore
they were covered with palm-leaves and with grass.
We continued on, and came to two other rivers, over
which we had to make bridges, in our usual manner,
by tying pine-trees together. Arrived at another Province, called Otoa, we found a town rather larger than
any we had seen to that time. We went thence to
towns of another province, which may be about two
days' march distant, where we took some persons not on
the look-out, they never having heard of us. The people
agreed to come and serve us peacefully for the return of

the captives, whom the Governor gave up, keeping only
a part as interpreters and guides, for the use of the way.

We were five or six days in going through this Province, called Chisi, where we were well supplied by the
Indians from their slender stores; and having marched
three days more without seeing any large town, we came
to the Province of Altapaha. Here we found a river
that had a course not southwardly, like the rest we had
passed, but eastward to the sea, where the Licentiate,
Lucas de Ayllón, had come; whence we gave still more
credit to what the Indian said, and we came to believe
as true all the stories that he had told us. This province
was thickly peopled, and the inhabitants all desired to
serve us. The Governor inquired of them for that
province, Cofitachyque, of which we came in pursuit;
they said it was not possible to go thither, there being no
road, and on the journey we should famish, there being
no food. We went on to other caciques, of the names
Ocuti and Cafaqui, who gave us of what they had to eat.
They said if we were going to make war on the Lady of
Cofitachique, they would give us all we should desire for
the way; but we should understand there was no road
over which to pass; that they had no intercourse, because
of their enmity, except when they made war upon each
other, which was carried on through obscure and intri-
cate parts, out of which no one would be expected to
issue, and that they were on the journey from twenty to
twenty-two days, eating in the time only plants and the
parched maize they took with them. Seeing our determination, they gave us eight hundred Indians to carry

31

our loads of clothing and provisions, and also others as guides.

We were taken directly to the eastward, and thus travelled three days. The Indian who deceitfully led us had said, that he would place us whither we were going in that time; and notwithstanding, towards the close, we began to discover his perfidy, the Governor did not desist from the course, but commanded that we should husband our provisions as much as possible, since he suspected we should find ourselves—which did actually come to pass—in embarrassment and want. We went on through this wilderness, and at the end of thirteen days arrived at some cottages. The Indians had now become so bewildered, that they knew not in what direction to turn. The road had given out, and the Governor went around to regain it, but, failing to find it, he came back to us desperate. He directed that the people should return some half a league to a great river, and there he began to give out rations of fresh pork from the hogs we drove with us, a pound to each man, which we ate boiled, without salt or other seasoning.

The Governor sent in two directions to find a path, or any mark indicating inhabitants—one person up the river to the north and northeast, and the other down along it to the south and southeast, and he allowed to each ten days in which to go and return. He that went to the south and southeastward came in, after being gone four days, with the news that he had come upon a little town having some provisions. He brought three or four people from it, who speaking with

our perfidious Indian, he understood them. This was no
little relief to us, because of the difficulty there is everywhere in the country of being understood; and once
more the guide repeated the falsehoods he had before
told us, which we believed, because we heard him talk the
language with those Indians. We directly set out, with
all our people, for that little village, to await there the
return of those who had gone in other directions to seek
for paths. We tarried four or five days, until all had
come together. About fifty hanegas of maize were found
in the place, and some parched meal; there were many
mulberry-trees loaded with fruit, and likewise some other
small fruits.

Thence we set out for the town of Cofitachique,
two days' journey from the village, seated on the banks
of a river, which we believed to be the Santa Elena,
where the Licentiate Ayllón had been. Having arrived
at the stream, the Lady of this town sent to us her
niece, borne in a litter, the Indians showing her much
respect, with the message that she was pleased we had
arrived in her territory, and that she would give us of
all she could or might possess. She likewise sent the
Governor a necklace of five or six strings of pearls.
We were furnished with canoes in which to pass over
the river, and the Lady gave us one-half of the town; but
after staying three or four days, she suddenly went off
into the woods. The Governor caused her to be sought,
and not finding her, he opened a mosque, in which
were interred the bodies of the chief personages of that
country. We took from it a quantity of pearls, of the

weight of as many as six arrobas and a half, or seven,
though they were injured from lying in the earth, and
in the adipose substance of the dead. We found buried
two wood axes, of Castilian make, a rosary of jet beads,
and some false pearls, such as are taken from this
country to traffic with the Indians, all of which we
supposed they got in exchange, made with those who
followed the Licentiate Ayllón. From the information
given by the Indians, the sea should be about thirty
leagues distant. We knew that the people who came
with Ayllón hardly entered the country at all; that they
remained continually on the coast, until his sickness and
death. In strife for command, they then commenced to
kill each other, while others of them died of hunger;
for one, whose lot it was to have been among them,
told us that of six hundred men who landed, only fifty-
seven escaped—a loss caused, to a great extent, by the
wreck of a big ship they had brought, laden with
stores. Having remained in the town of this Lady some
ten.or eleven days, it became necessary that we should
go thence in quest of a country which might furnish
food, as the quantity where we were was sufficient
only for the necessities of the Indians, and we, our
horses and followers, consumed it very fast.

Again we took the direction of the north, and for
eight days we travelled through a poor country, scarce
of food, until arriving at one called Xuala, where we
still found some Indian houses, though a thin population, for the country was broken. Among these ridges
we discovered the source of the great river whence we

had taken our departure, believed to be the Espiritu
Santo. We went on to a town called Guasuli, where
the inhabitants gave us a number of dogs, and some
maize, of which they had but little. From there we
marched four days, and arrived at a town called Chiha,
which is very plentiful in food. It is secluded on an
island of this river of Espiritu Santo, which, all the
way from the place of its rise, forms very large islands.
In this province, where we began to find the towns set
about with fence, the Indians get a large quantity of oil
from walnuts. We were detained twenty-six or twenty-
seven days to refresh the horses, which arrived greatly
fatigued, having worked hard and eaten little.

We left, following along the banks of the river, and
came to another province, called Costehe, the towns of
which are likewise on islands in the river, and thence we
went to Coça, one of the finest countries we discovered
in Florida. The Cacique came out in a hurdle to receive us, with great festivity and many people, he having
numerous towns subject to him. The next morning we
saw all the inhabitants, and having detained the Cacique,
that he might give us persons to carry our loads, we
tarried some days until we could get them. We found
plums like those here in Castile, and great quantities
of vines, on which were very good grapes. From
this we went to the west and southwest, passing
through the towns of the Cacique for five or six days,
until we came to another province, called Italisi. The
people being gone, we went to look for them. Some
Indians came to us, by whom the Governor sent to call

the Cacique, who, coming, brought to us a present of
twenty-six or twenty-seven women, skins of deer, and
whatever else they had.

From this point we went south, drawing towards the
coast of New Spain, and passed through several towns,
before coming to another province, called Taszaluza, of
which an Indian of such size was chief that we all
considered him a giant. He awaited us quietly at his
town, and on our arrival we made much ado for him,
with joust at reeds, and great running of horses, although
he appeared to regard it all as small matter. Afterward we asked him for Indians to carry our burdens;
he answered that he was not accustomed to serving any
one, but it was rather for others all to serve *him*.
The Governor ordered that he should not be allowed
to return to his house, but be kept where he was.
This detention among us he felt—whence sprang the
ruin that he afterwards wrought us, and it was why he
told us that he could there give us nothing, and that
we must go to another town of his, called Mavila, where
he would bestow on us whatever we might ask. We took
up our march in that direction, and came to a river, a
copious flood, which we considered to be that which
empties into the Bay of Chuse. Here we got news of the
manner in which the boats of Narvaez had arrived in
want of water, and of a Christian, named Don Teodoro,
who had stopped-among these Indians, with a negro, and
we were shown a dagger that he had worn. We were
here two days, making rafts for crossing the river. In
this time the Indians killed one of the guard of the

Governor, who thereupon, being angry, threatened the
Cacique, and told him that he should burn him if he
did not give up to him those who had slain the Christian.
He replied that he would deliver them to us in that town
of his, Mavila. The Cacique had many in attendance.
An Indian was always behind him with a fly-brush of
plumes, so large as to afford his person shelter from the
sun.

At nine o'clock, one morning, we arrived at Mavila,
a small town very strongly stockaded, situated on a plain.
We found the Indians had demolished some habitations
about it, to present a clear field. A number of the chiefs
came out to receive us as soon as we were in sight,
and they asked the Governor, through the interpreter,
if he would like to stop on that plain, or preferred to
enter the town, and said that in the evening they would
give us the Indians to carry burdens. It appeared to our
Chief better to go thither with them, and he commanded
that all should enter the town, which we did.

Having come within the enclosure, we walked about,
talking with the Indians, supposing them to be friendly,
there being not over three or four hundred in sight,
though full five thousand were in the town, whom we
did not see, nor did they show themselves at all.
Apparently rejoicing, they began their customary songs
and dances; and some fifteen or twenty women having
performed before us a little while, for dissimulation, the
Cacique got up and withdrew into one of the houses.
The Governor sent to tell him that he must come
out, to which he answered that he would not; and

the Captain of the body-guard entered the door to
bring him forth, but seeing many Indians present, fully
prepared for battle, he thought it best to withdraw
and leave him. He reported that the houses were filled
with men, ready with bows and arrows, bent on some
mischief. The Governor called to an Indian passing by,
who also refusing to come, a gentleman near took him by
the arm to bring him, when, receiving a push, such as to
make him let go his hold, he drew his sword and dealt a
stroke in return that cleaved away an arm.

With the blow they all began to shoot arrows at us,
some from within the houses, through the many loop-
holes they had arranged, and some from without. As we
were so wholly unprepared, having considered ourselves
on a footing of peace, we were obliged, from the great
injuries we were sustaining, to flee from the town, leaving
behind all that the carriers had brought for us, as they
had there set down their burdens.   When the Indians
saw that we had gone out, they closed the gates, and
beating their drums, they raised flags, with great shouting; then, emptying our knapsacks and bundles, showed
up above the palisades all we had brought, as much as to
say that they had those things in possession.   Directly as
we retired, we bestrode our horses and completely encircled the town, that none might thence anywhere escape.
The Governor directed that sixty of us should dismount,
and that eighty of the best accoutred should form in four
parties, to assail the place on as many sides, and the first
of us getting in should set fire to the houses, that no
more harm should come to us: so we handed over

our horses to other soldiers who were not in armour, that
if any of the Indians should come running out of the
town they might overtake them.

We entered the town and set it on fire, whereby a
number of Indians were burned, and all that we had was
consumed, so that there remained not a thing. We
fought that day until nightfall, without a single Indian
having surrendered to us—they fighting bravely on like
lions. We killed them all, either with fire or the sword,
or, such of them as came out, with the lance, so that
when it was nearly dark there remained only three alive;
and these, taking the women that had been brought
to dance, placed the twenty in front, who, crossing their
hands, made signs to us that we should come for them.
The Christians advancing toward the women, these
turned aside, and the three men behind them shot their
arrows at us, when we killed two of them. The last
Indian, not to surrender, climbed a tree that was in the
fence, and taking the cord from his bow, tied it about
his neck, and from a limb hanged himself.

This day the Indians slew more than twenty of our
men, and those of us who escaped only hurt were two
hundred and fifty, bearing upon our bodies seven hundred and sixty injuries from their shafts. At night we
dressed our wounds with the fat of the dead Indians,
as there was no medicine left, all that belonged to us
having been burned. We tarried twenty-seven or twenty-
eight days to take care of ourselves, and God be praised
that we were all relieved. The women were divided as
servants among those who were suffering most. We

32

learned from the Indians that we were as many as forty leagues from the sea. It was much the desire that the Governor should go to the coast, for we had tidings of the brigantines; but he dared not venture thither, as it was already the middle of November, the season very cold; and he found it necessary to go in quest of a country where subsistence might be had for the winter; here there was none, the region being one of little food.

We resumed our direction to the northward, and travelled ten or twelve days, suffering greatly from the cold and rain, in which we marched afoot, until arriving at a fertile province, plentiful in provisions, where we could stop during the rigour of the season. The snows fall more heavily there than they do in Castile. Having reached the Province of Chicaza, the warriors came out to interrupt the passage of a river we had to cross. We were detained by them three days. Finally, we went over in a piragua we built, when the Indians fled to the woods. After seven or eight days, messengers from the Cacique arrived, saying that he and all his people desired to come and serve us. The Governor received the message well, and sent word to him to do so without fail, and that he would present him with many of the things he brought. The Cacique came, having with him a number of persons, who bore him upon their shoulders. He gave us some deer-skins and little dogs. The people returned, and every day Indians came and went, bringing us many hares, and whatever else the country supplied.

In the night-time we captured some Indians, who, on
a footing of peace, came to observe how we slept and
guarded. We, unaware of the perfidy that was intended,
told the Cacique that we desired the next day to continue
our march, when he left, and that night fell upon us.
As the enemy knew whereabout our sentinels were set,
they got amongst us into the town, without being observed, by twos and fours, more than three hundred men,
with fire which they brought in little pots, not to be seen.
When the sentinels discovered that more were coming in
troop, they beat to arms; but this was not done until the
others had already set fire to the town. The Indians did
us very great injury, killing fifty-seven horses, more than
three hundred hogs, and thirteen or fourteen men; and
it was a great mysterious providence of God, that, though
we were not resisting them, nor giving them any cause
to do so, they turned and fled; had they followed us
up, not a man of all our number could have escaped.
Directly we moved to a cottage about a mile off.

We knew that the Indians had agreed to return upon
us that night; but, God be praised, in consequence of a
light rain, they did not come; for we were in so bad condition, that, although some horses still remained, we had
no saddles, lances, nor targets, all having been consumed.
We hastened to make them, the best we could with the
means at hand; and at the end of five days, the Indians,
coming back upon us with their squadrons in order,
attacked us with much concert at three points. As we
were prepared, and, moreover, aware of their approach,
we met them at the onset, beat them back, and did them

some injury; so that, thank God, they returned no more. We remained here perhaps two months, getting ready what were necessary of saddles, lances, and targets, and then left, taking the direction to the northwest, toward a Province called Alibamo.

At this time befell us what is said never to have occurred in the Indias. In the highway over which we had to pass, without there being either women to protect or provisions to secure, and only to try our valour with theirs, the Indians put up a very strong stockade directly across the road, about three hundred of them standing behind it, resolute to die rather than give back. So soon as they observed our approach, some came out to shoot their arrows, threatening that not one of us should remain alive. When we had surveyed that work, thus defended by men, we supposed they guarded something—provision perhaps—of which we stood greatly in need; for we had calculated to cross a desert of twelve days' journey in its extent, where we could have nothing to eat but what we carried. We alighted, some forty or fifty men, and put ourselves on two sides, arranging that at the sound of the trumpet we should all enter the barricade at one time. We did accordingly, carrying it, although at some cost, losing on our side seven or eight men, and having twenty-five or twenty-six more wounded. We killed some Indians, and took others, from whom we learned that they had done this to measure themselves with us, and nothing else. We looked about for food, although at great hazard, that we might begin our journey in the wilderness.

We travelled eight days with great care, in tenderness of the wounded and the sick we carried. One mid-day we came upon a town called Quizquiz, and so suddenly to the inhabitants, that they were without any notice of us, the men being away at work in the maize-fields. We took more than three hundred women, and the few skins and shawls they had in their houses. There we first found a little walnut of the country, which is much better than that here in Spain. The town was near the banks of the River Espiritu Santo. They told us that it was, with many towns about there, tributary to a lord of Pacaha, famed throughout all the land. When the men heard that we had taken their women, they came to us peacefully, requesting the Governor to restore them. He did so, and asked them for canoes in which to pass that great river. These they promised, but never gave; on the contrary, they collected to give us battle, coming in sight of the town where we were; but in the end, not venturing to make an attack, they turned and retired.

We left that place and went to encamp by the river-side, to put ourselves in order for crossing. On the other shore we saw numbers of people collected to oppose our landing, who had many canoes. We set about building four large piraguas, each capable of taking sixty or seventy men and five or six horses. We were engaged in the work twenty-seven or twenty-eight days. During this time, the Indians every day, at three o'clock in the afternoon, would get into two hundred and fifty very large canoes they had, well shielded, and come near the shore on which we were; with loud cries they would exhaust

their arrows upon us, and then return to the other
bank. After they saw that our boats were at the point
of readiness for crossing, they all went off, leaving the
passage free. We crossed the river in concert, it being
nearly a league in width, and nineteen or twenty fathoms
deep. We found some good towns on the other side;
and once more following up the stream, on the way
to that Province of Pacaha, we came first to the
province of another lord, called Icasqui, against whom
he waged severe war. The Cacique came out peacefully to meet us, saying that he had heard of us for
a long time, and that he knew we were men from
heaven, whom their arrows could not harm; wherefore,
he desired to have no strife, and wished only to serve us.
The Governor received him very kindly, and permitting
no one to enter the town, to avoid doing mischief, we
encamped in sight, on a plain, where we lay two days.

On the day of our arrival, the Cacique said that inasmuch as he knew the Governor to be a man from the
sky, who must necessarily have to go away, he besought
him to leave a sign, of which he might ask support
in his wars, and his people call upon for rain, of which
their fields had great need, as their children were
dying of hunger. The Governor commanded that a very
tall cross be made of two pines, and told him to return
the next day, when he would give him the sign from
heaven for which he asked; but that the Chief must
believe nothing could be needed if he had a true faith
in the cross. He returned the next day, complaining
much because we so long delayed giving him the

sign he asked, and he had good-will to serve and follow
us. Thereupon he set up a loud wailing because the
compliance was not immediate, which caused us all to
weep, witnessing such devotion and earnestness in his
entreaties. The Governor told him to bring all his people back in the evening, and that we would go with
them to his town and take thither the sign he had
asked. He came in the afternoon with them, and we
went in procession to the town, while they followed us.
Arriving there, as it is the custom of the Caciques to
have near their houses a high hill, made by hand, some
having the houses placed thereon, we set up the cross on
the summit of a mount, and we all went on bended
knees, with great humility, to kiss the foot of that cross.
The Indians did the same as they saw us do, nor more
nor less; then directly they brought a great quantity of
cane, making a fence about it; and we returned that
night to our camp.

In the morning, we took up our course for Pacaha,
which was by the river upward. We travelled two days,
and then discovered the town on a plain, well fenced
about, and surrounded by a water-ditch made by hand.
Hastening on as fast as possible, we came near and halted,
not daring to enter there; but going about on one side
and the other, and discovering that many people were
escaping, we assailed and entered the town, meeting
no opposition. We took only a few people, for nearly
all had fled, without, however, being able to carry
off the little they possessed. While we yet halted in
sight of the town, before venturing to enter it, we saw

coming behind us a large body of Indians, whom we supposed to be advancing to the assistance of the place; but
going to meet them, we found they were those we had left
behind, among whom we had raised the cross, and were
following to lend us their succour, should we need any.
We took the Cacique to the town, where he gave the
Governor many thanks for the sign we had left him,
telling us the rain had fallen heavily in his country the
day before, and his people were so glad of it that they
wished to follow and not leave us. The Governor put
him into the town, and gave him every thing found
there, which was great riches for those people—some
beads made of sea-snails, the skins of cats and of
deer, and a little maize. He returned home with them,
much gratified. We remained in this town twenty-
seven or twenty-eight days, to discover if we could take a
path to the northward, whereby to come out on the South
Sea.

Some incursions were made to capture Indians who
might give us the information; particularly was one un-
dertaken to the northwest, where we were told there were
large settlements, through which we might go. We went
in that direction eight days, through a wilderness which
had large pondy swamps, where we did not find even trees,
and only some wide plains, on which grew a plant so rank
and high, that even on horseback we could not break our
way through. Finally, we came to some collections of
huts, covered with rush sewed together. When the
owner of one moves away, he will roll up the entire
covering, and carry it, the wife taking the frame of

poles over which it is stretched; these they take down
and put up so readily, that though they should move
anew every hour, they conveniently enough carry their
house on their backs. We learned from this people that
there were some hamlets of the sort about the country,
the inhabitants of which employed themselves in finding
places for their dwellings wherever many deer were
accustomed to range, and a swamp where were many
fish; and that when they had frightened the game and
the fish from one place, so that they took them there
not so easily as at first, they would all move off with
their dwellings for some other part, where the animals
were not yet shy. This Province, called Caluç, had a
people who cared little to plant, finding support in meat
and fish.

We returned to Pacaha, where the Governor had
remained, and found that the Cacique had come in
peacefully, living with him in the town. In this time
arrived the Cacique from the place behind, at which we
had put up the cross. The efforts of these two chiefs,
who were enemies, each to place himself on the right
hand when the Governor commanded that they should
sit at his sides, was a sight worth witnessing.

Finding that there was no way by which to march to
the other sea, we returned towards the south, and went
with the Cacique to where was the cross, and thence
took the direction to the southwest, to another Province
called Quiguate. This was the largest town we found in
Florida, and was on an arm of the Rio Grande. We
remained there eight or nine days, to find guides and

interpreters, still with the intention of coming out, if possible, on the other sea; for the Indians told us that eleven days' travel thence was a province where they subsisted on certain cattle, and there we could find interpreters for the whole distance to that sea.

We departed with guides for the Province called Coligua, without any road, going at night to the swamps, where we drank from the land and found abundance of fish. We went over much even country and other of broken hills, coming straight upon the town, as much so as if we had been taken thither by a royal highway, instead of which not a man in all time had passed there before. The land is very plentiful of subsistence, and we found a large quantity of dressed cows' tails, and others already cured. We inquired of the inhabitants for a path in the direction we held, or a town on it, near or far. They could give us no sort of information, only that if we wished to go in the direction where there were people, we should have to return upon a west-south-western course.

We continued to pursue the course chosen by our guides, and went to some scattered settlements called Tatil Coya. Here we found a copious river, which we afterwards discovered empties into the Rio Grande, and we were told that up the stream was a great Province, called Cayas. We went thither, and found it to be a population that, though large, was entirely scattered. It is a very rough country of hills. Several incursions were made; in one of which the Cacique and a large number of people were taken. On asking him about the

particulars of the country, he told us that in following
up the river we should come upon a fertile Province,
called Tula. The Governor, desiring to visit there, to see
if it were a place in which he could winter the people,
set off with twenty men on horseback, leaving the remainder in the Province at Cayas.

Before coming to the Province of Tula, we passed
over some rough hills, and arrived at the town before the
inhabitants had any notice of us. In attempting to seize
some Indians, they began to yell and show us battle.
They wounded of ours that day seven or eight men, and
nine or ten horses; and such was their courage, that
they came upon us in packs, by eights and tens, like
worried dogs. We killed some thirty or forty of them.
The Governor thought it not well to stay there that
night with his small force, and returned on the way we
had come, going through a bad passage of the ridge,
where it was feared the natives would beset us, to a
plain in a vale made by the river. The next day we
got back to where the people lay; but there were no
Indians of ours, nor could any in the province be found,
to speak the language of these we brought.

Orders were given that all should make ready to go
to that province. We marched thither at once. The
next morning after our arrival, at daybreak, three very
large squadrons of Indians came upon us by as many
directions: we met them and beat them, doing some
injury, so much that they returned upon us no more. In
two or three days they sent us messengers of peace,
although we did not understand a thing they said, for

want of an interpreter. By signs we told them to bring
persons in there who could understand the people living
back of us; and they brought five or six Indians, who
understood the interpreters we had. They asked who we
were, and of what we were in search. We asked them for
some great provinces where there should be much provision (for the cold of winter had begun to threaten us
sharply), and they said that on the route we were taking
they knew of no great town; but they pointed, that if
we wished to return to the east and southeast, or go northwest, we should find large towns.

Discovering that we could not prevail against the
difficulty, we returned to the southeast, and went to a
Province that is called Quipana, at the base of some very
steep ridges; whence we journeyed in a direction to the
east, and, having crossed those mountains, went down
upon some plains, where we found a population suited to
our purpose, for there was a town nigh in which was
much food, seated by a copious river emptying into the
Rio Grande, from whence we came. The Province was
called Viranque. We stopped in it to pass the winter.
There was so much snow and cold, we thought to have
perished. At this town the Christian died whom we
had found in the country belonging to the people of
Narvaez, and who was our interpreter. We went out
thence in the beginning of March, when it appeared to
us that the severity of the winter had passed; and we
followed down the course of this river, whereon we found
other provinces well peopled, having a quantity of food,
to a Province called Anicoyanque, which appeared to us

to be one of the best we had found in all the country.
Here another Cacique, called Guachoyanque, came to us
in peace. His town is upon the River Grande, and he is
in continual war with the other chief with whom we
were.

The Governor directly set out for the town of Guachoyanque, and took its Cacique with him. The town was
good, well and strongly fenced. It contained little provision, the Indians having carried that off. Here the
Governor, having before determined, if he should find
the sea, to build brigantines by which to make it known
in Cuba that we were alive, whence we might be supplied with some horses and things of which we stood in
need, sent a Captain in the direction south, to see if
some road could be discovered by which we might go to
look for the sea; because, from the account given by the
Indians, nothing could be learned of it; and he got back,
reporting that he found no road, nor any way by which
to pass the great bogs that extend out from the River
Grande. The Governor, at seeing himself thus surrounded, and nothing coming about according to his
expectations, sickened and died. He left us recommend-
ing Luis de Moscoso to be our Governor.

Since we could find no way to the sea, we agreed to
take our course to the west, on which we might come out
by land to Mexico, should we be unable to find any
thing, or a place whereon to settle. We travelled seventeen days, until we came to the Province of Chavite, where
the Indians made much salt; but we could learn nothing of them concerning the west: thence we went to

another Province, called Aguacay, and were three days on the way, still going directly westward. After leaving this place, the Indians told us we should see no more settlements unless we went down in a southwest-and-by-south direction, where we should find large towns and food; that in the course we asked about, there were some large sandy wastes, without any people or subsistence whatsoever.

We were obliged to go where the Indians directed us, and went to a Province called Nisione, and to another called Nondacao, and another, Came; and at each remove we went through lands that became more sterile and afforded less subsistence. We continually asked for a province which they told us was large, called Xuacatino. The Cacique of Nondacao gave us an Indian purposely to put us somewhere whence we could never come out: the guide took us over a rough country, and off the road, until he told us at last he did not know where he was leading us; that his master had ordered him to take us where we should die of hunger. We took another guide, who led us to a Province called Hais, where, in seasons, some cattle are wont to herd; and as the Indians saw us entering their country, they began to cry out: "Kill the cows—they are coming;" when they sallied and shot their arrows at us, doing us some injury.

We went from this place and came to the Province of Xacatin, which was among some close forests, and was scant of food. Hence the Indians guided us eastward to other small towns, poorly off for food, having said that they would take us where there were other

Christians like us, which afterwards proved false; for they could have had no knowledge of any others than ourselves, although, as we made so many turns, it might be in some of them they had observed our passing. We turned to go southward, with the resolution of either reaching New Spain, or dying. We travelled about six days in a direction south and southwest, when we stopped.

Thence we sent ten men, on swift horses, to travel in eight or nine days as far as possible, and see if any town could be found where we might re-supply ourselves with maize, to enable us to pursue our journey. They went as far as they could go, and came upon some poor people without houses, having wretched huts, into which they withdrew; and they neither planted nor gathered any thing, but lived entirely upon flesh and fish. Three or four of them, whose tongue no one we could find understood, were brought back. Reflecting that we had lost our interpreter, that we found nothing to eat, that the maize we brought upon our backs was failing, and it seemed impossible that so many people should be able to cross a country so poor, we determined to return to the town where the Governor Soto died, as it appeared to us there was convenience for building vessels with which we might leave the country.

We returned by the same road we had taken, until we came to the town; but we did not discover so good outfit as we had thought to find. There were no provisions in the town, the Indians having taken them away, so we had to seek another town, where we might

pass the winter and build the vessels. I thank God
that we found two towns very much to our purpose,
standing upon the Rio Grande, and which were fenced
around, having also a large quantity of maize. Here we
stopped, and with great labour built seven brigantines,
which were finished at about the end of six months. We
threw them out into the water, and it was a mystery that,
calked as they were with the bark of mulberry-trees,
and without any pitch, we should find them stanch
and very safe. Going down the river, we took with us
also some canoes, into which were put twenty-six horses,
for the event of finding any large town on the shore
of the sea that could sustain us with food, while we
might send thence a couple of brigantines to the Viceroy of New Spain, with a message to provide us with
vessels in which we could get away from the country.

The second day, descending the stream, there came
out against us about forty or fifty very large and swift
canoes, in some of which were as many as eighty warriors, who assailed us with their arrows, following and
shooting at us. Some who were in the vessels thought
it trifling not to attack them; so, taking four or five of
the small canoes we brought along, they went after them.
The Indians, seeing this, surrounded them, so that they
could not get away, and upset the canoes, whereby twelve
very worthy men were drowned, beyond the reach of our
succour, because of the great power of the stream, and
the oars in the vessels being few.

The Indians were encouraged by this success to follow us to the sea, which we were nineteen days in

reaching, doing us much damage and wounding many
people; for, as they found we had no arms that could
reach them from a distance, not an arquebuse nor a
crossbow having remained, but only some swords and
targets, they lost their fears, and would draw very nigh
to let drive at us their arrows.

We came out by the mouth of the river, and entering
into a very large bay made by it, which was so extensive
that we passed along it three days and three nights, with
fair weather, in all the time not seeing land, so that it
appeared to us we were at sea, although we found the
water still so fresh that it could well be drunk, like that
of the river. Some small islets were seen westward, to
which we went: thenceforward we kept close along the
coast, where we took shell-fish, and looked for other
things to eat, until we entered the River of Pánuco,
where we came and were well received by the Christians.

LUYS HERNANDEZ DE BIEDMA.

34

APPENDIX.

TRANSLATIONS.

CONVEYANCE OF DOWER BY THE WIDOW OF PE-DRARIAS DÁVILA TO HERNANDO DE SOTO, IN CON-SIDERATION OF THE ESPOUSAL OF HER DAUGHTER.

BE it known to all who shall see this writing, that I, Doña
Ysabel de Bobadilla, wife that was of Pedrárias de Avila, deceased,
—be he in glory—Governor that was of Tierra Firme, my lord and
husband, declare, that inasmuch as, by the assistance of Our Lord
and His Blessed Mother, esponsals of marriage are concerted and
contracted, by words of assent, between Doña Ysabel de Bobadilla,
my legitimate daughter and of said Pedrárias, with you, Señor
Captain Fernando de Soto, being at this Court of their Majesties,
native and resident of the City of Badajóz, by these presents, henceforth I promise and obligate myself to give you, and do henceforth
give in dower and marriage with the said Doña Ysabel de Bobadilla,
my daughter, for her and for her goods of dower, that you may
keep and marry her with the consent and in the peace of the Holy
Mother Church of Rome, that is to say, all the cattle with their
young which the said Governor, my lord and husband, established
and left at Panamá, in Tierra Firme, with all the cottage, the slaves
who tend the cattle, the stud of horses with them in the fields, and
every thing else that to said round cottage and stock is in all or in
any wise belonging, with the increase of slaves, and whatever else
is thereto pertinent, which the said Pedrárias de Avila, by a clause
made of his will between living, in pure and perfect gift irrevocable
in favour of said Doña Ysabel de Bobadilla, my daughter, that she
thereby might the better and more honorably marry, as more fully

may be found in the clause referred to of said will, which I deem
here inserted and incorporated with the same force and vigour it
would have were it written out word for word; of the which I, for
what therein belongs to me and appertains, or that can appertain,
by reason of any right of dower, paraphernalia, and goods, acquired
during the matrimony existing between me and the said Pedrárias
Dávila, my lord and husband, as well in whatever other manner, I
consent publicly, and approve consent to the aforementioned dona-
tive made by Pedro Arias, and do so by good, lasting, and genuine
signature, for this and in all time of the world, for evermore . . .
Done at Valladolid, the 14th day of November, of the year 1536.

> One of the witnesses to this release was Juan de Añasco.   The document exists in full
> in the *Archivo de Indias*.

LETTER OF HERNANDO DE SOTO RESPECTING CON-
CESSIONS HE DESIRES SHALL BE OBTAINED FOR
HIM AT COURT.[1]

✠

VERY MAGNIFICENT SIR:

That which Your Worship is to favour me in is as follows:

Inasmuch as His Majesty has not ceded to Francisco Pizarro
more than two hundred and seventy-five leagues by Royal grant,
of the six hundred that the said Governor Pizarro holds from
Santiago, whence begins his government, to the mines of Callao,
which divide his territory from that of Don Diego de Almagro, as
will appear by an agreement made between them, must be taken off
from the beginning of his government to the town of San Miguel,
an extent may be of one hundred leagues, which region, from
said town to Panamá, supposing now His Majesty should be pleased
to grant it to me in government, is the most sterile and unprofitable of that country, although I am of opinion that by way of

---

[1] The original of these instructions, only the signature to which is in the hand-
writing of Soto, exists in the *Biblioteca Nacional*, at Madrid. It was no doubt written
while he was in Spain, in the year 1536 or 1537.

Quito there is good opening into the interior, whereby to serve His Majesty in the Provinces through which I came.

Your Worship, not being able to get what I have set forth, will try then for the government of Guatemala, with permission to make discovery in the South Sea, and for the title of Adelantado, with concession from His Majesty of the tenth part of whatever I may at my own cost discover in the sea, and conquer, with patent, and to my successors.

What Your Worship will send to the Señor Comendador, to be negotiated with His Majesty, is as follows:

The mantle of Santiago for Fernan Ponçe de Leon, and also for me.

All the Indians of Apportionment which said Hernan Ponçe de Leon and I hold by schedule from His Majesty, with other property in lands and houses,[1] in fee simple, and if possible with a title.

Let the government that may be got for me be in perpetuity if possible, and if not, then for the longest term Your Worship may be enabled to secure: And when you shall have acted on these instructions, and discovered where is the best chance of success, you will let me know how I am to treat with these Lords of the Council in the business, and what I am to write to the Señor Comendador, and when.

---

[1] The words *se an de dar*, to be given, are here driven through with a pen.

CONCESSION MADE BY THE KING OF SPAIN TO HER-
NANDO DE SOTO OF THE GOVERNMENT OF CUBA
AND CONQUEST OF FLORIDA, WITH THE TITLE OF
ADELANTADO.

[Translation made from a copy in the *Archivo de Indias* at Sevilla, rubricated by the Secretary Samano.]

THE KING.

INASMUCH as you, Captain Hernando de Soto, set forth that you have served us in the conquest, pacification, and settlement of the Provinces of Nicaragua and Perú, and of other parts of our Indias; and that now, to serve us further, and to continue to enlarge our patrimony and the royal crown, you desire to return to those our Indias, to conquer and settle the Province of Rio de las Palmas to Florida, the government whereof was bestowed on Pánfilo de Narvaez, and the Provinces of Tierra-Nueva, the discovery and government of which was conferred on Lucas Vazquez de Ayllón; and that for the purpose you will take from these, our kingdoms and our said Indias, five hundred men, with the necessary arms, horses, munitions, and military stores; and that you will go hence, from these our kingdoms, to make the said conquest and settlement within a year first following, to be reckoned from the day of the date of these articles of authorization; and that when you shall leave the Island of Cuba to go upon that enterprise, you will take the neces-sary subsistence for all that people during eighteen months—rather over than under that time—entirely at your cost and charges, with-out our being obliged, or the kings who shall come after us, to pay you, nor satisfy the expenses incurred therefor, other than such as you in these articles may be authorized to make; and you pray that I bestow on you the conquest of those lands and provinces, and with it the government of the said Island of Cuba, that you may from there the better control and provide all the principal and important material for the conquest and settlement, whereupon I have ordered to be made with you the terms and contract following:

First, I give you, the said Captain Hernando de Soto, power and authority, for us and in our name, and in that of the royal crown of Castilla, to conquer, pacify, and populate the lands that there are from the Province of the Rio de las Palmas to Florida, the government of which was bestowed on Pánfilo de Narvaez; and, further, the Provinces of the said Tierra-Nueva, the government whereof was in like manner conferred on the said Licentiate Ayllón.

Also, purposing to comply in this with the service of God our Lord, and to do you honour, we engage to confer on you the dignity of Governor and Captain-General of two hundred leagues of coast, such as you shall designate, of what you discover, so that within four years, to be reckoned from the time you arrive in any part of the lands and provinces before mentioned, you shall choose and declare whence you would have the two hundred leagues begin; that from where you designate they shall be measured along the coast, for all the days of your life, with the annual salary of fifteen hundred ducats, and five hundred ducats gratuity, in all two thousand, which you shall receive from the day you set sail in the Port of San Lúcar, to go upon your voyage, to be paid to you from the duties and profits to us appertaining in those said lands and provinces which you so offer to conquer and colonize; and in that time should there be neither duties nor profits, we shall not be obliged to order that you be paid any thing.

Also, we will confer on you the title of our Adelantado over the said two hundred leagues which you shall thus select and make known for your government in the said lands and provinces you so discover and colonize, and will likewise bestow on you the office of High-Constable (Alguazil mayor) over those territories in perpetuity.

Also, we give permission, the judgment of our officers of said province being in accord, that you build there as many as three stone fortresses in the harbours and places most proper for them, they appearing to you and to our said officers to be necessary for the protection and pacification of that country; and we confer on you the Lieutenancy of them, and on one heir for life, or successor whom you shall name, with the annual salary to each of the fortresses of one hundred thousand maravedis, which you shall enjoy from the time they be severally built and finished and enclosed, in the opinion of our said officers; to be done at your own cost, without our being obliged, or any of the kings who shall come after us, to pay you what you may expend on those fortresses.

Again, inasmuch as you have petitioned us to bestow on you some portion of the land and vassals in said province you would conquer and populate, considering what you have served us, and the expenditure you will meet from this time in making said conquest and pacification, we receive the petitions favourably: hence we promise to bestow on you, and by these presents we do, twelve leagues of land in square in the said two hundred leagues you shall designate to hold in government in the said territories and provinces before declared, which we command our officers of the said province to assign, after you shall have designated the said two hundred leagues, to include no sea-port, nor the principal town, and that with the jurisdiction and title we shall confer at the time we give you the deeds.

Again, as has been said, you have petitioned us, that for the better governing and providing of all the principal and important matters for the conquest and settlement of said territories and provinces, I should order that there be given to you with them the government of the said Island of Cuba, which, to that end, we deem well, and is our pleasure, for the time it shall be our will, that you hold the government of said island; and for thus much we will order to be given you our provision by which you will be obliged to have a Chief-Justice, who shall be a lawyer, to whom we shall require you to pay yearly on that Island the salary of two hundred *pesos* of gold; and we give to you five hundred ducats annual gratuity for the government of said Island, while you hold the same, to be paid from the duties and profits we may have from the province you have thus to conquer, pacify, and hold in government; and if there be none there, we shall not be obliged to pay you that, nor any other thing more than the two hundred *pesos* of the said Chief-Justice.

Also, we give you liberty and right that you from these our kingdoms and lordships, or from the Kingdom of Portugal, or Islands of Cabo Verde, or Guinea, do and may pass, or whosoever may exercise your power, to the said Island of Cuba fifty negro slaves, not less than one-third of them to be females, free of the import duties that of right may belong to us at said island, upon paying the license of two ducats on each to Diego de la Haya, which sum by our order he is charged to collect.

Again, also, we promise that upon your arrival in that country of your government, which you have thus to conquer and settle, we give liberty and right to whomsoever shall have your power, that you may take thither from these our said kingdoms, or from Portugal, or the Islands of Cabo Verde, other fifty negro slaves, the third part of them females, free from all duties.

Also, we concede to those who shall go to settle in that country within the six years first following, to be reckoned forward from the day of the date of these presents, that of the gold which may be taken from the mines shall be paid us the tenth, and the said six years being ended, shall pay us the ninth, and thus annually declining to the fifth part; but from the gold and other things that may be got by barter, or is spoil got by incursions, or in any other manner, shall be paid us thereupon one-fifth of all.

Also we give, free of import duty, to the inhabitants of that country for the said six years, and as much longer as shall be our will, all they may take for the furnishing and provision of their houses, the same not being to sell; and whatsoever they or any other, merchants or traffickers, sell, shall go free of duty for two years, and not longer.

Likewise, we promise that for the term of ten years, and until we command otherwise, we will not impose on the inhabitants of those countries any excise duty, or other tribute whatsoever.

Likewise, we grant that to said inhabitants may be given through you the lots and grounds proper to their conditions, as has been done, and is doing, in the Island of Española; and we also give you license, in our name, during the time of your government, that you take the bestowal of the Indians of that land, observing therein the instructions and provisions that will be given to you.

Again, we bestow on the hospital that may be built in that country, to assist the relief of the poor who may go thither, the charity of one hundred thousand maravedis from the fines imposed by the tribunal of that country.

Again, also, according to your petition and consent, and of the settlers of that country, we promise to give to its hospital, and by these presents we do give, the duties of *escobilla* and *relabes*, existing in the foundries that may there be made; and, as respects that, we will order our provision to be issued to you in form.

Also, likewise we will order, and by the present command and defend, that from these our kingdoms do not pass into said country, nor go, any one of the persons prohibited from going into those parts, under the penalties contained in the laws and ordinances of our letters, upon which subject this by us and by the Catholic Kings are given, nor any counsellors nor attorneys to exercise their callings.

The which, all that is said, and each thing and part thereof, we concede to you, conditioned that you, the said Don Hernando de Soto, be held and obliged to go from these our realms in person to make the conquest within one year next following, to be reckoned from the day of the date of this charter.

Again, on condition that when you go out of these our said kingdoms, and arrive in said country, you will carry and have with you the officers of our exchequer, who may by us be named; and likewise also the persons, religious and ecclesiastical, who shall be appointed by us for the instruction of the natives of that Province in our Holy Catholic Faith, to whom you are to give and pay the passage, stores, and the other necessary subsistence for them, according to their condition, all at your cost, receiving nothing from them during the said entire voyage; with which matter we gravely charge you, that you do and comply with, as a thing for the service of God and our own, and any thing otherwise we shall deem contrary to our service.

Again, whensoever, according to right and the laws of our kingdoms, the people and captains of our armaments take prisoner any prince or lord of the countries where, by our command, they make war, the ransom of such lord or cacique belongs to us, with all the other things movable found or belonging to him; but, considering the great toils and perils that our subjects undergo in the conquest of the Indias, as some recompense, and to favour them, we make known and command, that if in your said conquest and government any cacique or principal lord be captured or seized, all the treasures, gold, silver, stones, and pearls that may be got from him by way of redemption, or in any other manner whatsoever, we award you the seventh part thereof, and the remainder shall be divided among the conquerors, first taking out our fifth; and in case the said cacique or lord should be slain in battle, or afterward by course of justice, or in any other manner whatsoever, in such case, of the treasures and goods aforesaid obtained of him justly we have the half, which, before any thing else, our officers shall take, after having first reserved our fifth.

Again, since our said officers of said Province might have some doubt in making the collection of our duties, especially on gold and silver, stones and pearls, as well those that may be found in sepulchres, and other places where they may be hidden, as those got by ransom and incursion, or other way, our pleasure and will is, that, until some change, the following order be observed.

First, we order that of the gold and silver, stones and pearls that may be won in battle, or on entering towns, or by barter with the Indians, should and must be paid us one-fifth of all.

Likewise, that all the gold and silver, stones, pearls, and other things that may be found and taken, as well in the graves, sepulchres, *ocues*, or temples of the Indians, as in other places where they were accustomed to offer sacrifices to their idols, or in other concealed religious precincts, or buried in house, or patrimonial soil, or in the ground, or in some other public place, whether belonging to the community or an individual, be his state or dignity what it may, of the whole, and of all other, of the character that may be and is found, whether finding it by accident or discovering it by search, shall pay us the half, without diminution of any sort, the other half remaining to the person who has found or made the discovery; and should any person or persons have gold, silver, stones, or pearls, taken or found, as well in the said graves, sepulchres, *ocues*, or Indian temples, as in the other places where they were accustomed to offer sacrifices, or other concealed religious places, or interred as before said, and do not make it known, that they may receive, in conformity with this chapter, what may belong to them, they have forfeited all the gold and silver, stones and pearls, besides the half of their goods, to our tribunal and exchequer.

And we, having been informed of the evils and disorders which occur in making discoveries and new settlements, for the redress thereof, and that we may be enabled to give you license to make them, with the accord of the members of our Council and of our consultation, a general provision of chapters is ordained and dispatched, respecting what you will have to observe in the said settlement and conquest, and we command it here to be incorporated in tenor as follows:[1]—

*   *   *   *   *   *

Hence, by these presents, you, the said Captain Hernando de Soto, doing as aforesaid at your cost, according to and in the manner before contained, observing and complying with the said provision here incorporated, and all the other instructions we shall henceforth command you to obey, and to give with regard to that country, and for the good treatment and conversion to our Holy Catholic Faith of the natives of it, we promise and declare that to you will be kept these terms, and whatever therein is contained, in and through all; and you doing otherwise, and not complying therewith, we shall not be obliged to keep with you and comply with the aforesaid, nor any matter of it; on the contrary, we will order that you be punished, and proceed against you as against one who keeps not nor complies with, but acts counter to, the commands of his natural king and lord. In confirmation whereof we order that the present be given, signed by my name, and witnessed by my undersigned Secretary. Done at the town Valladolid, the twentieth day of the month of April, of the year one thousand five hundred and thirty-seven.

I THE KING.

---

[1] This Ordinance, first placed in the charter granted to Francisco Montejo for the conquest of Yucatan, dated the seventh day of December, of the year 1526, signed by the King, his Secretary, Francisco de los Cobus, Mercurinus cancellorius, fr. G. Epus. Oxemes, Dotor Caravajal, Epus. Canariensis, el Dotor Beltram, fr. G. Epus. Civitatem, was afterwards inserted in all like concessions, and is deemed to follow here.

ROYAL CEDULA PERMITTING JUAN DE AÑASCO TO TRAFFIC WITH THE INDIANS OF FLORIDA, SO LONG AS THERE ARE NO DUTIES ON IMPORTS IN THAT PROVINCE.

THE KING.

Inasmuch as thou on thy part, Juan de Añasco, our Comptroller of the Province of Florida, the government whereof I have conferred on the Captain Hernando de Soto, hast petitioned me to command that thou be permitted to traffic with the Indians of the Province, notwithstanding thou be our Comptroller there, or in such way allowed as might to us be deemed proper, we by this present do license and empower thee, so long as in that Province we shall not be paid the duties of almoxarifadgo, to bargain, contract, and traffic with the Indians thereof, alone or in company, as thou wilt, and shalt deem proper, as well in the things of these our kingdoms, as in those which in that country may be produced or may exist there; observing in respect thereof the ordinances that are or may be enacted by our Governor and officers of that Province, to the extent that neither thou nor the said company treat or contract with our exchequer, directly or indirectly, under penalty of forfeiture of our favour, and of your goods to the fiscal advantage of our Treasury. Dated at Valladolid, the fourth day of the month of May, of the year one thousand five hundred and thirty-seven.

I The King.

WILL OF HERNANDO DE SOTO.

In Dei Nomine, Amen.

Know ye who shall see this testamentary letter, that I, the Adelantado, Don Hernando de Soto, being of sound body and free mind, such as my Redeemer Jesus Christ has been pleased to bestow on me, believing firmly in what believes and holds the Holy Mother Church, in the most Holy Trinity, Father, Son, and Holy Ghost, three persons and one only true God, promising as a faithful Christian to live and die in His Holy Catholic faith, mindful of the blood that Jesus Christ shed for me as the price of my redemption, and endeavouring to repay and satisfy so great benefit, knowing that death is a natural thing, and that the more I shall be prepared for it the better will He be pleased, I declare that I commend my soul to God, who created it of nothing, and redeemed it with His most holy passion, that He place it among the number of the elect in His glory, and I order the body to the earth, of which it was made.

First, I command, should God take me from this present life on the sea, that my corpse be so disposed of, that it may be taken to the land wheresoever our Lord shall be pleased it shall come to port, and should a church be there, or should one there be built, that it be deposited therein until such time as there are arrangements for taking it to Spain, to the city of Xeréz, near Badajóz, where it be consigned to the sepulchre where lies my mother, in the Church of San Miguel; and in that church I order that of my goods a site and place be bought where a chapel be built that shall have for its invocation Our Lady of the Conception, in which edifice and work I desire there be expended two thousand ducats, one thousand five hundred in the structures and enclosure, and the five hundred in an altar-piece, representing the same Invocation of Our Lady of the Conception; and I order that vestments be made, with a chasuble, two dalmatics, an antependium and a cope, with three albs, and a chalice with its cover, both of silver, and two other chasubles for daily use, for which I direct there be paid of my goods other three hundred ducats; and I order that the mentioned vestments be of silk, of the color which to the patron and my executors, and to those of the said chapel, shall appear well; and I order that of my goods be bought a perpetual rent of twelve thousand maravedis, in good possession, which shall be given to a chaplain who shall say five masses each week for my soul, the souls of my parents, and that of Doña Ysabel de Bobadilla, my wife, and he shall be appointed by the patron of the chapel, with the understanding that should there be a clergyman of my line, who desires to be chaplain, it be given to him in preference to any other, and that he be the nearest of kin, should there be two or more.

Also, I order that if the body of my father or of my mother be in Badajóz, or in any other part whatsoever, not in that chapel, they be taken out and brought thence, and be entombed there where my body shall be, or should be placed, which is in the midst of the chapel, in such manner that the foot of the sepulchre adjoin the foot-stone of the altar; and thereon I order to be placed a tomb covered over by a fine black broadcloth, in the middle of which be put a red cross of the Commandery of the Order of the Knights of Saint Jago,[1] that shall be for use on week-days, and another pall of black velvet, with the same cross in the midst, with four escutcheons of brocade, bearing my arms; which escutcheons I wish and order to be likewise placed on the chapel, altar-piece, and railing, and vestments, in such manner as to the patron and executors shall appear most becoming.

Also, to the end that this chapel and chaplaincy be kept in repair and appointment, the chapel and the income alike, I order that Doña Ysabel de Bobadilla, my wife, be the patroness; and, after her, should God give me children, I desire the patron to be my eldest legitimate son, or my eldest legitimate daughter, should I have no male child, that they, or either of them, who shall be the patron, may buy the site for, and make the said chapel, and do all the foregoing appertaining to it, and buy the said twelve thousand maravedis, and appoint the chaplain. And should God not grant me legitimate sons or daughters, I order that after the lifetime of my wife, the patron be Juan Mendez de Soto, my brother, and after his life, his eldest son; and if he be without a male child, I order that the successor to that patronage be the eldest son of Catalina de Soto, my sister; and should she have no male child, let the successor thereto be the eldest son of Maria de Soto, my sister; and if it happen of the designated patrons there should be no issue male, I order the patronage to succeed to the next nearest of kin, being always male.

Also, in order that the chapel, and vestments, and rent for the chaplaincy, may always be available, and that in each year, on All Saints' Day, a mass be sung, and another on All Souls' Day, with its vigil, and offerings of bread and wine, there shall be a perpetual rent of five thousand maravedis, on good possessions, to be bought

[1] See page 223.

with my goods, and I order that they be used in no other way than for what is expressed.

Also, I order that on the day my body is interred, it be followed by the *curas* and clergy of the parishes, with their crosses, and by the orders there may be in the city aforesaid, and that there be paid them what is customary; and I require that each *cura*, with the clergy of their church, sing a mass on that day, and they be paid what is usual; and I order that on the same day thirty masses be said for me, and that there be paid therefor what is customary.

Also, I order that there be said twenty masses of *requiem* in the said chapel, for the soul of the Captain Compañon, and that what is usual be paid for them.

Also, that there be twenty masses of Our Lady of the Conception said in the chapel.

Also, I order that ten masses of the Holy Ghost be said in the chapel.

Also, I order that ten masses be said of All Saints in said chapel.

Also, I order that ten masses be said, five of them of the Passion, and five of the Wounds, in the aforesaid, my chapel.

Also, I order that sixty masses be said for souls in purgatory, in my said chapel; all which masses shall be said by whom my executors shall please.

Also, toward the completion of pious works, I order to each of them one real.

Also, I order for the redemption of captives, two reals.

Also, I order, that inasmuch as I gave Ysabel de Soto in espousal to Don Carlos Enrriquez, and it was understood should be given with her in marriage and for dowry whatever I might think best, I order that of my goods there be given to him three thousand ducats, which are the dowry of marriage of the said Ysabel de Soto, my cousin.

I confess to have received in dowry with Doña Ysabel de Bobadilla, my legitimate wife, seven thousand castellanos, of which, at the time of making this my will, I have received two thousand castellanos, the same being within my control; in Spain are deposited other two thousand in the House of Contratacion, and the remaining three thousand are in the possession of the debtor to whom was sold certain cattle in which the dowry was assigned.

Also, I admit that at the time I married Ysabel de Bobadilla, I sent her in marriage pledge six thousand ducats, all which, the seven thousand castellanos of dowry, as well as the six thousand ducats of *arras*, I order that she have and inherit of my goods, as her sole undivided property, that should belong to her of my said estate.

Also, I command that of my goods be given to my nephew, Pedro de Soto, five hundred ducats.

Also, I order that to a boy, who they say is my son, called Andrés de Soto, be given four hundred ducats from my goods.

Also, I order that to a daughter I left in Nicaragua, called Doña Maria de Soto, married to Hernan Nieto, be given one thousand ducats from my goods.

Also, I order to be given to Alonso Ayala, my mayordomo, from my goods three hundred ducats.

Also, I order that to Rodrigo Rangel, my secretary, be given, for the good service he has rendered me, three hundred ducats of my goods; to Castro, my carver, I order fifty ducats from my goods.

Also, I order two thousand ducats for the marriage of the maids of Doña Ysabel, who are Maria Arias, and Catalina Ximenes, and Mexia, and Arellano, and Carreño, which will be divided among them by Doña Ysabel de Bobadilla, my wife, as shall appear well to her, and as they shall have served her.

Also, I order to Doña Leonor de Bobadilla, in marriage, one thousand ducats, for the service that she and Nuño de Tobár have rendered, of which I desire she have five hundred, and he five hundred, to avoid delicacy or doubts.

Also, I order to Leonor de Bolaños two hundred ducats for her services.

Also, I acknowledge and declare that I have made a writing of companionship with the Captain Hernan Ponçe de Leon, in which are contained many things, as will appear by it, which was executed before Domingo de la (*illegible*), public notary, resident in Lima, and of that city, in the Province of Peru, which was amended and reaffirmed, with some additions, by another writing, made and exe-

36

cuted before Francisco Sepero, and Francisco de Alcocer, notaries of
His Majesty, in the town of San Christóbal, of the Havana, in the
Island of Fernandina, named Cuba, which I have present: whence
I say and declare, that of all the goods that to me belong, or can be
mine, of which I have no exact knowledge, I admit that of the
whole, one-half I possess are his; and of all goods whatsoever that
he possesses and has, the half are mine, by reason of the partner-
ship and brotherhood that we have formed, as contained in those
writings.

Also, I declare that, in the event my body cannot be had for
taking to Spain, for sepulture, as is set forth, it be no impediment or
hindrance to the founding of that chapel and the chaplaincy aforesaid; but that all be done as in this my will is expressed and declared.

Also, I order, that this my will being executed in the manner set
forth, of the remainder of my goods be purchased one hundred and
fifty thousand maravedis of perpetual rents, in good possessions,
which shall be joined with the other one hundred and fifty thousand maravedis of income which I have belonging to me of my
share in the royal revenues from silk, in the city of Grenada, which,
taken together, amounts to three hundred thousand maravedis, of
which I wish and order to be made two parts, one, being one hundred and fifty thousand maravedis, Doña Ysabel de Bobadilla, my
wife, to have and enjoy all her lifetime, and the other one hundred
and fifty thousand maravedis be employed yearly in marrying three
orphan damsels, daughters of some that be of my line, and to
the fifth degree, the poorest that can be found; the which shall be
employed by Doña Ysabel de Bobadilla, my wife, in their marriage,
on whom I confer all my power complete to that full object, and
they whom she shall elect and name, shall be elected and named as
though I myself had done so; and if it happen that damsels shall
not be found of my lineage to the fifth degree, I wish and order that
they be any other damsels, orphans, daughters of nobility, of the
poorest there may be in the city of Xeréz, near Badajóz, who likewise are to be selected and named by Doña Ysabel de Bobadilla, my
wife; and I order that after her days the said rent of one hundred
and fifty thousand maravedis I leave to her during life be united to

the other hundred and fifty thousand maravedis, being three hundred thousand maravedis of rent employed in the marriage of six damsels yearly, in the same manner as hereinbefore declared of the three, to each of whom shall be given fifty thousand maravedis for their dowry—the half in money, the half in apparel and furniture ; and for the better execution hereof, I leave for patrons and administrators of the three hundred thousand maravedis' rent, the very reverend fathers, the prior, or president, of the Convent of Santo Domingo, of the city of Badajóz, and the minister of the Convent of the Santisima Trinidad, of that city, and the prior of Sto. Agustin, of that city, and the guardian of San Francisco, which is within that city, who now are, or shall be, to whom I give my complete power to that end, and I order that the persons whom they name and designate stand named and designated as if by me; and I entreat them as favour, and charge their consciences, that this be done with all diligence, for it is in the service of Our Lord, mindful of all the foregoing contained above, that they be all six damsels of nobility of my line, the nearest of kin, and to the fifth degree, and should there be no relatives of my line within this grade, I desire they be daughters of nobility, orphan damsels, the poorest there are in the city of Xeréz, of Badajóz. And should there be no orphans that are of the poorest, I give such patrons the full power I have and possess, and of right belonging to me, to receive the said three hundred thousand maravedis, and have an administrator, that they may be collected, to whom shall be paid such salary for his trouble as they shall deem just ; and, that there may be memory of this, I desire that each of these reverend fathers have one thousand maravedis of alms, which, with what will have to be given the administrator, shall be taken from the said three hundred thousand maravedis.

And in order to make compliance with and protect this my will, and the bequests in it contained, I leave as my executors Doña Ysabel de Bobadilla, my wife, Captain Hernan Ponçe de Leon, Juan Mendez de Soto, my brother, and Gutierrez Garay de Cardeñosa, and, in default of him, his son Hernan Gutierrez Cardeñosa, to whom and to each I give *in solidum* all my complete power, with general administration, and all its incidences and dependences, accidences, annexes and connexes, so much, in such case as may be requisite, that without authority of judge or superior, but of their own inherent, they may enter upon those my said goods, and take of them all that may be necessary, and sell them at public outcry, or otherwise, at very low, or bad price, to comply with all the requirements of this my will, according as they are therein contained, discharging them conformably to law.

Made in the town of San Christóbal of the Havana, on the tenth day of the month of May, in the year of the birth of Our Redeemer Jesus Christ one thousand five hundred and thirty-nine.

EL ADELANTADO DON HERNANDO DE SOTO.

All in this will contained is correct, and was set forth in the presence of Señor Fray Juan de Gallegos, and Señor Fray Francisco de la Rocha.

FRAY JUAN DE GALLEGOS.
FRAY FRANCISCO DE LA ROCHA.

Besides this, and over what is set forth, I order that all the debts that it shall appear at any time I owe, by information or truth spoken, be paid from my goods; and inasmuch as I caused some soldiers to be quartered of my armament in the city of Santiago, and the other towns of this Island, the inhabitants of which gave them subsistence, if any thing because of this should be asked, let there be paid of my goods whatsoever shall appear I am indebted in this behalf.

Made on the said day of May, one thousand five hundred and thirty-nine years.

EL ADELANTADO DON HERNANDO DE SOTO.

Witnesses: { FR. JUAN DE GALLEGOS.
{ FR. FRANCISCO DE ROCHA.

Translated from a copy in the Lonja, at Sevilla, among the papers existing in the action of Ysabel de Bobadilla, widow, against Hernan Ponçe de Leon.

The name Maria de Soto seems not to be well transcribed from the original instrument, since the mention of Doña Mencia, as the sister of Hernando, is observed to occur several times among the voluminous papers in the suit, which is in conformity with what Salazar y Castro writes in his history of the House of Silva, that Maria Enriquez de Vargas brought with her in marriage the entailed estate of Manchada, with other lands from her parents, Don Alonzo Enriquez, Prefect of Badajóz, and Doña Mencia de Soto, sister of the Adelantado of Florida.

LETTER TO THE KING OF SPAIN FROM OFFICERS AT HAVANA IN THE ARMY OF SOTO.

[Original in the *Archivo General de Indias*, at Sevilla.]

On the envelope is written :—

✠

TO THE S. I. C. MAJESTY

OF THE EMPEROR AND KING OUR LORD.

H. I. C. M⁷.

WE gave relation to Your Majesty from Saint Jago de Cuba of the favourable beginning of our expedition, which, it appears, the Adelantado Don Hernando de Soto brought with his good fortune, wherewith to serve in the matter of which he comes in control. Suffice it to say, that he has thought best to look both into the state of the Island and the population, as Your Majesty is informed; but with great toil and cost to himself, as he wished to travel throughout, visiting the towns, which had much need of attention. As well has he been detained, at great expense with his soldiers, longer than he wished, while providing himself, without loss of time, in every particular useful for his conquest, managing aptly in all matters, and setting every thing in complete order.

We inform Your Majesty, that to-day, on the eve of departure, he has large vessels in port, two caravels and two brigantines, in all nine sail, having lost two since our arrival. He carries in them two hundred and thirty-seven horses, besides some of relief; three hundred and thirty foot, as well as those mounted; in all, five hundred and thirteen men, without the sailors. With these go more abundant subsistence than could have been gotten out of Spain for an armada. There are three thousand loads of cacabi, twenty-five hundred shoulders of bacon, and twenty-five hundred hanegas of maize: moreover, there are beasts on hoof for the settlement, and for the butcher, to be in readiness on the return of the vessels, through which we are to receive large supplies. With this object, the Adelantado has bought many grazing farms, at the cost of much money, to be employed solely in affording us sustenance.

In order that Your Majesty may entertain good hopes of that country of Florida, we report, that directly upon our arrival here, in order that Juan de Añasco might go with fifty men to look for some port on the coast, he was elected to be the royal Comptroller; and although he passed through many hardships, because of the winter, he found the most convenient place that could be desired very near, only some seventy-five or eighty leagues from this land, inhabited and very secure. He brought four of the Indians, as interpreters, who are so intelligent that they already understand us, after a manner, and give grand expectations of that country, so much so, that all depart joyfully and contented.

The bearer of this letter is the Captain Hernan Ponçe de Leon, companion of the Adelantado, who has been a witness to all this, and is a person of whom Your Majesty can be informed in whatsoever may most interest you.

We will say no more at present, save that on arriving in the land of Florida, we will, by Divine pleasure, take particular care to give a very long relation of all that shall hereafter occur.

Our Lord guard and increase the S. I. C. life of Your Majesty with augmentation of more and greater kingdoms and lordships, as the servants of Y. M. desire.

From the town of San X°bal of the Havana, the eighteenth day of May, of the year 1539.

From Y. S. I. C. M'ᵃ

　　　Servants, who your Imperial feet kiss.

JUAN	JNO. DE AN	LUIS FERNANDEZ
GAYTAN	ASCO	DE BIEDMA
Rubrica.	*Rubrica.*	*Rubrica.*

FAC-SIMILE OF SIGNATURES TO FOREGOING DOCUMENT.

LETTER OF HERNANDO DE SOTO AT TAMPA BAY TO
THE JUSTICE AND BOARD OF MAGISTRATES IN
SANTIAGO DE CUBA.

VERY NOBLE GENTLEMEN:

THE being in a new country, not very distant indeed from that
where you are, still with some sea between, a thousand years
appear to me to have gone by since any thing has been heard from
you; and although I left some letters written at Havana, to go off in
three ways, it is indeed long since I have received one. However,
since opportunity offers by which I may send an account of what it
is always my duty to give, I will relate what passes, and I believe
will be welcome to persons I know favourably, and are earnest for
my success.

I took my departure from Havana with all my armament on
Sunday, the XVIIIth of May, although I wrote that I should leave
on the XXVth of the month. I anticipated the day, not to lose
a favourable wind, which changed, nevertheless, for calms, upon our
getting into the Gulf; still these were not so continuous as to prevent
our casting anchor on this coast, as we did at the end of eight days,
which was on Sunday, the festival of Espiritu Santo.

Having fallen four or five leagues below the port, without any one
of my pilots being able to tell where we were, it became necessary
that I should go in the brigantines and look for it. In doing so,
and in entering the mouth of the port, we were detained three days;
and likewise because we had no knowledge of the passage—a
bay that runs up a dozen leagues or more from the sea—we were
so long delayed that I was obliged to send my Lieutenant-General,
Vasco Porcallo de Figueroa, in the brigantines, to take possession of
a town at the end of the bay. I ordered all the men and horses to
be landed on a beach, whence, with great difficulty, we went on
Trinity Sunday to join Vasco Porcallo. The Indians of the coast,
because of some fears of us, have abandoned all the country, so that
for thirty leagues not a man of them has halted.

At my arrival here I received news of there being a Christian in

the possession of a Cacique, and I sent Baltazar de Gallegos, with
XL. men of the horse, and as many of the foot, to endeavour to
get him. He found the man a day's journey from this place, with
eight or ten Indians, whom he brought into my power. We
rejoiced no little over him, for he speaks the language; and although
he had forgotten his own, it directly returned to him. His name is
Juan Ortiz, an hidalgo, native of Sevilla.

In consequence of this occurrence, I went myself for the Cacique,
and came back with him in peace. I then sent Baltazar de Gallegos,
with eighty lancers, and a hundred foot-soldiers, to enter the
country. He has found fields of maize, beans, and pumpkins, with
other fruits, and provision in such quantity as would suffice to subsist a very large army without its knowing a want. Having been
allowed, without interruption, to reach the town of a Cacique named
Urripacoxit, master of the one we are in, also of many other towns,
some Indians were sent to him to treat for peace. This, he writes,
having been accomplished, the Cacique failed to keep certain
promises, whereupon he seized about XVII. persons, among
whom are some of the principal men; for in this way, it
appears to him, he can best secure a performance. Among
those he detains are some old men of authority, as great as can
be among such people, who have information of the country farther on. They say that three days' journey from where they are,
going by some towns and huts, all well inhabited, and having many
maize-fields, is a large town called Acuera, where with much convenience we might winter; and that afterwards, farther on, at the distance of two days' journey, there is another town, called Ocale. It is
so large, and they so extol it, that I dare not repeat all that is said.
There is to be found in it a great plenty of all the things mentioned;
and fowls, a multitude of turkeys, kept in pens, and herds of tame
deer that are tended. What this means I do not understand, unless
it be the cattle, of which we brought the knowledge with us. They
say there are many trades among that people, and much intercourse,
an abundance of gold and silver, and many pearls. May it please
God that this may be so; for of what these Indians say I believe
nothing but what I see, and must well see; although they know, and
have it for a saying, that if they lie to me it will cost them their

37

lives. This interpreter puts a new life into us, in affording the means of our understanding these people, for without him I know not what would become of us. Glory be to God, who by His goodness has directed all, so that it appears as if He had taken this enterprise in His especial keeping, that it may be for His service, as I have supplicated, and do dedicate it to Him.

I sent eighty soldiers by sea in boats, and my General by land with XL. horsemen, to fall upon a throng of some thousand Indians, or more, whom Juan de Añasco had discovered. The General got back last night, and states that they fled from him; and although he pursued them, they could not be overtaken, for the many obstructions in the way. On our coming together we will march to join Baltazar de Gallegos, that we may go thence to pass the winter at the Ocale, where, if what is said be true, we shall have nothing to desire. Heaven be pleased that something may come of this that shall be for the service of our Divine Master, and whereby I may be enabled to serve Your Worships, and each of you, as I desire, and is your due.

Notwithstanding my continual occupation here, I am not forgetful of the love I owe to objects at a distance; and since I may not be there in person, I believe that where you, Gentlemen, are, there is little in which my presence can be necessary. This duty weighs upon me more than every other, and for the attentions you will bestow, as befits your goodness, I shall be under great obligations. I enjoin it upon you, to make the utmost exertions to maintain the repose and well-being of the public, with the proper administration of justice, always reposing in the Licentiate, that every thing may be so done in accordance with law, that God and the King may be served, myself gratified, and every one be content and pleased with the performance of his trust, in such a manner as you, Gentlemen, have ever considered for my honour, not less than your own, although I still feel that I have the weight thereof, and bear the responsibility.

As respects the bastion which I left begun, if labouring on it have been neglected, or perhaps discontinued, with the idea that the fabric is not now needed, you, Gentlemen, will favour me by having it finished, since every day brings change; and although no occasion should arise for its employment, the erection is provident for the

A

well-being and safety of the town: an act that will yield me increased satisfaction, through your very noble personages.

That our Lord may guard and increase your prosperity is my wish and your deserving.

In this town and Port of Espiritu Santo, in the Province of Florida, July the IX., in the year 1539.

The servant of you, Gentlemen.

EL ADELANTADO DON HERNANDO DE SOTO.

This document, which exists in copy only, written in a firm, clear hand, is to be found in the *Archivo de Indias*, and doubtless is that which accompanied the letter of the Licentiate Bartolomé Ortiz, dated at Santiago, the eighth day of November, 1539, addressed to the Emperor and Council of the Indias. In it he says:

"Directly as the Governor left here I fell sick in bed, and remained so three months, on which account I could not finish the bastion and bulwark he commenced. * * * It may be a month since the Governor of this Island wrote from the Port of Espiritu Santo to the Board of this City, stating his arrival in Florida, and its occurrences, a copy of which I send. He strongly urges the completion of the bastion at this port, but the magistrates oppose it; and, contrary to my commands, have ordered the assessment to cease, which is necessary for this purpose, and the following up of the wild Indians. * * * "

Notwithstanding the character in which the letter of the Adelantado is copied, the transcript seems to be faulty in omissions, and affords several evident mistakes of words.

LETTER TO CHARLES V. FROM THE JUSTICE AND BOARD
OF MAGISTRATES OF SANTIAGO DE CUBA, GIVING A
STATEMENT OF OCCURRENCES ON THE ISLAND.

[Original in the *Archivo General de Indias* at Sevilla.]

On the envelope is written :—

TO THE SACRED IMPERIAL CATHOLIC MAJESTY,

THE EMPEROR KING OUR MASTER.

S. I. C. M.

On the seventh day of June, of the present year, the Adelantado
Don Hernando de Soto arrived at this port with five ships, bringing
six hundred men for the conquest of Florida. He laid before us a
provision bestowing on him the government of this Island, which we
receive as favour. Being mindful that he goes to serve Your Majesty in the settlement of that country, his people have been enter-
tained among the inhabitants of the place in the best manner possible, and he now makes ready for his departure. May our Lord
guide him thither, and give the success most for His service and that
of Your Highness.

According to Your Majesty's command, he presented for his
Chief Judge the Licentiate Bartolomé Ortiz, a civilian, long resident in these parts, of whom we hope that he will see the inhabitants receive good treatment, with considerations of justice and
honour.

On the 5th of April just past, a French vessel, having seventy-
eight men, entered this port, with the intention of robbing the city,
at a time when it pleased God there should be found here a vessel
belonging to Diego Perez, resident of Sevilla, which opposed her,
the two with bombards fighting together a day and night, each
killing three or four men for the other, the most of the townspeople
in the mean while going to their farmhouses and bringing together
their women and property, as in the city there was no military
defence or support of any sort. With this resistance, that vessel
went out and went off. Now we have news that she sailed to San

Noval of the Havana, on this Island, burned all the town, the church inclusive, taking a certain amount in gold, the property of persons deceased, and another of the Crusade, with one hundred and fifty dollars, the proceeds of gate duties, belonging to Your Highness, besides doing other injuries to individuals. When she left this city, they said she would return; and as it may be that these or some other Frenchmen might dare as much, we resolve to make this known to Your Majesty, that the remedy may be applied in affording the protection of some artillery with which to make defence at the wharf, and give that security which a half dozen of large calibre and a dozen culverins we think sufficient to insure. These we beg that Your Highness will order to be sent to us, and the necessary ammunition from the House of Contratacion in Sevilla, with the haste possible; for if this town be burned or destroyed, the Island is ruined, and the injury is great. God will not permit that the Church and other stone edifices shall be consumed. They have cost much to erect, and could not be rebuilt in a long time.

We likewise make known to Your Majesty that, eight months since, twenty or thirty wild natives insurged, and have committed many atrocities, killing Christians, Spaniards, negroes, domestic Indians, and herds, and setting farms on fire. Although this Board has from the first sent a force against them, which killed many, they continue to do harm; and the Adelantado, having got this information, directly upon his arrival in this city sent out a troop of Spaniards, with negroes and tame Indians, at the cost of the assessment we have made here; and having also ordered out another party, from the town of San Salvador, the two are now in their pursuit. We hope these may be overtaken and chastised, that the evil may cease. Nothing has been heard as yet. Since there are no arms here nor on the Island, and standing in much need of some, it will be necessary that Your Highness require that from Sevilla there be provided for us as many as fifty thousand maravedis, the half for crossbows, shafts, strings, and appurtenances, the other half in lances and bucklers. We ask Your Majesty will order that the money be laid out in the Contratacion of Sevilla, and the arms sent to us in the first ship that comes to this city, when directly as they arrive we will pay the royal officers the amount thus spent.

Money has been requisite to make this war upon the Indians, who do so great mischief, and to protect us from the French vessels. The Board, being without any for the purposes, was obliged to raise as many as three hundred dollars gold by assessment of the community. We entreat that Your Majesty be pleased to deem the act properly done, the greater part being paid by the principal persons of the Island ; and that, should one or two hundred more be found necessary, Your Highness will favour us by directing that we be authorized and empowered to raise the sum, which, beyond our great obligations, is a necessary measure for the welfare of the land.

From what has been already said, it may be seen how greatly this Island and people need that Your Majesty should order that they be favoured and assisted, lest every thing be lost, and they go away to Florida, Peru, and other parts to find support, which occasion, to many residents, appears to be at hand. Should Your Highness be pleased to permit that all the gold which is got by the Indians and negroes pay the tenth part during seven or eight years, the mines would be sought out and worked unattended by the frauds and deceptions practised at the time of melting the metal, many perjuring themselves in statements that it is got by the negroes, when it is procured by Indians. So small is the quantity obtained, because of the hindrance, that it does not annually amount to thirteen thousand dollars; and, making this concession, every one would strive to discover mines, and not cease to look after gold, as many have done, to engage in fields of other labour and pursuits, whence the income of Your Majesty is less, and the inhabitants continue very poor.

We entreat that it may serve Your Highness to command this favour : that a stone fortress be directed to be built in the Havana ; and all the citizens of this place, with the residents, beseech that, in consideration of the want also here of one for defence, it serve you to direct that a fortress be built at this port, to be a permanency in the Island, so that, though many French vessels come, it may be able successfully to prevent their entrance here. This fabric would be the avoidance of many evils, put the inhabitants in heart to remain and settle here ; or otherwise, Your Majesty may be assured that this city is in danger of being pillaged and burned, whenever it is the disposition of the French that it should.

The Bishop of the Island arrived here ten or twelve days after the Adelantado came; consequently we have rejoiced much, his presence giving us great consolation, and we trusting in God that it will be very profitable, both for the Island and its inhabitants. As he writes to Your Majesty, nothing remains to be said more than refer to what he states.

Sacred I. C. Majesty our Master. Be the Imperial person of Your Majesty preserved, and your dominion enlarged, as we your vassals desire.

From the City of Santiago, of the Island of Fernandina, the XXVI. day of July, of the year 1539.

From Y. S. I. C. Majesty's humble vassals, who kiss your royal feet and hands.

JUAN DE LA TORRE.

INO. ARMANSA.

LOPE HURTADO.

ANDRES PARADA.

THORIBIO DE CASTRO.

By order of the Justice and Board of Magistrates:

X°VAL DE TORRES,

Notary Public, and of the Board.

MEMOIR OF THE NAMES OF PERSONS WHO CAME
FROM FLORIDA, WHO THEY ARE, AND OF WHAT
COUNTRIES NATIVE.

FROM SEVILLA.

Balthasar de Gallegos.
Rodrigo de Gallegos.
Jno. de Añasco.
Xpóval Espindola.
Trugillo.
Jno. Lopez Chachon.
Fuentes.
Villalobos.
Algalin, shoe-maker.
Bartholome Ruiz, stocking-maker.
Porras.
Tristan.
Coria.
Jno. de Mesa.
Morales.
Ynistrosa.
Rodon, sword-cutler.
Gº. Cartuyo, sailor.
Carrançe.
Galindo.
Alonso.
Rui Garcia, from Santlúcar Barrameda.
Jno. Diaz, from Sanlúcar.

FROM BADAJÓZ.

Pedro Calderon, and two sons.

Arias Tinoco, and two brothers, sons of Cardeñosa.
Luis Bravo, son of Balthasar Bravo.
Juan de Vega.
Balthasar Gen. notary.
Jno. Xuarez, companion of Luis Bravo.
Jno. Guttierrez.
Francisco Sanchez.
Andres Sanchez, brother.
Hernando de Vega.
Juan Gª. Rueda.
Jno. Carrion, tailor.
Ximon Perez.
Rodrigo Alonso.
Jno. Ruiz, carpenter.
Hernan Mauzera.
Atanasio.
Villalobos.

FROM XERÉZ AND VILLANUEVA.

Alonso Vasquez, and Rodrigo Alvarez, his brother, from
    Xeréz.
Gonzalo Vazquez, from Villanueva.
Alonso Blasco, his brother.
Diego Garcia, brother of a prebend of Badajóz.
Jno. Carrasco, tailor.
Two Franciscos Vazquez.
Alonso de la Parra.
Alonso Botellon.
Pero Nuñez de Prado, from Llorena.
Jno. Gonçalez Alor.
Gonçalo Mendez.
Alonso Gomez.
Bacan de Xeréz.
Aguillar de Villanueva.
Gonçalo Alonso.
  38

FROM BURGUILLOS.

Zambrano.
Two Vargas.
Bolaños.
Andres Perez.
Francisco Perez.

FROM ZAFRA, ALMENDRALEJO, AND SEGURA.

The General Luis de Moscoso, and two brothers.
Gonzalo Quadrado.
Francisco de Tapia.
Jno. Coles, tailor.
Sayago, tailor.
Cortes, from Almendralejo.
Pero Alonso del Azuchal.
Rangel, from Almendralejo.
Ortiz, his brother.
Villegas, from Almendralejo.
Alonso Caro, from Almendralejo.
Andrez Marin, from Almendralejo.
The Father Pozo, from Segura.
Almendron, brother, from Segura.
Perez, farrier, from Segura.
Portillo, brother, from Segura.
Galvan.
Maçucles.
Madrigal.
Calçada.
Cornejo.
Francisco Martynez.
Pedro de Figueroa.

FROM MEDELLIN.

Alonso Caro.

Garcia de Godoy.
Jno. de Amarilla.
Go. Martin.
Redondo.
Sagrado.
Saualria.
Alonso Gutirrez.
Favian Rodriguez.

Alvaro Nieto.
Jno. Nieto, his brother.
Domingo Landero, his brother.
Diego Sanchez.
Alonso Gutierrez.
Jno. Garcia Pechuga.
Caldera.
Jno. Fernandez.

The Bachelor Herrera.
Verdejon.
Guzman.
Lope de Acuña, from Yllescas.
Rodrigo Corona, trumpeter.
Villagarcia, from La Mancha.
Castro del Castro, from Garciamuñóz.
Jno. Gaitan, from Talavera la Reina.
Treasurer of this Armada.
Carranz. from Torrejon.

Biedma, factor of this armament.

Rayo.
Francisco de Lera, tailor.
Cañete.
Jno. Rodriguez Lobillo, from Ronda.
Alonso de Torres.
Jno. Lopez Çabarron.
Another Jno. Lopez.
Carrion.

FROM CASTILLA LA VIEJA.

Tiedra, of Salamanca.
Pedro de Torres, from Medina del Campo.
Bonifacio, from Valladolid.
Luis Daçe.
Gin.
Alonso Hernandez.
Miranda de Soria.
Pedro de Soria.
Bustillon.
Baeça.
Verdugo.
Val de Olivas.
Pozo Salmeron.
Bautista and his brother.
Salamanca, tailor.
Tapia.
Calva Rasa.
Villegas, from Plazencia.
Velasco.
Ortiz.
Castro.
Alvañes.
Velasquez.
Salazar.
Salduendo.
Villa Roel.

Carrion, from Carrion de los Condes.
Valderas, from Leon.
Morales, from Soria.
Sancho de Torres.
Agostin.
Valtierra.
Jno. de la Calle, shoe-maker.
Jno. Duarte.
Diego Gallego.
Gaspar de Aguilar.
Diego de Oliva.

Don Antonio, brother of the Marquis.
Reinoso.
Marban, notary.
Another Marban.
Alonso Goncalez.
Jiraldo.
Otaco.
Argote.
Maestre Jno.
Castrejon.
Osorio Garcia.
Castreros.

Juanes de a Vedi, seaman.
Miguel.
Pedro de Aroca.
Tolosa.
Min. Alrianes.
Jno. Perez.

Agostin.
Martucho.
Peria.
Bernaldo, calker.

THE AILING WHO REMAINED AT PANAMÁ.

Jno. Ruis, from Sevilla.
Enrriquez, from Astorga.
Viceinte Martinez.
Arias, a Galician.

FRIARS AND CLERGYMEN.

Three Friars.
One Clergyman, French.

FROM THE MOUNTAINS, AND STRANGERS.

Sin Ventura Salazar, from the Mountains.
Silvera, a Galician.
Sant Jorje, also.
Moreno, also.
Pedro de Rybera, also.
Hortuño, a Portuguese.
Jno. Cordero, also.
Alonso Gutierrez, also.
Pegado and his son, also.
Anton Martinez, also.
Manuel de Torres, also.
Gavian Lopez and his brother, also.
Domingo Sardina, also.
Jno. Alvarez, also.
Alvaro Alfonso, also.
Antonio Velazquez.
Jorge Matheos.
Viota, from Aragon.

Gº, a Galician.

Jno. Sedeños.

Jacome.

Antonio, a Galician.

Miguel de Audirrela.

This document, which, from the folds and look of the paper, appears to have been carried in the pocket some little time, is to be found in the *Archivo de Indias*, without any mark or indication of its origin, source, or authority. In the heading, "The alling who remained at Panamá," there is probably in the proper name a mistake for Pánuco. The number of persons is two hundred and twenty-one.

LETTER TO THE KING FROM THE VICEROY OF NEW SPAIN, WITH TESTIMONY IN BEHALF OF GARCIA OSORIO, SOLICITING THE ROYAL FAVOUR.

His Catholic Majesty:

At the request of Garcia Osorio, resident of the city, evidence has been taken in this Royal Audiencia, wherewith to inform Your Majesty touching his rank, merits, and past services, of his marriage with the daughter of a *conquistador*, and of the state of want he is in, to pray Your Majesty will favour him with some berth, that may become vacant in the Royal Treasury here, or in other way that may offer.

Besides this testimony, taken according to the order newly provided and commanded by Your Majesty, was received this official one on the subject. There appears from it that Garcia Osorio is a native of the City of Astorga, and housekeeper in this of Mexico, married to Doña Ysabel Marmolejo, daughter of Francisco Marmolejo, one of the first conquerors of this city, and of New Spain; and that he went in company with the Adelantado, Hernando de Soto, to Florida, where he was through the occurrences, in person, with arms, horses, and Spanish servants; and that he served Your Majesty likewise well, as a good soldier, in Italy, at the taking of Tunis, and also in the expedition to France; that to employ himself in Your Majesty's service he sold his patrimony, the town of Moleçuelas, in the kingdom of Castilla, and that he is a person of good standing, son of an hidalgo and man of quality.

Aside from what appears in the testimony, the Royal Audiencia deems Garcia Osorio a person of nice honour and character, reliable of trust, and, as such, some offices, of mayor and chief alcalde, have been given to him by me, the Viceroy, with one of which he is at present provided. In him combine qualities that make it desirable, with the pleasure of Your Majesty, that what can be given to him should be.

The foregoing letter in the *Archivo de Indias* at Sevilla, signed with the rubrics of the Viceroy, Don Luis de Velasco, and the *Oydores* of the Royal *Audiencia*, is from testimony taken in the year 1560, in New Spain, at the request of Garcia Osorio, a citizen of Mexico, concerning his merits, &c., wherein, as witnesses to the fact of the death of his brother, Francisco Osorio, in the march of Soto, appear Luis Daça, Diego de Silvera, Juan Lopez Cacho, Joan de Ganies, Francisco de Castrejon, and Gonçalo Mendez de Soto, merchant, all which are names to be found on the roll, or memoir of returned soldiers.

Castrejon swore that the brothers appeared in the expedition "like gentlemen, as they were, and with the consideration due to that grade were respected as such; they bore arms, and supported horses and Spanish soldiers at their own cost, and the said Garcia Osorio was captain of the arcabusiers, toiling, both he and his brother, to their best ability, in the service of His Majesty . . . ."

MEMORIAL OF ALONSO VAZQUEZ

TO THE KING OF SPAIN, PETITIONING FOR CERTAIN PRIVILEGES, AND
PERMISSION TO RESIDE IN FLORIDA, TOGETHER WITH THE TESTI-
MONY OF PERSONS AS TO HIS SERVICES IN THE ARMY OF HER-
NANDO DE SOTO, DURING THE INVASION OF THAT PROVINCE.

[MEMORIAL.]

His Royal Majesty:

Alonso Vazquez, native of the city of Xeréz, near Badajóz, says,
that in the year thirty-eight, gone by, he was with the Governor,
Don Hernando de Soto, in the armada brought together to go upon
the discovery of Florida, whither he went, the said Alonso Vazquez,
as soldier; and after they were arrived he was in the service of
Your Majesty in the exploration more than six years, during which
time he held command of over forty men, conferred for his good
example and his conduct; and thus he entered upon that first discovery accomplished in the province, where, in all that offered, he
served loyally and well, as likewise did his brother Rodrigo Vazquez, who accompanied him, enduring much hardship and hunger;
and he was injured of many wounds, was shoeless, and without
clothing; besides that he spent, in the aid he undertook to render the
Licentiate de la Gasca, in horses, in negroes, and arms, more than a
thousand ducats: And, in consideration of such his services, being
of the first that explored that Province of Florida, as will appear
from this memorial he presents; and knowing the country to which
he would return, taking with him his wife and household to live,
remain, and serve there (which is like what should be earliest done
for the royal interest, that persons should go thither who have been
in the country and know its character): and to the end of its
prosperity and of sustaining it, he asks and entreats that Your
Majesty be pleased, because he is of the first discoverers and conquerors, to command that your royal order issue to your Governor
and other justices (¹) in that province to give in *encomienda* Indians

39

of *repartimiento* due to his services and condition, whereby he may make support.

Also he begs that there be given him the command of a regiment of the chief city that shall be established there. (¹)

Likewise, also, that license be ordered to issue permitting him to go to that province and taking his wife and household, four nephews of his, and two women belonging to his wife, and two men.(²)

Also, he begs that he be favoured with permission to transport eight slaves for his use, free of all duties, in consideration of their services.(⁴)

Also, that license be ordered to issue to him that he may transport a female slave of the India of the King of Portugal, which is of Brazil, and two girls, her children.(⁵)

Likewise, he says, that his said brother, Ro. Vazquez, was with him in the conquest, and remains in Florida, and that the Governor gave him the post of Alguazil-Mayor of the field and of the principal city that should be established; and he desires that upon his arrival, an equal privilege be extended to him,(⁶) since he goes to remain and to serve Y. M.; in the giving of which he will be favoured.

GONZALO DE ORIBE.

On the margin are these original memoranda of the Orders in Council:

(¹) Recommendation.

(²) It is not permitted that the regiment should be there provided.

(³) Not being of the forbidden, and giving bonds that they go direct to Florida, and reside in the country ten years.

(⁴) According to the practice.

(⁵,⁶) Not allowed.

[PETITION.]

In the city of Xeréz, near Badajóz, the twelfth day of the month of June, one thousand five hundred and sixty years, before the magnificent Lord-licentiate Avila, Alcalde-Mayor of this said city, appeared Juan Guillen, householder thereof, and presented a power and a writing, and an interrogatory, which is the following:

Witnesses: SALVADOR MACON,
        DIEGO HERNANDEZ.

VERY MAGNIFICENT LORD:

I, Alonso Vazquez, native of the city of Xerez, appear before Your Worship, and say that respecting certain services that I have rendered to His Majesty, Don Felipe, our master, in wars and conquests, for the preservation of my rights in perpetual remembrance I find it necessary to take certain evidence. Accordingly, I ask and beg of Your Worship that you take the testimony of witnesses, which to that end I shall present, examining them by an interrogatory submitted, interposing therein through all your authority and initiatory decree, that the evidence to be taken in the matter shall everywhere find entire credence throughout and for whatsoever it should be most required . . . Your Worship I implore.

THE BACHELOR BAEÇA.

The Letter of Authority to be found in the Original is here omitted.

[INTERROGATORIES.]

I. First: if they know the aforesaid Alonso Vazquez?

II. Also, if they know, and is it also true, that in the year one thousand five hundred and thirty-eight, he went from Spain to the discovery and conquest of Florida, in the armament of Don Hernando de Soto, brought together by the consent and order of His Majesty, the said Alonso Vazquez going as a soldier known and admitted to be in the service of the King?

III. Also, if they know that the Adelantado Hernando de Soto debarked at Santiago de Cuba, and there and in the Havana he tarried a year, that said armament might be properly fitted out; and if the said Alonso Vazquez debarked with him, having been likewise in those towns the full time of a year, and at his own cost and maintenance?

IIII. Also, if they know that with that captain's rank the said Alonso Vazquez went to Florida, where he remained from five to six years with the said Adelantado?

V. Also, if that, directly after they debarked, the fidelity of said Alonso Vazquez being known, the Captain Juan Ruyz Lobillo gave him thirty, forty, and even as many as eighty men in charge, which he kept for a long time?

VI. Also, if at the end of twelve days, more or less, the said Alonso Vazquez went with Baltasar Gallegos, captain in the forces of that discovery, in the first entry made into the country, the Governor and the rest of the people remaining at the port?

VII. Also, if they went to a Province called Paracuxi, they found inhabited, and heard that it was a country abundant and plentiful in food; and that all the men, among whom was the said Alonso Vazquez, and his brother Rodrigo, who ever accompanied him in the service of His Majesty, suffered very great hunger for the space of a month, in which time they ate nothing but the green stalks of maize, suffering extremely?

VIII. Also, if the said Captain Baltasar de Gallegos sent to call the Governor Soto, in consequence of the news they had, who having come they went inland, among them being the said Alonso Vazquez, and Rodrigo his brother?

IX. Also, if, marching through that country with great toil and hunger, they arrived at a marsh, where they remained three days without eating, until, getting through it and coming out, they arrived at a province called Ocal, where there was some food, and the said Alonso Vazquez, and his brother, with the rest of the people, were somewhat restored?

X. Also, if there the greater part of all the rest did not fear to enter the country, and told the Governor not to go forward, because in that direction a Governor named Narvaez had already been lost, and that they should return to embark?

XI. Also, if the Governor said that he desired to make the discovery of the country at the risk he might, and left in that place Luis de Moscoso, in command of all the camp?

XII. Also, if the Governor having told Alonso Vazquez that he should remain with the people of the camp, he answered that he should do little good to the King were he confined to incursions of little danger, and that his intent was entirely to serve His Majesty, and did not wish to remain at the camp, but to go on the enter-

prises; and that he did do so, going with the Governor, and explored the country, getting good news, in consequence of which, the
people sent for and uniting with them, they directly marched inland?

XIII. Also, if in Mauvila the friendly and peaceful Indians
planned to destroy them all, and did indeed kill fifteen or twenty
men, and wounded one hundred and fifty; and if they know that in
breaking down the palisade, where the Indians were in strength,
many wounds were received by Alonso Vazquez, and particularly
one in an ankle, which was broken by it, whence were extracted
many bones, and which for more than a year could not bear his
weight?

XIV. Also, if, at the time of the cry, in the affair of Tula, when
the Indians fell upon them in mass, the Captain Juan Rruyz Lobillo
did not say to Alonso Velazquez, and to two other soldiers, that
they should go out and ascertain if the Indians were coming, while
he put on arms; that he went with those soldiers, and saw the
Indians and strove manfully with them, so that they were kept back
until Captain Vasconcelos sallied with the cavalry and defeated
them?

XV. If that, in the affair of Chicazulea, in the savanna, in
another affray, he resisted courageously; doing all to him that was
possible as a brave soldier, zealous of His Majesty's service, as likewise did his brother Rodrigo?

XVI. Also, if in the five or six years which the said Alonso
Vazquez was in Florida, with the rest, he did not undergo great
hunger and fatigue, bearing arms, unshodden, unclothed, as is public
and notorious, in the toil and suffering that was undergone in the
discovery of that land, in which he was through all?

XVII. Also, if all the while he had a company under his command, he kept the men well satisfied; and so much so, that, upon a
time it being taken away from him, thereupon at once the soldiers,
aggrieved at it, of themselves returned to ask it for him, so that in
a month it was restored, and he remained with it, ever after being
liked, affable, and conversable, was by the Governor himself liked,
and by other captains and gentlemen was liked, honoured, and
respected, and so was he held in the general intercourse?

XVIII. Also, if they know that, after he came with the survivors to Mexico, dressed in skins, in the succour which the Doctor de la Gasca asked, the said Alonso Vazquez went out with his brother Rodrigo, spending in horses, arms, and negroes, more than a thousand ducats?

XIX. Also, if he knows that the said Alonso Vazquez always kept in those parts a horse and groom, ever employing himself in the service of His Majesty faithfully and manfully?

XX. Also, if in all the different rencounters, Indian fights, and on whatsoever occasions that presented for the serving of His Majesty, the said Alonso Vazquez was not ever to be found among the first, from his own free and spontaneous will, being in that conquest from the beginning until the end?

XXI. Also, if in the pacification and colonization of that country, which His Majesty has desired and attempts, would Alonso Vazquez be of avail, from having travelled over and seen it, and knowing it as well as the best; could he be of great use to His Majesty from the certainty of what appears, that of those who have been in Florida, not more than three or four men have returned there, and none so capable as Alonso Vazquez, whence they know that he would greatly benefit the royal service were he in that country; for, besides knowing it all very well, is he not a man of excellent judgment?

XXII. Also, if all the foregoing is public and notorious, stating the reasons of the knowledge in such manner as to afford credence?

And thus propounded, the Alcalde-Mayor foregoing ordered that the witnesses be brought, intended to be examined, and commanded their testimony to be taken.

[TESTIMONY.]

Witness. Then in the city of Xeréz aforesaid, on the fourteenth day of the month of June of the said year, the said Juan Guillen, in his behalf presented as a witness DOÑA YSABEL DE SOTO, wife of Don Carlos Enriquez, deceased, of said city, of whom the oath being taken in due form, answered to the foregoing questions as follows:

I. To the first inquiry, she said that she has known the said

Alonso Vazquez for a long time; she is neither his relative nor enemy, and she may be forty years of age, a little more or less.

II. That she knows what is stated: And being asked how she knows it, says: Because she was in that armada with the Captain Don Hernando de Soto, her uncle, who went as Adelantado to Florida, at the time that is mentioned, and with Don Carlos Enriquez, her lord, who accompanied him; and in which went Alonso Vazquez, as soldier, to the port of Havana, and thence he went to Florida; because she witnessed this to Havana, where she remained and saw him embark; and hence her knowledge.

III. That she knows what is stated to be true, because she witnessed it as aforesaid.

IV. That she saw Alonso Vazquez embark, and heard it said that he went to Florida with other people; and that he continued in that expedition until it came out by way of Mexico; which she heard Ana her serving-woman say, who went in it, and also many other persons with whom she has since spoken.

V. That she has so heard from many who were in the armada.

VI. That she does not know of this, beyond what she has said.

VII. That she knows only what many have said of the hunger they underwent.

VIII. That she had heard it said of him, by many of the expedition, and by the Adelantado himself, that he was beloved of him.

IX., X. That she has only heard it said by those persons.

XI. That she does not know it.

XII. That she only knows it so far as she supposes that Alonso Vazquez would have gone with the Adelantado, because he liked him much, and was on good terms with him.

XIII. That she has heard it said by Ana Mendez, her servant, who was there.

XIV., XV. That she does not know it.

XVI. That she was not present; and therefore does not know it except from hearing it said by persons who were there, and from letters that were written to her from Florida, concerning the trials that were undergoing.

XVII. That she reaffirms what she has said; that Alonso Vaz-

quez is a respectable man, and that it appears to her that it should
be as the inquiry states, since he was honoured by the Adelantado,
who liked him, and was liked by every one.

XVIII. That they came out of Florida into Mexico, and were
dressed in skins; for this witness was among them: of the rest she
knows nothing.

XIX., XX. That she knows no more than she has already stated.

XXI. That (*because of the things stated*), it appears to her that
any employment given him by His Majesty would be well bestowed.

XXII. That what she has stated is true, and what she knows of
the matter upon which she is sworn, and signs it with her name.

                                        DOÑA YSABEL DE SOTO.

After the foregoing, on the sixteenth day of the month aforesaid,
Juan Guillen presented JUAN BOTELLO, householder, of the town of
Villanueva de Varcarotta, being and dwelling in the valley of Mata-
moros, who being duly sworn, &c., answers as follows:

I. That he knows Alonso Vazquez by sight, intercourse, and
conversation; that to the general questions, he is about forty-seven
or forty-eight years of age, of no relationship to Alonso Vazquez,
nor do any of the prohibitions contained forbid his testimony.

II. That he knows what is asked is so; that he was in the armament, and in the same ship where Alonso Vazquez went as soldier;
and hence his knowledge.

III. That the Adelantado debarked at Santiago de Cuba; and
there, and at Havana, and on the island, he was a year getting ready
the armada; where Alonso Vazquez also was, at his own cost and
maintenance. . . .

IV. That he knows it, for the reasons that he has stated.

V. That Captain Juan Ruyz Lobillo put thirty or forty men
under the charge of Alonso Vazquez, and, witnessing his ability, he
gave him others, taken from another soldier, so that he had near
eighty men, though the number is not exactly enough remembered
to be sworn to, from the long lapse of time since then.

VI., VII., VIII., IX., X. That he knows the facts stated, from
having been present.

XI. That he knows it as one of the men going in the advance.

XII. That he, at the time the said Alonso Vazquez spoke the words, was not in the advance, and does not know.

XIII. That he knows Alonso Vazquez was struck by an arrow in the ankle at that fight, of which he remained lame for a long time; and this he knows, because he was present throughout.

XIIII. That he knows what is stated, for he was there present; and that though he only looked out for himself, Alonso Vazquez was a soldier of high character, and should have behaved well, for that he did everywhere.

XV. That in Chicaça, at the savanna, the Indians gave them battle, in which they sorely used many soldiers; and not being at that part where Alonso Vazquez was, but only present, for the Indians entered the town on three sides to engage them; still, he heard it said that he had behaved like a valiant soldier.

XVI. That he knows the truth of what is asked; but so great were the toils, and so excessive, that no man can find tongue to utter them, nor memory to recite them.

XVII. That the company of soldiers was taken away from Alonso Vazquez; but being a man of such worth, and affable, and they being so satisfied with him, that themselves asked the Governor that he would again put him over them, which he did; of which he has knowledge as a soldier, being present.

XVIII. That he desired and was assigned to go, as was his brother, to the assistance of the Doctor de la Gasca, in Peru, when the news came that aid would not be needed: and in so much he could not have failed to spend much money—how much, the witness is unable to say.

XIX., XX. That he reiterates what he has said.

XXI. That the being of Alonso Vazquez in Florida would be important, from his knowledge of the country; having travelled in it and having a knowledge of the Indians, of how they are to be treated, and how protect themselves in the settlement of the country. And this is what he knows of the matter, which he signs with his name.

He presented ANA MENDEZ, serving-woman of Doña Ysabel. . . .

I. That she has known Alonso Vazquez for a long time; that she is about thirty-one years of age, is not a relative.

40

II. That she knows the truth of what is said; for the Alonso Vazquez went in the armada, herself with Doña Ysabel de Soto, her mistress. . . .

III. That she knows the truth of the statement, having witnessed. . . .

IV. That Alonso Vazquez was there; she saw him, that he was among the men; that she was in all that took place at that time in Florida. . . .

V. That she knows the truth of the inquiry; Alonso Vazquez being a worthy man, the captain set him as chief officer of the squadron over the people at sea.

VI. That she reaffirms her statements, and of the rest knows nothing.

VII. That she knows its truth, as she witnessed it all.

VIII. That the truth is stated; for that she was present, and there went there the said Alonso Vazquez, and Rodrigo his brother.

IX. That she remembers crossing that swamp, there being much water in it, in places reaching to the knee, in others to the waist, and thence over the head, which they went through with much labour in three days; but has no recollection whether they passed the time without food or not.

X. That she knows it; for that she was present, and there was fear as stated.

XI. That she does not remember, but declares anew what she has stated.

XII. That she remembers it; that it was so.

XIII. That it is true; that she saw them fight and the Indians kill there Don Carlos, her master, and Alonso Vazquez was wounded by an arrow in an ankle, and was a long time lame.

XIV. That she heard some soldiers of Florida say it.

XV. That she does not remember with regard to the matter.

XVI. That it is true, and she was present.

XVII. That it is true that Alonso Vazquez was well beloved by all the people of the armada.

XVIII. That they went from Florida to Mexico, wearing skins; that she was with them, and the rest she does not know.

XIX., XX. That she says what she has said, and the rest she does not know.

XXI. That he knows well the Provinces of Florida; is a man respected, and from having been there, will better understand the things that will avail. . . .

XXII. That she repeats, &c.

(Unsigned ; witness being unable to write.)

He presented Gonzalo Vazquez, resident of this city, dweller in the town of Matamoros, who was duly sworn:

I., II. That he has known the said Alonso Vazquez, for about the last twenty years; that he is fifty-four years of age, more or less; is not a relative. . . .

III. That he knows it; because Alonso Vazquez debarked with the rest of the soldiers of the armada, where stated, and was there at his own expense during the time mentioned.

IV. That he knows the truth of it; that he witnessed it; that he was in the company of Captain Juan Bruyz Lobillo; that they were there the full time.

V. That it is true; that Alonso Vazquez had charge of and commanded the men, in number more or less as stated; that he set the watches, and performed the other offices usual in military service.

VI. That he knows the facts; because he went with Baltasar de Gallegos and with the other soldiers to a country called Paracoxi, in Florida; Alonso Vazquez was with them and his brother Rodrigo, of which he was a witness—all going together.

VII. That it is true that they all endured the privation of food that is said, and they ate nothing but the stalks of corn, boiled or uncooked.

VIII., IX. That he knows it because he was present.

X. That he had heard it said: that it was talked about among the soldiers; but did not hear it from the Governor or the Captains.

XI. That he knows it, because he went with the people the Governor took with him, and returned with the rest of the soldiers to where Luis de Moscoso was; and breaking up the posts they united, and went on through Florida, advancing. Alonso Vazquez and his brother Rodrigo being of the company.

XII. That he does not know; that he did not hear him say it.

XIII. That he knows it; he was wounded in an ankle.

XIV. That he does not recollect.

XV. That they both behaved like good soldiers, as well there as at other places; for he found himself often with them.

XVI. That he knows it all; he was himself present.

XVII. That Alonso Vazquez associated with men of high standing; was beloved of all; and of the rest is ignorant.

XVIII. That they came there to Mexico habited in skins, when the Doctor de la Gasca sent for men, and an equipment was got ready to go to his assistance, that was not called into use; some soldiers in making ready, Alonso and Rodrigo Vazquez were of the number, could not have failed to spend much.

XIX. That Alonso Vazquez stood well there, and was respected. . . .

XX. That he was among the soldiers, ever doing his duty, of which the witness was an observer.

XXI. That he would be of great use in Florida. . . .

XXII. That he reaffirms; and it is what he knows of the matter. . . .

This memorial and petition exists in the *Archivo de Indias*, with two certified copies of the testimony taken at Xeréz de los Caballeros, from which many redundancies and repetitions have been allowed to drop in making the translation.

INDEX.

LIST OF SUBSCRIBERS.

1 JAMES LENOX;   New York.
2 ANDREW BROWN;   Middletown, N. J.
3 THEODORE S. PARKER;   Hoboken, N. J.
4 JOHN V. L. PRUYN;   Albany.
5 ERASTUS CORNING;   Albany.
6 CHARLES I. BUSHNELL;   New York.
7 NEW YORK STATE LIBRARY;   Albany.
8 JOEL MUNSELL;   Albany.
9 HENRY H. KIMBALL;   Boston.
10 ROBERT H. WATERMAN;   Albany.
11 ALMON W. GRISWOLD;   New York.
12 FRANCIS B. HAYES;   Boston.
13 GEORGE FOLSOM;   New York.
14 S. ALOFSEN;   Jersey City, N. J.
15 SAMUEL L. M. BARLOW;   New York.
16 ABRAM E. CUTTER;   Charlestown, Mass.
17 FRANK H. LITTLE;   Albany.
18 WILLIAM F. FOWLE;   Boston.
19 ALFRED WILD;   Albany.
20 JOHN A. McALLISTER;   Philadelphia.
21 MELANCTHON M. HURD;   New York.
22 THOMAS H. MORRELL;   New York.

23 WILLIAM D. MAXWELL;   New York.

24 AUG. TOEDTEBERG;   Brooklyn, N. Y.

25 WILLIAM GOWANS;   New York.

26 WILLIAM L. ANDREWS;   New York.

27 ROBERT LENOX KENNEDY;   New York.

28 GEORGE BRINLEY;   Hartford.

29 JOHN F. McCOY;   New York.

30 BENJAMIN R. WINTHROP;   New York.

31 CHARLES B. COTTEN;   New York.

32 PENNSYLVANIA HISTORICAL SOCIETY;   Philadelphia.

33 HENRY B. DAWSON;   Morrisania, N. Y.

34 ELIAS DEXTER;   New York.

35 N. H. JORALEMON;   Hoboken, N. J.

36 JAMES T. GIBERT, M. D.;   New York.

37 FERDINAND J. DREER;   Philadelphia.

38 JAMES M. BRUCE;   New York.

39 SAMUEL G. DRAKE;   Boston.

40 T. A. BISHOP;   New York.

41 CHARLES H. HART;   Philadelphia.

42 SAMUEL S. PURPLE, M. D.;   New York.

43 HENRY T. DROWNE;   New York.

44 WILLIAM A. WHITEMAN;   Philadelphia.

45 JOHN FOWLER, JR.;   New York.

46 MERCANTILE LIBRARY ASSOCIATION;   New York.

47 ELI FRENCH;   New York.

48 J. M. READ, JR.;   Albany.

49 FRANCIS S. HOFFMAN;   New York.

50 RICHARD W. ROCHE;   New York.

51	George Clasback;	New York.
52	J. K. Wiggin;	Boston.
53	H. R. Stiles, M. D.;	Brooklyn, N. Y.
54	Henry Bradstreet;	New York.
55	John M. Keese;	Rhinebeck.
56	William E. Sedgwick;	Lenox, Mass.
57	J. H. Hickcox;	Albany.
58	William Brotherhead;	Philadelphia.
59	Alexander Farnum;	Providence.
60	W. Elliot Woodward;	Roxbury, Mass.
61	John M. Bradstreet;	New York.
62	Freeman M. Josselyn;	Boston.
63	C. B. Richardson;	New York.
64	Joseph Sabin;	New York.
65	George W. Wales;	Boston.
66	J. P. Putnam;	Boston.
67	Edward Dexter;	New York.
68	Robert Lenox Banks;	Albany.
69	G. A. Somerby;	Boston.
70	Charles E. West;	Brooklyn, N. Y.
71	William T. Horn;	New York.
72	T. A. Emmet, M. D.;	New York.
73	Henry A. Whitney;	Boston.
74	John S. H. Fogg, M. D.;	Boston.
75	E. B. O'Callaghan, M. D.;	Albany.